THE
STORY OF EVIL

Volume I: Heroes of the Siege

Tony Johnson

Printed in the United States of America.
This is a First Edition Print – January 2013

ISBN-13: 978-1481909273
ISBN-10: 1481909274

Map of Element

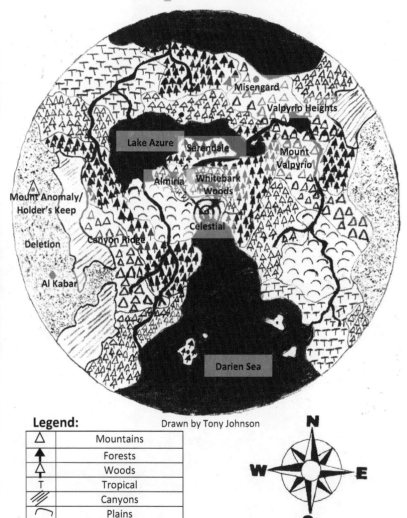

Drawn by Tony Johnson

Legend:

△	Mountains
▲	Forests
⌂	Woods
T	Tropical
⫽	Canyons
⌒	Plains
⣿	Desert

Map of Celestial

Drawn by Tony Johnson

Legend:

1	The Castle/The King's Tower
2	The Courtyard
3	The Castle Wall
4	The Arena/Stadium
5	The Inner Wall
—	Main Road
~	Fluorite River/Aqueduct
●	Warriors' Watchtower
X	Catapult
U	Cesspool

Dedication

Dedicated to my family: Dad, Mom, Ted, Ben, Dawn, and my dog and best friend, Rudy. To my grandparents and extended family. To all the friends I have met in my life. And to any family and friends, who I have yet to meet, awaiting me in the future. There, that covers everyone. I treasure the memories I have of each and every one of you and look forward to the future ones we will make together. I love you all.

Author's Note

Since I started developing *The Story of Evil* series around the age of 12, it has been my dream to see it published. The fact that you are holding this book in your hands and reading these words means my dream has come true.

Heroes of the Siege marks the beginning of a long journey I hope you will join me on. I believe I have an amazing story to tell. Action, adventure, suspense, betrayal, mystery, horror, drama, and romance await you in this epic tale of good versus evil.

Thank you for taking the time to read this book, it means more to me than you will ever know.

Welcome to ***The Story of Evil**...*

Tony Johnson

"As long as there is darkness, there will be light to fight it."

Prologue

Once upon a time there lived two gods. One was good; the other was evil. Nothing else existed except for them. The two gods were polar opposites, but they both agreed on one thing: they each wanted to create a world and fill it with their creations. Both gods used an equal amount of their own power to create a colorful planet crafted out of five elements: fire, wind, water, electricity, and earth. They named the world Element.

The good god inhabited Element with people who became known as the four races: Humans, Elves, Giants, and Dwarves. The four races exhibited the qualities of the good god. They were caring, compassionate, and loving. Everyone was created equally and each race respected the others. The good god gave his people intelligence, the capacity to retain knowledge, and the ability for all members of the races to communicate through a universal language.

The people found it easy to survive off the land. Building fires, using plants for food and medicine, and hunting animals were all instincts that were quickly learned. Creative inventions and ideas were spread throughout the world. Some of these included the six simple machines: lever, wheel and axle, pulley, incline plane, wedge, and screw. These tools helped the people to build more than just crude shelters to live in. They began to build houses. Houses turned into villages. Villages turned into towns. And towns turned into huge cities with castles. The four races were a civil people who lived in order and thrived together in the communities they built.

The evil god chose to populate Element with monsters. There were two types of monsters: Anthropomorphic Monsters (monsters vaguely resembling the four-limbed shape of the people of the four races) and Animal Monsters (monsters shaped like large and twisted versions of common animals). Monsters were the exact opposite of the good god's four races. They were chaotic, wild, violent, and cared only about their own survival.

Whereas the people were all created equally, the monsters were made unequally in a pyramid caste system. Many were weak, while only a few were truly powerful. Some could speak and understand the universal language used by the four races, but all the majority of monsters could only communicate through guttural noises. Since the monsters lived in a world of survival of the fittest, many of the weaker monsters pledged their allegiance to serve a stronger monster in exchange for safety and protection. This resulted in the formation of monster clans. Opposing clans of monsters often battled for territory, food, pride, or simply for the thrill of battle. Occasionally, clans would join alliances to form an army.

While the good god's creations were given the ability to communicate with each other and build cities, monsters were given the ability to harness the elemental powers of the planet. Anthropomorphic Monsters could turn whatever metal their body was touching into the element they possessed. Whatever weapon(s) and armor they were equipped with could be turned elemental, giving them advanced abilities in battle.

Animal Monsters and other monsters that could not wield weapons or wear armor were able to use their bodies as a conductor of their element. Some could blast their element from their mouth. Others could turn their skin, fur, or feathers into their element without causing harm to their bodies.

3

Most monsters could only control one of the five elements. Some of the stronger monsters had the ability to attack and defend with multiple elements. There were even a small handful of monsters that were so powerful they could command elements in their general vicinity and control them according to their will without even needing to physically touch them.

The four races and the monsters could not get along. The two sides were constantly at war. The people wanted to live safely and peacefully in their establishments, separated from the unforgiving and barbaric way of life that the monsters embraced.

The monsters believed that the good god's creations were inferior to them and that the members of the four races should be enslaved. It would be the job of the people to build the weapons, armor, and architecture that only members of the four races could create. The idea of a monster's perfect world was having the people harvest the crops, hunt the animals, and prepare enough food to feed everyone, while they lived safely fortified from enemy clans and armies.

With no peaceful solution, monsters constantly attacked the villages, towns, and cities while the people tried to defend themselves and their establishments. Although monsters were often successful at capturing villages and towns, the cities provided a tougher challenge. The monsters knew that controlling cities offered better protection against opposing clans rather than living in the open wild. Any city with a castle was a highly contested and targeted territory. But monsters could never get a force large enough to successfully siege a city unless two or more clans decided to join together and form an army. Even if they had the numbers, their weak strategies of attack often handicapped the success they envisioned.

No matter where a person lived, whether in a small village or a major city, at any moment they knew an attack was imminent. Even though the people outnumbered monsters 3:1 worldwide, the monsters knew they were more powerful because of their ability to harness the powers of the elements.

After countless years of struggle between the people and the monsters, one monster rose to absolute power. No army had ever come close to reaching the number of monsters under his command. He was the evil god's largest and strongest creation – Draviakhan. Draviakhan was a five-headed dragon of immense power. Each of his five menacing dragon's heads could shoot out blasts of one of the elements. His jet black scales mirrored the evil that was inside him. The Imperial Dragon, as he was called, had twelve wings jutting out of his back to give his four thousand pound body the ability to not only fly, but to agilely glide underwater.

Draviakhan led his massive army throughout Element and killed any monster that would not join his cause (if the monster was lucky enough to be offered the choice). But his real target was the good god's creations. Draviakhan ordered his army to kill women and children and keep men alive as slaves. The strategy ensured a limited population for the future generations of the good god's people. They would never be able to revolt.

Tens of thousands of the members of the four races were mercilessly slaughtered as Draviakhan's army rampaged through every establishment they encountered. A trail of mass destruction was left behind them as they pressed forward through Element.

Warriors from every race united, coming together from throughout the world to battle Draviakhan and his army. On the Pastoral Plains, "The First Great Battle" commenced. Wives and children anxiously waited for a return that never came.

Draviakhan and his forces littered the valley with the bodies of their enemies. The First Great Battle was considered the single most horrific day in history for the four races.

Soon after the crippling defeat, the once stable respect between the Humans, Elves, Giants, and Dwarves was severed from the pressure of the defeat and culmination of years of destruction.

A rift grew between the four races. Slowly, over time, they seceded from each other. Moving away from collected populations of people was the best defense against Draviakhan. If they were all spread out, they would be harder to find, which meant fewer would be killed. Humans went one way, Elves the opposite, and the Giants and Dwarves followed in similar fashion. North, south, east, and west, the good people split apart in every direction. Cities and towns were left abandoned. Only memories remained. The strategy was effective in lengthening the lives of people, but it did nothing to stop the enemy. Every day was spent in fear as the scattered races wondered how long it would take before they were found in their new locations.

One day, Draviakhan's monsters came across a small, self-sustaining farm located at the western base of the Canyon Ridge Mountains. Every breathing creature was killed, except for one young man. He was the one person the monsters should have killed. His name was Oliver Zoran; the one who would eventually kill Draviakhan. Oliver had escaped death, but watched as his father, mother, brothers, sisters, animals, house, and land were all completely destroyed. Everything he had known and loved was gone forever. In that moment, he vowed to himself and to the good god that before he died, he would end the life of the Imperial Dragon.

Oliver traveled across the entire world with nothing more than a sword and shield, a horse, and a mysterious egg. He battled and defeated any monster that blocked him on his path to vengeance. On his journey, the good god gave him the powers of each of the five elements. The abilities that were once only wieldable by monsters now empowered his armor,

6

sword, and shield. It was in using these new-found powers that Oliver Zoran was able to defeat and kill Draviakhan, ending hundreds of years of pain and suffering for the four races. What stood remaining of the Imperial Dragon's army cowered in fear at the young man who had just beheaded (five times) their powerful leader.

Zoran's quest became a widely told story that served as inspiration and motivation for people worldwide. The abandoned villages, towns, and cities began to be repopulated. New and better cities were built over the ruins of old ones.

Zoran established the Celestial City on the Pastoral Plains. The greatest city in history would be built on the place where the warriors of the four races had been so devastatingly defeated. It featured a magnificent castle; the largest one ever created. In the highest tower, the dragon slayer sat on his golden throne, underneath his golden crown with the new name of King Zoran.

King Oliver Zoran led his kingdom into a time of peace and prosperity that surpassed everything gained before Draviakhan's arrival. But although the evil god's darkest creation had been defeated, evil had not been completely destroyed. The time of peace was only temporary. The war was far from over. Soon, the ultimate villain would rise up and challenge King Zoran's reign over Element.

This is *The Story of Evil*.

Chapter 1

The crowd roared with excitement as they cheered for their hero, Stephen Brightflame. Steve was only three points away from winning his semi-finals match in the Warriors' Jousting Tournament. He closed the visor of his red helm and kicked his heels into the sides of his armored horse, Clyx. The hearts of thousands of collective fans beat faster and faster as the thoroughbreds raced towards each other. Steve's blue cape whipped behind him as Clyx's speed increased. Steve lowered his heavy red and blue lance. The colors swirled down the shaft in a dizzying spiral.

The sharp crack of splintering wood rang through the entire stadium and was quickly replaced with a chorus of cheers. Steve had landed a devastating blow on his opponent's chest, denting his polished yellow armor.

Two more points till victory.

The Warriors' Joust was the most popular sporting event of the year. The warriors were a well-respected class amongst the civilians in the kingdom. They served as the law enforcement in all the villages, towns, and cities on Element. Each year, every town sent their best jouster to the Celestial City to compete in the prestigious tournament.

The Celestial City was the capital of Element where King Zoran reigned over his kingdom. At some point early in its establishment, Celestial (sometimes called the Circle City) became the unofficial central point of the world. Maps always featured the grand city in their center. Just south of Celestial's walls was the deep blue Darien Sea. It was filled with huge wooden ships; their giant, puffy, white sails canvassed the bay like clouds. Large ships from faraway places docked in the Darien Bay and then sent their smaller lifeboats upriver into the city. This was the easiest way to access merchant shops to sell, trade, and buy supplies for their own cities before taking it all back downstream to their sail ships.

North of the city was the Whitebark Woods, which transformed into dense forests before reaching Lake Azure. To the west lay the Prairie, with its rolling hills and valleys. The snowcapped Valpyrio Heights Mountain Range ominously stood to the east of Celestial. These mountains were home to Element's only volcano, Mount Valpyrio. The melted snow and ice of Valpyrio Heights formed a large lake high in the mountains. The lake emptied out through one of the largest waterfalls in the world and became the Fluorite River. The Fluorite River flowed through the downward-sloped Evergreen Forest and Whitebark Woods and ran into Celestial - as the city's main water source - before emptying out into the Darien Sea.

In the center of Celestial was King Zoran's castle. It was the largest, tallest, and most beautiful castle on all of Element. Its many towers appeared to touch the heavens as its colorful red and blue flags flapped in the comforting breeze that swept east to west across the city. No matter where you were in Celestial, you could look up and see the castle. You could even be miles away outside the city's outer wall and still be able to catch a glimpse of at least the King's Tower. According to travelers, one of the most breathtaking sights in the world was looking down from the eastern Valpyrio Mountains and into the large valley called the Pastoral Plains that the Celestial City was built in.

Other than the amazing scenic beauty that the Circle City provided, it was also the center of culture and commerce.

Many people traveled from far away to experience the city's famous landmarks, museums, restaurants, shopping, and other attractions. The tender hospitality Celestial residents gave to visitors only added to the charm of the city. You would have to try hard to find someone who was not constantly smiling and always optimistic. Visitors always left Celestial with a heartwarming feeling. It wasn't hard to understand why Celestial was both the most highly populated city and the most visited city on all of Element.

The best time to visit Celestial was during the Annual Warriors' Tournaments. Thousands of people from all over the world flocked to the Circle City to watch competitions between warriors held over two days, once a year. Some of the tournaments included Warriors' Archery, Warriors' Combat, Warriors' Melee, and everyone's favorite, the Warriors' Joust.

The weekend was not just about competition, fun, and excitement, it was also an opportunity to celebrate how far the four races had come since the dark days of Draviakhan's reign. The warriors were the central focus of the festivities and rightly so, since they were the ones that risked their lives to protect civilians and prevent monster attacks.

Stephen Brightflame grew up in Celestial. He had earned the privilege and honor to proudly represent his hometown in the Warriors' Joust. Steve removed his helm as he trotted Clyx around, playfully encouraging the crowd's support. He couldn't contain his excitement as he smiled to the spectators. Steve had one of those bright smiles that made people instantly like him.

"This is amazing," Steve said out loud to himself. He knew moments like these were meant to be treasured as they would not last forever. If he won the Warriors' Joust, he would automatically be invited to represent Celestial again for next year's tournament. But if he lost, he would have to again go through the grueling rounds of Celestial's qualifying matches, competing against warriors who also dreamt of being in the position he was currently in.

Steve still couldn't believe he had been the victor of the Celestial Qualifiers. He had a shaky start, but ended up making it to the final round, called the ladder round. He started as the lowest seed, but ended up defeating everyone he challenged. What was even harder for Steve to believe was the fact that he was currently just one match away from the Championship Joust in the actual tournament. Ever since he was a child, he dreamed of becoming the worldwide champion jouster of the warriors, but he never believed it would actually happen.

The crowd noise was deafening; even the people who lived in the houses surrounding the arena were hanging out their windows, watching the action, and adding to the cheers. Everywhere he looked Steve saw pennants of Celestial's colors of red and blue being waved back and forth through the air. The colors matched his specially designed and perfectly fitted jousting armor. Steve was wearing all red, while Clyx was in blue. The two colors combined to form a cooperative team between man and horse.

As Steve looked around the stadium at the smiling, cheering faces, his eyes caught the face of a beautiful woman. She smiled at him. He nodded back with an attractive smile of his own. It caused six ladies around that area to think the smile was meant solely for them, making all of their hearts flutter.

The woman Steve was focused on held up her arm and stuck out two fingers towards him. With the pointer and middle finger of her right hand, she held both straight up, high above her head. Steve smiled at her and nodded.

Two points. That was all he needed before he won and moved on to the championship match.

Steve galloped over to his side and put his jouster's helm back on. He was handed a new lance from one of his four faithful squires. These young boys held him in the highest

11

regard. They tried to emulate Steve's every action and mannerism. Boys wanted to be like him, and girls were in love with him. This was the kind of attention the hometown jouster got from civilians. Everyone put their hope in him to win the golden trophy.

Clyx was just as popular. Steve was a stable boy for the warriors when he met the stallion for the first time. He had just fed the warhorses their dinner when he heard an odd clicking sound. He quickly turned around to see where the noise had come from. Steve realized it was coming from the newborn colt with short, light brown fur, crunching on his food. Every time the animal took a bite of the hard food, his jaw clicked. That was the day Steve named him Clyx.

When Steve rode the brown stallion through the city to the entrance of the arena on the mornings of his Qualifier's matches, boys and girls would run up and give Clyx a carrot, just to hear the funny noise.

Steve had never met a more loyal horse than Clyx. He had ridden him countless times on his patrols in the city and in battles against monsters outside the city. Steve rode Clyx for his jousting matches in the Celestial City's qualifying rounds. He had competed in eight jousts held over the past two months as Celestial looked for the warrior who would represent them in the Warriors' Jousting Tournament.

After winning the Qualifiers, Steve was offered a different horse. A special purebred was always pedigreed years beforehand specifically for Celestial's jouster. Somewhere there was a horse being bred for the tournament ten years down the road.

Steve had declined the breeder's offer. Clyx was a stallion warhorse. He wasn't entirely agile or super-fast, but together they had a connection and a bond. Steve and Clyx had willpower that knew no ends. Sometimes that quality triumphs over physical attributes. No one could convince Steve to abandon his trusty steed. All Steve would say was, "Together we have come this far, and together we will go as far as we can."

During the tournament, people kept saying Clyx's build was not meant for jousting and that Steve was just getting lucky wins. Celestial was considered the underdog and everyone expected their next match to be their last. But Steve and Clyx never lost. They were currently in their eleventh match of the Warriors' Joust.

Steve turned and faced his opponent, preparing for the next encounter. But before he raised his lance to show the flagman he was ready, Steve stopped. He noticed something odd in the crowd. He looked around and saw that everyone was holding up two fingers. That woman's signal had been contagious. *Two points.* Steve would have responded to the crowd by holding up two fingers of his own, but in one hand he held his lance and in the other, Clyx's reins. So instead, he just lifted his lance high above his head, pointing it to the blue sky, polka-dotted with fluffy white clouds. This elicited another eruption of cheers.

When Cyrus, Steve's opponent, received his lance from his own squires and signaled he was ready, the flagman slowly walked to the middle of the arena with his flag held even. As the two warriors anxiously awaited the raise of the flag, a bleeding Celestial warrior with two arrows stuck in his chest ran out into the middle of the arena yelling, "We're under attack! We're under attack!"

Steve heard the screams from the crowd before he noticed the dark shadows on the sand filled arena floor. Along with every audience member, his gaze glanced towards the sky.

Flaming boulders began raining down around everyone.

People ran in panic in any direction possible. A boulder crushed a row of wooden stands that people had been sitting in and were trying to escape from. They were lost in the wreckage, being burned alive as the shattered wood caught fire. Other

13

flaming boulders crashed into the buildings surrounding the arena, the very ones the people were looking out of to watch the jousting match. Some of the houses toppled over onto the escaping civilians. The smell of smoke filled the air as flames engulfed anything that could be set on fire. Unfortunately, half of the stadium was made entirely out of wood.

Clyx spun in a complete circle while bucking. The exciting joust turned instantly chaotic made him nervous. Steve almost fell backwards off his horse, but managed to tighten his grip on the reins and stay mounted. He patted his wild horse between the ears, trying his best to compose his friend. Clyx stopped bucking, but his neighing and tail wagging were still excessive as his wide brown eyes watched in horror at the commotion surrounding him.

Steve's blue eyes matched his horse's expression, although they were hidden behind the visor of his helm. Steve did all he could to try and remain calm, but his heart was racing in a panic. He, Clyx, and everyone else in the arena knew what was happening.

Monsters were beginning an assault on the Celestial City.

Chapter 2

Steve noticed three of his four squires standing near his horse. He didn't want to imagine what had happened to the missing one. Each boy had been entirely faithful in being his squire, tending to both his and Clyx's needs for the duration of the tournament. One was tasked with supplying Steve with lances. Another constantly waved Celestial's red and blue banner. The other two held his weapons: his sword and shield.

My sword bearer is the one missing, Steve realized. Without being told, the squire carrying Steve's shield reached up and handed it to the warrior. *Even during an attack, here they are, standing by my side; ready and waiting.*

Then Steve saw the fear in their eyes. The boys weren't really beside him to obey his orders. They were looking to him to protect them during the attack. Stephen Brightflame was their hero, their role model. If anyone could keep them safe it was this warrior they held in such high regard.

Steve scanned the smoky arena through the small slits in his visor. He pointed his lance to the closest exit. "Get out of the open!" he yelled from the top of Clyx. His voice went unheard by the three boys on the ground, but they knew what he meant by the direction of his pointed lance.

Steve watched them run for their lives as a flaming boulder crashed into the arena floor not more than thirty feet from him. He used his shield to cover his eyes as an avalanche of gritty sand shot up and covered him and everything in the surrounding vicinity.

That was too close. Just like his squires, Steve needed to get to cover too, but it was hard to move fast on a horse when the crowd was wildly running every which way.

Right when he started to follow the boys, Steve realized flaming boulders were not his biggest worry anymore. He watched a group of monsters come through the eastern exit. It was the same exit the three young squires were headed for.

"Minotaurs," Steve said under his breath as he saw the two sharp horns jutting out of each of their heads. Minotaurs were Anthropomorphic Monsters. Like the people of the four races, they walked on two legs and had free use of their arms. Three of them entered into the arena. They were equipped with axes and wearing armor that looked too small for them. Undoubtedly, it had belonged to a group of warriors they had killed in the past. Monsters had trouble making their own armor and weapons, so they would steal them from the bodies of dead warriors they had killed.

Two of the minotaurs had short black fur covering their bodies. The other one had brown. It was the same type of short fur that Clyx had. Also similar to horses, minotaurs had rippling muscles in their limbs. They were considered very aggressive monsters that did not have much skill or technique in using their weapon. Battle usually consisted of them picking a target and hacking away until it stopped moving, before doing the same to the next enemy.

Minotaur's heads looked like an angry bull's head had been plopped on top of their body. They had large snouts, little ears, and beady eyes. Males had sharp, straight horns sticking out from the top of their head. Females' horns were spiraled, comparable to ram's horns.

The three male monsters were wildly swinging their axes at anything that moved. Upon seeing the group of three defenseless squires, one of the beasts smiled and targeted them with his attack. The boys saw the minotaurs, turned around, and started sprinting back to Steve. But they were not fast enough. These monsters could take one step for every four of the small boys' steps. Even if it were Steve running away, he doubted he could escape one of the muscle-bound monsters on foot.

One of the squires was a victim of the monster's weapon. Luckily, the boy had not seen the flaming axe being swung at his head since he was running away.

At least he died without pain. That was the only positive Steve could come up with in the moment. But Steve's optimism was quickly replaced with reality. *What does it matter? Either way the boy's dead.*

The squire murdering minotaur had control over the element of fire. Steve could see that the breastplate it wore was glowing with red and orange flames, the same color as its axe. As the monster squared its feet to deliver a killing blow to the two remaining children cowering in front of him, Steve kicked his heels into Clyx harder than he ever had before and raced to save them from a similar fate.

Steve smashed his lance into the beast's unarmored face, feeling the entire skull give way as it was easily crushed inwards. The fire on both the armor and the axe vanished the same moment the monster fell to the ground, dead. Still in a full sprint on his blue armored horse, Steve launched headfirst off Clyx, holding his shield above his head for protection. He crashed into the brown furred minotaur, shield first. The two looked like a giant ball of brown and red as they rolled over and over each other in the sand.

Steve ended up on top and repeatedly smashed the pointed bottom of his triangular shield into his enemy's throat. He didn't stop until a geyser of red blood sprayed up and hit him in the face. Steve wiped it off with his gauntlet armored forearm and threw away his battered shield. He sat in the sand, next to the dead monster's body, and took a moment to catch his breath.

The warrior looked around for the remaining two squires and saw they had moved to both sides of the eastern exit and were waving to people, showing them the way out of the arena. For a moment, he smiled at the sight: two children who stood risking their own safety just in an attempt to bring what little order they could to the chaotic scene. *They will make great warriors if they survive the rest of this day*, Steve thought being both optimistic and pessimistic.

He rolled out of the way as a giant electrically charged axe slammed into the sand, right where his head had just been. The final minotaur in black fur was standing above a weaponless Steve. The monster was furiously mad. Steve realized the other black one he had killed with his lance must have been a close relation. He preferred to think they were lovers. Quite possibly it could have been both. Since monsters did not have morals, it did not matter to them if it was family who pleased them in that way. Warriors often made jokes at the expense of monsters. Incest was prevalent in many of the punch lines.

Steve lay on the ground with no weapon or shield for protection. He looked up at the minotaur, preparing to die as his enemy raised a sparking lightning axe and started to bring it down for the easy kill.

Chapter 3

Steve breathed a sigh of relief as someone impaled the armored monster from behind. The tip of a sword entered through its back and came out of its chest. Steve rolled out of the way as the dead minotaur almost fell down on top of him.

"And with that I take the lead! Five points to four," a warrior yelled over the deafening sounds of the battle and roaring flames. He stepped forward and pulled the sword out of the monster. Steve looked up and grabbed the arm of his best friend Tyrus Canard, who pulled him up off the ground.

"Cutting it close that time, huh?" Steve shouted back as he removed his restrictive jouster's helm and held it to his side.

"I wanted you to see how helpless and vulnerable you are when I'm not around to save you," Ty smiled back.

"What would I do without you?" Steve said, feeding Ty's pride.

"I don't know. I wouldn't want to live in a world without me," Ty said, shrugging his shoulders.

Steve and Ty were as close as brothers could be without sharing the same bloodline. They were both orphans who had been adopted by the same warrior, Titus Thatcher. Steve had been abandoned by his parents at the age of two and Tyrus' parents had been murdered when he was only a child. Titus Thatcher had been close friends with Ty's warrior father, Caesar Canard, and served as godfather to Ty and his older brother Darren.

Warriors often had godparents set up for their children because they knew they were in the most dangerous profession. They wanted to make sure their children were provided for in case they were killed in action.

Steve and Ty grew up together and rarely left each other's company. The two warriors had had many adventures together fighting monsters and always seemed to barely find their way out of hopeless situations.

Ty joked around a lot on the battlefield, especially during close encounters with death. Steve didn't mind it because he knew humor was Ty's way of dealing with the stressors of battle. He had even come to realize that laughing along with Ty (or at Ty) seemed to help ease his mind as well.

Some warriors used humor in the stressful situations of battle for multiple reasons. One was because in being so close to death, all warriors preferred having the last living memory of a fallen brother to be one in which he was smiling. They also used humor as a way to mask the emotions they felt in battle situations. If Ty could have seen behind Steve's mask of a smile, he would have noticed that Steve was just as scared as everyone else that was running from the arena.

"Brightflame!" Steve exclaimed as Ty handed him the weapon he had used to kill the minotaur.

"I know how much that sword means to you," Ty said.

Steve looked up and down his sword as he held it out in his hand, examining it as if it was a precious jewel. He had entrusted it to his eldest squire while he jousted; the first squire who wasn't with the other three after the attack began. As soon as Steve grabbed the weapon, he winced in slight pain. The coil around the hilt was warm.

"Why is this hot?" he asked, looking at Ty. Steve knew the answer as soon as he asked the question. The emotion in Ty's face told Steve that he didn't need to ask about the squire's condition when Ty had retrieved the sword from him. Steve knew one of the flaming boulders was the cause of the boy's death. The fact that Ty had given him only the sword, and not the leather sheath the boy carried the sword in, made sense. *Metal doesn't melt as easily as leather.*

"You didn't hear any warning horns from the outer watchtowers did you?" Steve asked another question, quickly trying to get his mind off the subject of the dead child. He didn't know if he missed hearing the attack alarm being sounded because of the noise in the arena.

"No, there was no alarm. I have no idea how the catapults got close enough to launch into the city without being noticed by the patrolling warriors."

"I've got a bad feeling about this, Ty," Steve said, looking around at the surrounding chaos.

"As do I." Ty nodded, feeling the same pit in his stomach.

The boulders had achieved their purpose because the monsters had broken down enough of the inner wall that they were now easily entering Celestial. The other purpose of the flaming boulders was to set the city on fire. That goal was accomplished as well. All around Steve and Ty, the wooden parts of the stadium were engulfed in flames. As the two brothers stood there, a whole side of the arena collapsed, sending embers swirling high into the air. They both knew it was time to keep moving. They were warriors. It was their job to protect the city and to save the lives of the civilians.

"Where are you headed?" Ty asked.

"To protect the castle," Steve said as he nodded to the north, where the top of a castle tower was now visible through the caved-in side of the arena. "What about you?"

Ty pointed up to the sky. Steve looked up and saw monsters flying high overhead in the sky. Immediately, Steve knew that Ty was going to fight the monsters in the air. This was one of the most dangerous duties of the warriors, but one that Ty had been trained in and was skilled at.

"Be safe, brother," Steve told Ty before they embraced in a hug.

Ty pulled away and responded with his typical witty humor, "What's the fun in being safe?" before running off and disappearing into the heavy smoke.

Steve breathed out a quick two noted whistle, the first note high, the second higher. Clyx perked up, looked in Steve's direction, and began to trot over to him. The stallion had run over to a small spot of the arena where the smoke hadn't reached yet. Steve grabbed his horse's reins and rubbed him between the nose and eyes to calm him down again.

"Easy, boy...easy," Steve said, soothing his horse so he could safely mount him. "I need you to be good, okay? It looks like today's excitement has only just begun."

"Jouster!" someone interrupted, yelling in a nervous and shaky voice. Steve hurriedly led Clyx over to where the sound came from. Steve didn't see anyone other than a dead jousting horse on the ground with blood pouring out of a huge gash through its armor. The voice called out again. "Brightflame!"

Underneath the dead horse Steve saw his jousting opponent. The man's leg was awkwardly bent. Steve winced, imagining the pain. *His foot must have gotten caught in the stirrup when the horse went down. A leg should not bend in that direction*, Steve thought. It looked like it had snapped right out of the jouster's pelvis, almost like his leg was coming directly out from the side of his hip. Steve couldn't even tell if the leg was attached to the rest of the jouster's body or not. There was a growing pool of red, soaking into the sand underneath the warrior.

Steve knelt down next to his dying warrior brother. They may have been jousting opponents, but all warriors were part of a brotherhood. It was a connection that grew even closer in one's final moments. Steve clasped the shoulder of the injured warrior in a caring embrace. His face was pale and his breathing was too shallow for someone who should be in excruciating pain.

"What's your name, friend?" Steve asked as calmly as he could manage.

"Cyrus. Pleased to meet you, Stephen Brightflame, but this may be the shortest friendship the both of us will ever know."

Steve nodded reluctantly. "You know my name?"

"Of course, it's all I heard while I was here. This city loves you. You would have won the championship for them. You're an excellent jouster," Cyrus said.

"That's only if I would have beaten you. We never finished our match."

"That's right, I was just about to make my comeback," Cyrus said as he laughed sarcastically. The laugh turned into a cough of blood that trickled from his mouth.

Steve didn't know what to say. He wasn't going to lie and tell him he was going to make it out of here alive, because both he and Cyrus knew that wouldn't be true. The dying warrior turned his head and spit blood into the sand and then wiped his mouth.

Steve realized that Cyrus looked to be only two to three name days older than him. *He's too young to die.* Steve shook his head sideways as he thought that if one of the boulders followed even a slightly different trajectory, it could have been Clyx dead with him trapped and bleeding out underneath his horse. He remained silent as Cyrus used his remaining strength do deliver his final words.

"You know I was born in this city? I grew up here. Then I met a girl from Casanovia. We moved there after we got married. She's there now, pregnant with my child. Her name is Emma."

"Any other family? Your parents?" Steve asked in a caring voice.

"No, I...I never knew my parents. Emma and our baby are the only family I have. Please send word of my love to them."

"I will do it in person. I promise you."

"Thank you. You know I always wanted to die in Celestial. Place of birth, place of death. Makes everything come full circle, doesn't it?"

Steve knew it was a rhetorical question, but even if he had answered, Cyrus wouldn't have heard it. Cyrus succumbed to his injuries and died. Steve reached out his hand and closed the warrior's open eyelids.

Steve stored the promise he had just made in the back of his mind before standing up and looking at his horse. "You ready, boy?" Steve took it for a "Yes," when Clyx snorted. He put his jouster's helm back on and mounted his horse, sliding into the leather saddle. With reins in one hand and Brightflame in the other, he took a moment to look around.

There were broken boulders on the arena floor and in the stands. Half of the arena seating was carved out of stone. The other half was made of wooden bleachers. Almost all of the bleachers had burned down. Bodies lay scattered everywhere. Some were missing limbs. People were crawling on the ground in pain, taking in their final breaths or worse, screaming their final screams. Others had been burned and charred black, to a point of unrecognizable gender.

A screeching phoenix monster above the open aired stadium spiraled out of control. One of its wings was frozen solid in ice. It crashed down into a pile of debris. The screeching stopped on impact. Steve smiled, looking back at it as he galloped out of the death filled arena. His smile turned upside down when he saw a dead warrior lying next to the phoenix. *I guess it wasn't an enemy monster,* he bitterly thought.

Steve exited out of the eastern side of the arena and analyzed the scale of destruction. Now that his view of the city wasn't blocked by the walls of the stadium, he could see much more of the devastation. The flaming boulders had wreaked havoc on the section of Celestial he was in. There were huge pillars of smoke rising up from buildings all around him that had collapsed or been completely burned down. Steve followed the pillars with his eyes and looked up to the sky. Amazing colorful blasts of elements were being shot between enemy and friendly flying monsters, exploding into a bright flash when a target was hit.

Ty will be up there within minutes. Steve thought about where his own duty as a warrior would lead him. In the far distance, high above the buildings, he saw the top of the King's Tower. He lashed his reins against Clyx and headed north for his destination, the castle.

Along the way, he used Brightflame to cut down monsters from behind that were also headed to the castle. Some of them he killed seconds before they were about to kill a Celestial civilian. People were running and screaming in the streets. Many were limping or bloody. Some were carrying the lifeless bodies of loved ones. Everyone was trying to get into the protection of their homes and avoid the death and destruction from being out in the open.

Steve was trying to put the pieces together and understand the attack as he rode. *Why didn't the warriors in the outer towers sound their alarm horns? The monsters must have gotten catapults into the farmlands to launch their flaming boulders into the city. They should have been seen from miles away.* Somehow, monsters were already in the city. For the first time in Celestial's history, the enemy had made it past the inner wall.

The inner wall was one of three fortifying walls in the Celestial City. The other two walls were the castle wall and the outer wall. The outer wall separated the wilderness from the farmlands. It marked the end of the actual circle of Celestial. It was the shortest of the three walls, at only ten feet high. It was high enough so that monsters or wild animals would not be able to vault over it without ladders or some sort of aid. The next wall was the inner wall, which separated the farmlands from the buildings of the city. It stood at fifty feet and was much thicker than the outer wall. The castle wall was the partition between the city and the castle. This barrier was the tallest and thickest, standing at a massive seventy-five feet high.

Just like how the three barrier walls grew from shorter (on the outside) to taller (closer to the castle), the buildings of Celestial were built similarly. From far away, the Circle City was shaped like a giant tent. The buildings around the edge were shorter, but gradually inclined as they moved closer towards the King's Tower (the highest point of the castle and the exact center point of the city).

The farthest buildings from the castle, closet to the inner wall, were the smallest and shortest. This was the largest section of the city that featured the most houses. They belonged to the less fortunate residents. That was not to say they were poor though, because compared to any other city in the kingdom, they were financially blessed.

Tiny snakelike dirt roads maneuvered in between the small houses, alleyways, and dead end streets. If someone didn't know where they were going, they could easily get lost in the tangled maze.

The closer you got to the castle, the wider and larger the roads grew, just like the houses. There were fewer of these larger and taller buildings of course because the circumference of the circle got smaller the further you traveled inwards, towards the center. Celestial was designed purposefully with the better looking houses located where they were, so that the people who headed from the edges of the city to the center would be able to see the possibility of luxuries acquired after a life of hard work.

Further in, closer to the castle, was the next ring of the city. It had cobblestone streets rather than dirt. These buildings were even taller than the last section. This was the business, education, and commerce section. Families walked here and stayed for eight hours each day for work. Adults went to their careers while their children went to school. About fifty percent of the population worked in this part of Celestial. The other half headed in the opposite direction and worked the farmlands on the other side of the inner wall or in the ocean if they lived near the south.

Steve could see from where he was that parts of the inner wall had been demolished. Catapulted boulders had broken through parts of it. Monsters were aggressively entering through the openings. They were also coming in over the inner wall by way of ladders. From the top of the wall came the loud clanging of metal on metal. Steve watched as warriors were overrun by monsters. There were too many for them to handle. Countless monsters kept coming over the barrier. Even more came in on flying monsters, easily slaying the few warriors who attempted to stop them.

Maybe there are too many breaches. For a moment, Steve considered turning around and heading to the wall, but he couldn't. He had his orders. His duty was to go to the castle.

Steve had been in battles since he officially became a warrior at the age of seventeen. He had grown accustomed to scenes of chaos, but what he was witnessing today was different. This was not an ordinary attack. Monsters were never in groups this large or organized. This was a full scale assault that the warriors were unprepared for, especially on this weekend when they were allowed to relax a little more than usual and enjoy the festivities and celebration.

This is what it looks like to be taken over by monsters. The moment Stephen realized that was the moment he began to fear. He knew this day would go down in the history books. Either the monsters would successfully siege the Celestial City and take control away from the people, or the warriors would prevent the largest monster attack ever known. He hoped the result would favor the warriors, but from what he was seeing so far, it looked like it would be the first option. He removed that thought from his mind as soon as it entered because it was his job to try to prevent that, even at the cost of his own life. As a warrior, he was a primary target for the attacking monsters.

Steve wasn't scared to die. Chances were that if he died today, it would mean that the city was taken. *I don't want my life to pointlessly end in vain.* Steve could not imagine any scenario in which he would still be alive in a monster controlled city. Even if he was the last warrior versus an army of monsters, he would fight them with every last ounce of strength until he could not physically lift Brightflame anymore. He would rather die fighting to save Celestial, than live to see his city fall.

Unfortunately, before the end of the day, all Steve would see was darkness.

Chapter 4

Steve was nineteen, having just had his nineteenth name day four months ago. He was in the prime of his life. Steve was not the smartest, strongest, funniest, handsomest, or most charming man, but he tried not to compare himself to others. He had an unproven theory that when the good god created his people, he gave each person either a lot of one personality strength or a little of many different personality strengths. Because of this, some people were good at doing certain things, while others weren't. Steve knew some people who were good at mathematics, but didn't have an ounce of creativity. Other people had a high level of intelligence, but were socially awkward and difficult to have conversations with.

Steve was happy with who he was and felt that he had a personality that had a little bit of everything. He was the complete package. You couldn't get much more average than Stephen Brightflame. Most people didn't want it that way. Most people wanted to be unique. Being unique meant being remembered. For example, an athletic person would be very popular because he or she would be known as "the most physically gifted person." Steve would never say it out loud, but why would that person be known as the "most athletic" rather than the "least intelligent?" People tended to focus on the positives in people. After thinking about it, he realized that was better than the implications of the opposite. Having people focus on the best parts of themselves helped their self-confidence and increased overall happiness.

Steve tried his best to see everything from both an optimistic and a pessimistic point of view. As a warrior, he had been trained to always visualize the full picture along with the good and bad consequences, regardless of personal feelings. Besides, being popular was not important to Steve. He would rather have few very close friends, than a lot of people that only knew his name. By the end of the day, he would come to realize he had both.

Out of the four races, Steve belonged to the Human race. Humans were known for their good communication, public speaking, and leadership abilities, but were prone to sicknesses if they were not physically fit. If there was a race considered to be the opposite of Humans, it would be the Elves. Elves did not have the aptitude for being great leaders or having a silver tongue like Humans. You would rarely see a person of Elven decent leading warriors on a battlefield. They understood tactics and strategy as well as anyone else, but it was not their fortitude to draw them out and enforce them. The strength of Elves was that they had good metabolisms, were very healthy, and were not easily infected with disease.

Giants and dwarves were exact opposites. Giants were known for their size and physical strength, but they lacked the talent of building and blacksmithing that the Dwarves were renowned for. Dwarves were the exact opposite of Giants in that they were the smallest of the four races and were not as strong as Giants. Usually the weaknesses of each race were the butt ends of lighthearted jokes told by members of opposite races.

All four of the races had different lifespans. The lifespan of an Elf was the longest at about 150 name days. At 75 years, Giants had the shortest life expectancy. Dwarves (sometimes called halfmen) tended to live until around the age of 125. Humans had an average lifespan of 100 years. Steve knew, in his line of duty as a warrior, that his life expectancy was much,

much shorter than the one century average. Still, a day did not go by that he would have been willing to trade in his adventurous life for anything different.

Standing tall at 6'4, Steve was still a head and shoulders shorter than the minotaurs he and Ty just defeated in the arena. He had heard of some Giants who stood over the heights of minotaurs at eight feet tall. However, unlike the monsters who seemed to survive longer the larger they were, Giants had a short lifespan for their size.

Steve's years of training as a warrior had taken him to his peak physical fitness level. He had a strong upper body. His arms were well-toned and muscular, due to having to carry a sword in his right hand and a shield in his left every day. He could run with all that extra weight for three miles before having to slow his pace.

As he made his way towards the castle, it seemed like Clyx was moving, but their destination never got closer. He wished he was already inside the castle because every couple of blocks it was one heartbreaking sight after another.

First there was a screaming man engulfed in flames rushing out of his burning house. He stopped right in front of Clyx yelling, "Help me! Help me!" There was nothing Steve could do as the man stumbled into the Fluorite River, burning alive. The cold, refreshing water could not save him from the severity of the burns he had already received. Steve watched as the man fell into the river. He saw a puff of smoke and heard a sizzle, but the man was motionless, floating, face down in the water.

Next, Steve felt a lump in his throat as he saw civilians standing in the street, pointing up at a burning building. Two people on fire jumped out of their windows from the top floor of their four story apartment to end their scorching pain. Their bodies hit the hard street with a sound that should never be allowed to enter ears. Steve felt like he was spending an eternity staring at each death he saw, when in reality he was looking away or closing his eyes from the gruesomeness as soon as it happened.

The sound of bells ringing snapped Steve back into the chaos ensuing at regular speed. The bells were coming from the castle, meaning that its draw bridges would be going up in five minutes. The job of the warriors in the event of an attack was to hold off monsters as long as they could so that as many civilians as possible could flee to the castle or to the warriors' watchtowers for shelter. Located in the center of the city, the castle was considered the safest place to be. However people felt safe enough to go back to their homes and bolt their doors.

The sudden ringing of the bells meant the monsters had successfully breached and advanced far enough into the city that the warriors now had to retreat into the safety of the castle or the watchtowers. Steve had only heard the sound in city-wide test drills. Hearing the bells now and knowing it was not a test, made everything so much more real. *Retreat.* Steve hated that word. *It means giving up. It means failure.*

The castle bells must have inspired Clyx to run faster because he started sprinting as if his tail was on fire. Steve ducked down behind Clyx's head, creating less wind resistance and making himself and the horse more aerodynamic. The only time he would sit up was when he was using Brightflame to slice open monsters.

The enemy's numbers grew smaller and smaller as more and more people appeared in the streets closer to the castle. *The monsters have not advanced this far yet.*

Steve was heading through a large merchant section of Celestial. Sellers were packing up their merchandise, bundling up their tents, and heading home or to one of the watchtowers, whichever was closer. There were even more vendors and shoppers than usual because of the weekend's events. Everyone was trying to act as calm as possible.

In the practice drills held once a year, civilians were walked through what to do and told not to panic. The drills worked well, because everyone Steve saw in the scattering crowds was being civil to one another. There was no pushing. People were not selfishly trying to save themselves at the cost of others. There were even brave Celestial natives who stood at street corners and collected tourists who were visiting the city and did not know where to go. *They are leading them back to their own homes for protection.* Steve also noticed that the quick-thinking crowd had left an aisle in the street open so that warriors could quickly get to where they needed to be.

Clyx was sprinting as fast as he could, considering he was wearing heavy jousting armor. The buildings were quickly whizzing by when a huge flaming boulder was launched behind Steve. He never saw it coming until it was too late. The boulder stayed in one piece as half of it crashed into the front of a building, sending stone debris flying through the air. The other half of the boulder smashed through the cobblestone street, creating a crater in the ground only a few feet from Steve.

Even though Steve was on his horse, he felt the shock of the impact through his saddle. The blast launched Clyx and him upwards, sending them barrel rolling through the air. Steve was ejected from the saddle in midair. He briefly saw the blue sky, with little colored dots of flying monsters among the clouds, followed by sideways buildings. Then his head smashed hard into the stone street.

If he hadn't been wearing his red jouster's helm, his brains would have painted the street red and purple. He removed the broken helm and angrily cast it aside. The impact made a sharp metal edge cut open his forehead. Blood was running down and getting into his eyes.

Steve was surprised he hadn't been knocked unconscious, but almost wished he had been because he felt horrible. The ground was swinging back and forth as he was on his hands and knees, trying to get his bearings. It slowly began to adjust beneath him, but now Steve felt like his stomach was swinging back and forth. A rush of nausea ended with him throwing up a vile greenish color from his stomach. *There's the breakfast I had this morning.* He watched between his hands as it slowly spread around the stones of the cracked cobblestone street. Steve tried to remain as still as possible until the unstable ground finally came to a rest.

There was a high pitched ringing in his ears. Every fifteen seconds, when the castle bells rang, the chime bounced around inside his skull, making the ringing even more painful. Steve realized he could not hear anything out of his right ear. He reached up his right hand and touched it, only to find his fingers covered in the blood that was pouring out from inside his ear.

Steve lifted himself up slowly and looked around, trying to get reoriented to his surroundings. Next to him was a huge boulder. A third of it was sunken into the cobblestone street in a huge crater. The building it had hit was already a raging inferno. Steve could feel the heat coming from it, even being on the far side of the cracked street. Many other people had been launched by the impact of the boulder. Some were starting to stir, but most lay motionless. Broken wood, stone, and glass from the building were scattered all across the damaged road.

As Steve's eyes continued to scan over the wreckage, they darted back to where he saw the sun gleaming off moving blue armor, struggling to move under a pile of rubble.

"Clyx!" Yelling the name sent a jolt of pain through his head. Steve dizzily stumbled over to where his horse lay on his side. He was badly injured, Steve could tell, by the rapid rising and lowering of his abdomen and a steady stream of blood flowing down his side. Clyx was snorting in pain while he struggled to get up, wildly moving his head and kicking his legs. But the center of his body didn't lift off the ground. Steve quickly brushed off the debris that covered his horse, trying to find the source of injury.

Then he saw it.

Clyx had been impaled straight through, from shoulder blade to shoulder blade, by a sharp piece of splintered wood.

The horse's eyes looked back at his master. They were watery from the pain he was feeling. Despite the pain, the stallion was struggling to get up, wanting to continue to serve his master. Steve gently petted Clyx's head to relax him. The horse began to breathe more calmly, and stopped trying to move, as if Steve's touch had let Clyx know that he didn't need to suffer much longer.

"You were a great horse, buddy," Steve said. Memories flashed through his mind of seeing the colt born in the stable, naming him Clyx, training him, taking him into battle against monsters on countless missions, having children feed him carrots, and then winning the Celestial Qualifiers and advancing far into the abruptly ended tournament. Steve had known Clyx before he even met Ty. Clyx was his oldest friend and best companion. The stallion took in one long breath, and then slowly let out all of the air from his lungs.

The adventure filled life of Clyx, the carrot loving warhorse, had come to an untimely end.

Chapter 5

The head-aching sound of the ringing castle bells let Steve know he had no time to mourn over the loss of his animal friend, even though that was all he wanted to do. The constant buzz in his left ear had subsided, but remained in his right ear, where blood continued to flow out of. He tried to open his mouth as wide as he could. Sometimes he could feel his ear pop by doing that. But it didn't work this time. He could hear nothing in his right ear except for the annoying buzz.

As Steve sat on the ground, he took off all of his lower armor except for his low cut, red steel boots. With the set of greaves protecting his shins and the cuisses protecting his thighs both removed, Steve would not have to continue traveling with the extra weight. It didn't matter when he wore it while riding Clyx, but now that Steve was walking on his own, and on a time limit, he needed to be as light as possible. He wished he didn't have to remove the defense providing armor in case he was attacked by monsters, but it was a worthy compromise, all things considered.

Steve also unclasped his blue warrior's cape that hung from the back of his plate armor. Capes were an optional part of the warrior outfit. Steve usually didn't wear one, but he was today since he thought it would look cool flapping behind him as he jousted on Clyx. Now, as he realized, it only felt like a tight encumbrance, annoyingly chaffing his neck.

The warrior staggered as he walked. Everything was blurry. He had hit his head very hard on the stone street, and was feeling the effects of a concussion. It was the second one he had had in his life. They were not fun. Buildings seemed to grow tall and then short, wide and then narrow. He walked over to the buildings and put his right hand up against them, dragging his fingers along their sides. Touching something stable seemed to help his balance and stopped everything from jumping around.

Out of his good ear, Steve could hear the thundering impacts behind him as flaming boulders continued to slam into buildings. *How have they launched so many?* Twenty had crashed down since the attack began, and that was only on one side of the Circular City.

Monsters have never had that kind of ammunition, let alone the artillery to fire it. Celestial had twelve of their own catapults, spaced evenly around the city, just inside the inner wall. No matter what direction an enemy invaded from, Celestial always had every catapult ready and loaded. Steve heard the snap of a catapult somewhere from the east. The sound was a sign of hope for Steve. Warriors were still fighting.

Maybe monsters haven't broken into the city from the east. Either that or some warriors are not retreating. Even though the castle was sounding the call to retreat, warrior commanders were given the option to have their clans continue to fight if they could still do damage to the enemy without risking too many of their own men's lives.

Between how far Steve had traveled on Clyx and the distance he had dizzily stumbled, he had made it far enough towards the center of the city to get himself out of range of the monsters' flaming projectiles. That meant that there were no more burning buildings, which meant no more smoke. It was easier to breathe as he picked up his walk into a jog and his jog into a run.

Steve was unsure if he would be able to physically make it all the way to the castle after hitting his head. The dizziness and nausea were beginning to leave him, but there was an odd feeling of a dull ache in the back of his head that beckoned him to fall asleep. *My only option is to head to the nearest watchtower.*

The warriors' watchtowers were evenly dispersed all around Celestial. Even among the taller buildings of the city, these towers reached at least three times higher towards the sky. Still, they were great lengths shorter than the magnificently high towers of the castle.

There were twelve watchtowers in total. Four of them were located outside the inner wall, rising high from the farmlands. Each one was equally spaced apart and served as a distinct mark for the north, south, east, and west. The south tower was unique in that it rose out of the Darien Bay, and also served as a lighthouse for incoming ships.

From the four outer watchtowers, warriors watched over the workers in the fields to make sure there were no monster attacks from the surrounding wilderness. It wasn't easy for a monster to get to the civilians before they were spotted. Beyond the outer wall there were miles of empty plains surrounding Celestial. Whether a monster came north from Whitebark Woods, east from Valpyrio Heights, south from the Darien Sea, or east across the Prairie, they would be seen long before they even reached the farmlands. Warriors would blow into their tower's large warning horn if they spotted even one monster. The long and deep *vaarooom* sound could be heard by anyone in the farmlands. It even reached the ears of civilians in the city. After hearing the alarm, field workers would retreat into the watchtower for safety while warriors would be sent out to deal with the enemy.

The watchtowers not only served as a lookout, but also as an armory where every type of weapon was stored. Even off duty warriors were always on duty. If there was ever a major attack (as it was today), they were required to equip a weapon and armor at the nearest tower and help out if needed. King Zoran commanded that every warrior be assigned a role to play in the defense of the city if there was an attack, despite the fact the city had never been penetrated before.

There were eight towers that stood on the inside of the inner wall (within the city). Warriors from these towers watched over Celestial for any signs of fire or disasters. They also watched the four outer towers for distress signals.

Each tower had five to ten warriors on guard day and night. Every warrior had to spend at least one day, every fortnight, in their assigned tower. It was a boring job, because usually the street patrols took care of any problems in the city, but the warriors made the most of their time in their watchtower. It served as a therapeutic day and allowed each warrior to relax his stress filled mind from the difficulties of his job. If a person couldn't find a warrior on street patrol, they would always be able to alert the warriors stationed in the nearest watchtower if a crime had been committed or if they saw something dangerous about to occur.

The watchtower Steve was closest to was led by Commander Ostravaski. Steve didn't know Commander Ostravaski personally, but out of the twelve commanders in charge of each watchtower, he was said to be the strictest. Rookie warriors always dreaded being assigned to his tower. Warriors were not allowed to switch where they were drafted to when they graduated from Warrior Training.

Steve turned and entered into the plaza Commander Ostravaski's watchtower was in. The tall stone tower loomed over all the buildings surrounding it. Civilians were funneling in through the large set of doors.

Steve was in a plaza called "Big Square." It was one of four main road plazas in Celestial. The three others were called Oval Plaza, Diamond Plaza, and Little Square Plaza. Out of all four, Big Square was the largest and most heavily trafficked. It was considered an iconic landmark of Celestial.

Through the center of Big Square Plaza ran the Fluorite River. In the night, the water was an amazing sight because the riverbed was full of Fluorite Crystals. Fluorite Crystals were glowing energy crystals that came in every color. They were very common, so they weren't worth a lot, but they were beautiful to look at. The crystals illuminated the Fluorite River, giving the water a subtle glow and sparkle as it winded all the way to the castle.

The Fluorite River supplied most of Celestial's freshwater, but it did not reach the entire city. To correct this, when the city was first built, a long aqueduct was created that carried water from the northwestern part of Lake Azure, all the way down to Celestial. The aqueduct was built at a gradual decline (so that the water always flowed downwards), and used conduits to get through the hills of the Evergreen Forest that blocked its path. A city between Lake Azure and Celestial called Almiria was responsible for the treatment and sanitation of the water to make it drinkable, before it continued to flow down the aqueduct. The aqueduct ran diagonally through the Circle City on huge stone pillar arches, starting in the northwest corner before exiting into the Darien Sea from the southeastern corner. If people did not have immediate access to river water, they would be able to obtain their water from the aqueduct.

Ostravaski's Tower (as it was called by civilians) was one of two watchtowers that the aqueduct ran directly through. The aqueduct was a part of the actual tower. A lot of people had headed to one of these two towers during the siege. If an attack was bad enough, and they thought they might be trapped inside the tower for an extended period of time, they knew the aqueduct would provide an infinite supply of water.

Steve ran towards the warriors' watchtower which stood only 100 feet away. About halfway to the tower he heard a great sucking in of air above him. He looked up and saw an injured brown dragon shoot an elemental blast out of its mouth. The brown ball of energy crashed into the bottom of the watchtower. The direct impact took out a huge chunk of the stone wall. The brown dragon was brought down within the minute by an onslaught of arrows from warriors in the tower. It had known it was dying and wanted to make one last major attack. The dragon fell down onto the top of the aqueduct, bounced off, and crashed down hard onto the plaza's stone floor.

Distant screams brought Steve's attention back to the tower. The entire cylinder fortress above the puncture hole twisted, ripped, and separated from the base. It began falling over like a tall tree that had been chopped down by a lumberjack. It was slow at first, but then the fall seemed to speed up. Warriors patrolling the top of the tower fell far down to the ground, as the floor they were standing on slowly tilted from horizontal to vertical.

The shadow of the falling tower covered Steve. He sprinted across the plaza, trying to avoid being crushed by it. If he would have turned backwards and tried to outrun its height, he would have been dead before even clearing half of the tall tower. As it were, he didn't even know if he was fast enough to outrun the width as it came down. Behind him he could hear the terrible sound of the crumbling tower with just his left ear. The flat stones underneath his feet began to shake like an earthquake as the sound of destruction got louder and closer.

Steve did not turn around to look. He had enough trouble focusing on what was in front of him because of the dust that had been kicked up from the debris. It caused a dark, dense cloud of gray to spread over the plaza. Then Steve noticed another obstacle.

Ostravaski's Tower was pulling down the connected aqueduct with it as it fell. Across the entire plaza, the aqueduct columns were being torn from their foundations. Steve was trapped between the falling tower behind him and the collapsing aqueduct in front of him. He couldn't go back and he couldn't stop. His only hope was in continuing forward. He sprinted towards the aqueducts and crossed under one of the giant arches. Huge stones crashed down all around him.

Steve kept sprinting forward, dodging and vaulting over the fallen debris and rubble. He felt like one of the parkour entertainers who raced through streets and on the tops of buildings doing acrobatic flips and daring leaps.

Steve glanced back for the briefest of seconds behind him. He had successfully gotten past the trajectory of the fallen warriors' watchtower. Through the dust he saw its thousands of bricks scattered across the plaza floor. But while looking back, he also saw that the main frame of the aqueduct arch he had just passed under was coming down on top of him in one large piece.

Steve jumped through the air in full sprint and dove down into the Fluorite River. The arch of the aqueduct plunged down into the water after him, just a few feet away. The force of the weight of the crashing stone bricks pushed the river away from it. Steve tumbled along with the huge wave, crashing into burned, dead bodies bobbing up and down as they were all carried along by the river. He was propelled 100 meters, all the way to the other side before hitting the bank.

The drenched warrior threw Brightflame up onto dry land and then used both his hands to pull himself up. He tried to catch his breath, but all he could breathe in was the expanding dust that filled the air from the crumbled debris of the watchtower and aqueduct that had spread across the plaza and over the river.

How many people took shelter in that tower? How many people just died? The thoughts raced through Steve's mind as he looked back at the wreckage he was almost a part of.

After a fit of trying to catch his breath and choking on the dust, he stumbled north on the road that ran parallel to the river and led directly to the castle. Steve's hearing was barely at half capacity and now that the dust stung against his eyes, he felt vulnerable with his lack of main senses. He walked far enough to get out of the reach of the lung clogging dust.

Hearing the castle bells at closer intervals beckoned for his feet to cycle faster. Steve looked up at the insanely large castle not even a half a mile down the road in front of him. It was always a majestic sight to see, especially as he was on the castle's face side.

He looked behind him to see the wreckage of Commander Ostravaski's Tower. The ruins started to appear through the settling dust. Also appearing in the dust was a horde of monsters. Some of them were stopping and picking up weapons and armor out of the tower's rubble, but most were sprinting towards the castle. The two bridges that spanned the river and connected Big Square to the road Steve was on were bottlenecking the monsters, but they were still closing in on Steve faster than he could run.

The castle bells sounded again. They could not have been any more frequent, which meant the castle drawbridges were about to be raised. As soon as the monsters crossed a certain part of the road Steve was on, the drawbridges went up. No exceptions.

Anxiety filled Steve's mind as he knew it was going to be a race to the castle before it was closed. He was tired from all the running, but he had to resume at full speed for the final half mile. If he didn't make it to the castle in time, he would have nowhere to go except to turn back to the monsters, where a quick death awaited. Civilians were also running to the castle ahead of him, emerging from side streets and sprinting up the main road. All of them ran for their lives towards the only hope of life they had left, inside the protecting fortress of the castle.

Steve saw a woman ahead of him fall down dead, an arrow lodged in the back of her head. What looked to be her husband turned back for her, but he was shot and killed as well.

An ice blue tipped arrow grazed underneath Steve's jaw. Four inches higher and it would have been fatal. The flash of another arrow flew past his right side, but he did not hear it make a whizzing sound because of his bad ear. Looking back over his shoulder, Steve saw that a few monsters had equipped bows and arrows and were aiming at him and the civilians. He also saw that some of the monsters were twice as fast as he was at his sprinting speed. Monsters who hadn't stopped to shoot had already gained half the distance to him.

There is no way I can outrun them. I won't even make it a quarter mile before they catch up to me. Steve took a deep breath and looked at the civilians sprinting up the road in front of him. *I'm already dead, so why not buy time for them?*

Before Steve could turn around and engage in an already defeated battle, an onslaught of arrows rained down from the castle wall. The thud of the metal tipped arrows slamming into screaming monsters changed Steve's mind. Archer warriors were prolonging the time Steve had by creating a small window of separation. Steve continued running forward, as a couple of warriors fell in line alongside him from side streets.

A Giant warrior running next to Steve was hit by an arrow. Steve looked back and saw the injured man grasping at the injury, wincing in pain. He had been shot in the calf and could barely walk. Without a second thought, Steve ran back towards the approaching enemies to help the man. When he turned around, he saw a yellow tipped arrow headed right for his head. He quickly dodged his head to the side and felt the breeze of the electrically charged arrow sail by. Steve had always had good instincts, but he knew the move he just made was simply a lucky reflex.

He slid down next to the injured man. He was a warrior from another city because his armor was silver and green, instead of Celestial's customary silver, red, and blue. The Giant yelled in a deep voice, "No! What are you doing? Save yourself!"

"What?" Steve yelled back. He hadn't heard the man over his throbbing left ear, his deaf right ear, and the loudness of the castle bells. Being so close to the castle, Steve realized how loud the bells really were. He had forgotten they were made to be heard from outside the city walls. Even if Steve had heard the man's refusal for help, he wouldn't have changed his course of action. Steve lifted up the wounded soldier, who must have weighed about one hundred and thirty pounds more than him.

The Giant placed his hand on the shorter warrior's red shoulder spaulder. Steve served as a crutch for the Giant to get pressure off his injured leg. The two went as fast as they could towards the castle, but it was staggeringly slow. The drawbridge had already started to creak as its chains slowly began to pull it up. The warriors could not risk letting even one monster onto the drawbridge. All the monsters would have to do would be to freeze the large chains with a monster that had the water element and then break them by smashing them with a weapon. The drawbridge would stay down, allowing monsters to enter the castle courtyard freely.

Steve knew any warrior would feel bad to have to deny access when a brother was so close to safety. The only solitude they might find if he and the Giant died would be to shift the blame to them and say, "The bells gave them enough of a warning. It was their fault they didn't make it to the castle on time."

Steve wished he was a Giant like the man he was escorting. He could use a Giant's size and strength in this situation. The two men were moving too slowly. A fast green orc had caught up to them. Undoubtedly he had used his element of wind to increase his speed. The monster was preparing to swing his weapon into the backs of the unknowing warriors, when an arrow entered into his forehead. More of the castle archers had come and were standing on the wall above the drawbridge and in the two towers on either side of it. Now that the monsters were closer, they could all pick off the ones of their choosing instead of just launching arrows wildly into the horde.

The Giant hopped as high as he could on his uninjured leg as Steve heaved him up with a push from his other side. It was just enough of an effort to get him on top of the rising drawbridge. Steve threw Brightflame up onto it since he had no sheath to carry it in.

The drawbridge was quickly rising higher and higher. Steve reached up, but it was just out of reach. He quickly took a couple steps back and prepared for a running jump. If he missed, he would fall down into the sharp spiked and alligator infested moat below him. The alligators were not fed that often.

Steve sprinted forward, and planted his foot dangerously close to the edge of the cliff where the cobblestone road dropped off into the moat. He used every muscle in his right leg to launch himself as high as he could. The fingers of his left hand didn't get high enough to reach the edge of the drawbridge. Luckily, a split second later, he shot up his right arm and caught on with his right hand. He hung on by one arm with all his strength as the bridge continued to be raised.

Steve looked back to see the monsters, but before noticing them, he saw a Dwarf warrior running for the bridge. The Dwarf's small strides didn't allow him to run as fast as the other warriors. With a face full of fear, he was standing at the edge of the cliff, right where Steve had just been. Steve held out his free hand and yelled, "Jump!"

Their arms met and they both gripped their fingers around each other's forearms so tightly it would leave bruises. Steve had caught him. Rather, they had caught each other. Steve was glad this was just a Dwarf. He would not have been able to catch the weight of a Human, Elf, or Giant with just the one hand. Still, as soon as he caught the Dwarf he knew the sudden extra weight was too much. The Dwarf had felt Steve's body give a little bit when he had latched on. Steve's right hand started to slip from the drawbridge. If he didn't drop the Dwarf, they would both fall to their deaths.

"LET ME GO!" the halfman yelled. A warrior would always end his life before taking a fellow brother down with him. Steve declined the man's advice. He would never forgive himself if he allowed his grip to loosen and the Dwarf to fall. As he looked down at the little man, his gaze moved past him and down to the iron spikes jutting up out of the murky green water. Sadly death would not be instant. He would be impaled by a spike and unable to move, and then he would have to endure being eaten alive by the alligators.

Steve felt his hand holding the drawbridge slip again. For a brief second only the tips of his four fingers held onto the edge. He cried out in agony at the pain of his inadequate strength.

And then he lost his grip.

Chapter 6

A large hand quickly reached over the ledge and caught Steve's arm as he fell. With all of the strength in his massive right arm and shoulder, the Giant lifted up both the Human and the Dwarf, who Steve had never let go of. The Dwarf got up high enough that he was able to reach up and get both hands on the edge of the ledge and pull himself up. The Giant helped pull Steve up the rest of the way as Steve's arms felt like jelly from soreness. The three rolled down the slope of the drawbridge and into the castle's courtyard. They heard the pelting of arrows into the other side of the drawbridge, where they had just been hanging.

"Thank you for saving my life." The Dwarf and the Giant simultaneously said, as Steve picked Brightflame up off the ground.

"You would have done the same for me," Steve replied. The massive drawbridge was raised the rest of the way and made a loud clunk as it locked into the wall. Four massive iron portcullises were then dropped behind it. The bars on each gate went horizontal, vertical, and then crisscrossed in opposite directions. It would be impossible for any monster to break through their defenses. If any monsters did, they would still have to cross the courtyard and then get through the even thicker portcullis that led into the actual castle.

A doctor came rushing over to the warriors, the last three to make it into the courtyard. She looked down at the Giant's leg. "We need to get that arrow out. Come, I'll show you where we are treating warriors." The attractive female doctor got under one of the Giant's shoulders. The Dwarf hurried under the other one to help. The Giant had to awkwardly crouch to bring himself down to their level.

Steve thought about joining them and getting treatment for his concussion and the injuries to his ear and forehead, but he hated going to doctor's for help. His pride told him it was a sign of weakness if he admitted he was physically hurting.

Steve watched as the warriors and the doctor headed off together to a medical tent. Before they were out of sight, the Dwarf turned around and nodded to Steve in silent appreciation. Steve tipped his head back in acceptance. That was the last time he ever saw the Giant and the Dwarf.

Steve walked down the courtyard's main central path. Tributaries that stemmed from both sides of the path led walkers through beautiful gardens and magnificent fountains. There were also huge bushes and blocks of granite carved in the form of legendary heroes. The courtyard was open to the public at any point during the day. People would often come to this scenic place to read, write, or have a picnic. It was normally a beautiful and peaceful place, but today it was anything but serenity. There was not a civilian in the courtyard that was not physically or emotionally in pain. The wounded were being treated by what few doctors and surgeons had made it inside the castle wall. If a warrior was too injured and could not make it to one of the tents that were set up sporadically around the courtyard, they would just stay in one spot and call out for help.

The grunts and groans of warriors, men, women, and children in agonizing pain filled the air. Doctors rushed around barking orders. Steve couldn't imagine the decisions they were faced with. The goal of the limited amount of surgeons was to save as many people as possible. They had to determine which injuries were not life threatening enough that their time would not be wasted if they worked on them. Walking away from someone meant that they were leaving that person to die. The doctors would move on to someone they were sure could pull through. Anyone who wasn't injured was either trying to aid the medically trained civilians, crying uncontrollably, or consoling their friends, families, and even complete strangers about the loved ones they had lost.

Steve looked down and tightened his grip around Brightflame in his hand. He often found himself subconsciously touching his sword whenever he was saw civilians in pain. Brightflame was somewhat of a reminder that he was their protector. It was his responsibility to use the power that his sword gave him to defend the weak.

Trying to ignore the pain all around him, Steve walked on. He ran up a large set of stone steps two at a time and jogged up onto the large stone platform. Sometimes this raised stage was used for plays and musical events. Civilians could come and sit in the courtyard and watch. It would not be the last time today that Steve would find himself on the stage.

He walked across the large stone platform, under the iron barred portcullis, and through the large doors of the castle. Only invited guests were admitted past this point and into the actual castle. Average warriors like Steve were not even allowed in unless the city was under attack.

Steve had only been invited to the castle once before. After a warrior won the Qualifiers and became Celestial's official entrant for the Warriors' Jousting Tournament, they were invited to a special banquet. Steve politely declined the invitation because he wanted to celebrate along with the civilians in his hometown section in Celestial rather than in the castle. The children who drew pictures of him jousting and saved up their allowances to buy carrots for Clyx were his real fans. They were the ones who supported him over the other warriors and served as his main inspiration to win. Steve figured if there was anyone he wanted to celebrate with it was them.

The day after he won the Qualifiers, a large party was held in the closest plaza near Steve's apartment in the arena district. Everyone he knew from his life up to that point came out to support him and wished him luck in the upcoming tournament: Titus Thatcher, Ty, Darren, all of the warriors from his watchtower, and all of his neighbors in the local community. It was a very happy time of celebration. Steve could not think of any time he smiled more or laughed as much as he did that night with his family and friends surrounding him.

Everyone that came brought their best dishes of food. It was more than enough to fill the bellies of everyone in attendance. Even the stray dogs, cats, and street orphans, who had come to see what all the commotion about, were freely given a hearty amount. Steve used the opportunity of having so many people in attendance to auction off the lances and armor that he wore throughout the Qualifiers. The earnings were all given to local charities that Steve was burdened for.

The highlight of the day's events was a miniature jousting tournament for the children. The warriors from Steve's watchtower spent the entire previous night setting up a tiny arena out of hay bales. Young boys felt like the warriors they dreamed of being as they were given miniature ponies to ride and flimsy rubber lances to joust with. As a reward for participation, all of the participants were given toy replicas of Steve's sword, Brightflame. They were also all given front row seats for Steve's first match in the Warriors' Jousting Tournament.

Steve held a belief that there are winners and losers in competition, and because of this, not everyone deserves to be rewarded with the same prize. He wanted the champion of the mini-joust to receive something special. So Steve decided that the winner would become his forth squire and be the one to carry Brightflame in its sheath while he was jousting. Sadly, that boy was one of the squires who had died.

Steve was the last warrior to enter into the castle. The portcullis was dropped and the giant doors were closed behind him. He looked around the magnificent entrance lobby. The rest of the warriors numbered around seventy-five. That number should have been many, many times higher. The men stood in tight circles, whispering about what was going on and the horrors they had seen within the past hour.

A figure in a shining gold and silver armored suit walked down the long straight staircase leading up to the further stories of the castle. The voice of the man interrupted all of the conversations as he stopped and stood on the stairs, overlooking the warriors in the lobby.

Sir Lambert was the Supreme Commander of the warriors of Celestial. His rank and title were shown by the amount of gold he wore on his armor. He was King Zoran's right hand man. Steve was convinced along with most warriors, that Sir Lambert was the smartest man in the kingdom. He planned attack raids against monsters and devised intricate battle strategies that never failed. He pitted the strengths of his men against the weaknesses of the monsters they fought. Lambert had helped design the defenses of Celestial including the warriors' watchtowers. He had also created the city's defense plan in case of a surprise attack; the plan that Steve and the rest of the city had just followed.

"Archers to the walls. Aerial warriors, saddle whatever monsters are left in the high stables of the castle towers."

Steve was surprised at the Supreme Commander's calmness as he called out orders to the warriors in the lobby, telling them which parts of the castle they would be designated to. Steve found it odd that he did not spend any time explaining the attack.

As soon as a warrior heard their area of expertise called, they headed off in that direction, not waiting for the remaining orders that did not pertain to them. To the warriors who were not archers or fliers, Sir Lambert pointed to each huddled group and sent them off to different sections of the castle.

Everyone had received their orders and was running to their positions, except for Steve, who stood alone with his back to the huge doors he had just come through. He started to follow behind the closest group of huddled warriors heading towards a back end of the castle. Right before they entered into a hallway to exit the lobby, a hand tightly grabbed Steve's shoulder, forcing him to stop.

"You're coming with me, warrior."

Chapter 7

Steve turned around and looked up at the tall Sir Lambert, who stood three inches higher even though he was still considered a Human like Steve.

"Your name, warrior," the deep voice that marked the man's old age asked in a statement. There was a hint of gruffness in his raspy throat that made him sound angry. In truth, he was a gentle, caring man. The only time he did not show any mercy was towards monsters while he created the warriors' attack plans.

"Brightflame, Stephen Brightflame, Supreme Commander." Steve felt like a small, insignificant warrior as he nervously reached to shake Lambert's outstretched hand, trying to keep his own hand steady.

"I thought I was the Supreme Commander," Lambert said.

Steve was so awestruck it took him an awkwardly long time before he understood the joke. He finally smiled, hoping he didn't look like a fool to this great man he respected.

"Follow me, Stephen," the Supreme Commander grinned, playing off Steve's nervousness as if he hadn't noticed.

As he led Steve up the stairs of a nearby tower, Sir Lambert realized that he recognized the warrior's name. "Brightflame? The jouster?" he asked, not turning around as Steve followed behind him.

"Yes sir, that's me," was all Steve said.

The Supreme Commander gave out a grunted chuckle, finding it humorous that of all the warriors, it happened to be Celestial's jouster who he had selected to follow him. "I saw what you did out there," he said.

Steve instantly thought he had done something wrong by the accusatory sound in the Supreme Commander's voice.

"I watched you from the archers' wall as you saved the life of those two men at the risk of your own. Your actions were truly valiant."

"It was my responsibility as a warrior." Steve replied, letting out a sigh of relief. A part of him was wondering if he was in trouble for doing something wrong.

"Yes, but few men can make that kind of decision in that quick of a moment. We need that kind of fearlessness today."

"Fearless? I was full of fear," Steve admitted.

The Supreme Commander weighed Steve's words for the next five steps up. "True fear stops or slows down the actions your heart tells you to take. Your heart wanted to see your warrior brother survive. Without even thinking, you went back to help them even with the monsters shooting at you. What you felt was not fear, you were just scared. The difference between fear and being scared is the difference between life and death in those quick moments of instinctive choice," Sir Lambert philosophized.

Steve saw the wisdom in the Commander's words and nodded, even though the Supreme Commander wasn't facing him.

"As you may have realized, this is more than a regular attack." Sir Lambert gestured outside a small window in the tower, not taking the time to look out of it as he continued to walk up the stairs.

Steve took a glance through the curved open window. The image caused him to stop in his tracks. The view he saw would stick with him for the rest of his life. It was his first chance to see the magnitude of the destruction of the attack from an aerial view. He had known it was bad from what he experienced en route to the castle, but what he saw from high in the tower - it put everything in perspective.

He was standing in one of the two towers at the face of the castle, looking south. He saw the collapsed watchtower of Commander Ostravaski spilled across the large plaza with pieces of the aqueduct jutting sharply up out of the Fluorite River. Other buildings in his view were tipped over or had been completely leveled. He could see the large oval shape of the arena, far off in the distance. Instead of an oval it now looked more like a horseshoe because of the large section that had collapsed.

Steve looked up and saw dragons, phoenixes, gryphons, and warbirds teaming up and killing what was left of the warriors on friendly monsters. *I hope Ty isn't among them.*

A warrior was blasted off his dragon and lifelessly cartwheeled through the air before disappearing behind buildings in the distance. His monster was then viciously torn to shreds. Monsters absolutely despised other monsters that had turned sides and served the good god and his people. Few things gave them more pleasure than killing traitors.

Fires blazed in buildings all around the south, sending pillars of smoke rising up high in the sky. Past the smoke and flames, Steve could see that only one of Celestial's catapults was being used out of the two viewable from his location. Warriors were firing either one large boulder or many tiny boulders out into the advancing monster army. They were rushing to get off as many shots as they could. Even though the castle bells of retreat had sounded, they remained steadfast.

The warriors manning the trebuchet catapult must have believed they would be overtaken within minutes just like the warriors on the catapult further down the curved outer wall. Being too late to retreat to the nearest watchtower, they put their final breaths to good use and used them to kill as many monsters as they could with their projectiles.

Beyond the inner wall and the fields behind them, was the harbor. Dozens of massive ships were burning. Some were already halfway below the waters, pulling the rest of the ship down with it, to the dark bottom of the Darien Sea.

Steve turned away from the scene of destruction he saw through the window. He ran up two steps at a time to catch up to Sir Lambert. They exited onto a fourth story of the castle. Before continuing, the famous warrior turned around and spoke to Steve.

"I need a man like you to help provide an extra guard for the king. I am temporarily promoting you to knighthood, Stephen Brightflame."

Steve was speechless. "What?" he asked, half laughing and half in shock. At first he thought he had misheard the Supreme Commander. The Guardian Knights were an elite club whose job was to protect the royalty. There were only twelve of them. All were dubbed official knights and civilians were ordered to show them respect by calling them "Sir."

It had always been Steve's dream to be one of the twelve knights, one of the twelve guardians of the king. He had never heard of a temporary knight before, but if anyone had the authority to give him his new title, it was the leader of the Guardian Knights, the Supreme Commander.

Steve found justification in accepting the position he felt unworthy of. *If this is the Supreme Commander's wish then who am I to deny this warrior of legend?*

"You heard me true," Sir Lambert confirmed. "Forgive me for not taking the time to dub you officially, Sir Brightflame."

"It's only formality," Steve agreed as he tried to hide his excited smile. Thank you for the honor, Supreme Commander."

"You've earned it," Sir Lambert said, already turned around and walking again. He continued to lead Steve further into the large castle.

He seemed so composed and commanding before, calmly barking out orders. But up close, his eyes give away his nervousness. Whatever is happening, it can't be good.

Steve followed closely. They walked at a fast pace through wide and narrow corridors and through large and small rooms. Some were quickly opened by the workers who stood by them, others by a large set of keys the Supreme Commander could easily take off and then reattach to his belt. Steve began to get a headache trying to mentally figure out which compass direction he was facing.

He was convinced Sir Lambert could read his confused mind, when the man blurted out, "We're almost there." He opened a set of large iron trimmed wooden doors with his keys. A giant spiraling staircase was revealed to be on the other side.

Steve knew where they were headed as soon as he looked up and saw how high the staircase reached. He had just entered the famous King's Tower, the highest manmade building in the entire kingdom. From the top, it was said you could see for hundreds of miles on a clear day. The tower from base to tip was exactly 1000 feet.

The second tallest man-made structure in the world was a tower in a city called Misengard. That tower was only 625 feet tall, so the King's Tower was quite an architectural feat. That was the reason it was so notoriously popular. People came from far away to Celestial just to catch a glimpse of it.

As he followed in an endless upward, circular motion, Steve noticed beautiful paintings on the stone walls. All along the inside of the tower were intricate drawings and paintings of the stories of legend told in chronological order. All of the tales Titus Thatcher had told him as a child were depicted here. He had forgotten that Thatcher had told him long ago about how the stories could be seen on the stones of the King's Tower.

"They're amazing aren't they?" Sir Lambert asked Steve. Again, he was not even facing Steve as he talked, but somehow he knew the warrior was in awe of the paintings. "It's ironic isn't it? The depictions of the heroes of legend form the base of the most iconic building in the world. If it wasn't for their sacrifices and victories on the battlefield, who knows if this tower and this city would be here today?"

"Yeah, it's something isn't it?" Steve responded. *That was a stupid answer. I shouldn't have even said anything. I wish I knew a fun fact or something about one of these stories, but I doubt there is anything I know that he doesn't.*

Steve was very self-conscious about everything he said in front of (or behind, as he was) this man he admired. He wanted to make a good impression rather than embarrass himself. He turned his eyes back to the paintings. It was like watching the story play out of a hero against a villain. As soon as one ended, another began. The pictorials were just like how his mind imagined them as a child.

Steve smiled as he saw some of his favorites: the first warrior, mighty Atomis; the first friendly monster, a dragon named Frostbite and her warrior rider, Sima; and the legend of the White-Armored Warrior.

The Supreme Commander purposely did not strike up a conversation. He allowed the captivated, newly knighted warrior to marvel at the beautiful renditions of history. These were the men and women who paved the way for Steve to be in the position he was in today: a free Human, living in the greatest city on Element, who was allowed to choose whatever profession he wanted.

The last painting was of King Zoran and his legendary battle against Draviakhan. Steve slowed down and ran his fingers along the wall. Out of all the legends, this was his favorite and by far the most important.

After Oliver Zoran's story, the paintings ended. Only the gray stones of the castle tower remained. *Room for future legends,* Steve thought.

"We're almost there," Sir Lambert exhaled. He was past his seventieth name day, but was a man with the body of someone twenty years younger. Even if he were only fifty, he still would have been winded from the mountain of a staircase hike. Steve himself began to feel sore as each step was a repetition of the previous one, time and time again. His thighs and calves ached as he ascended further.

How is Sir Lambert keeping up this pace at his age? The man's body must be as strong as they say his mind is.

To distract himself from the boring, repetitive steps, Steve began to count each of the steps before he reached a window. He had determined there were fifty steps between each of the windows. As he briefly looked out each one, he saw the buildings far below getting smaller and smaller with each pass. The wind grew fiercer, whipping through the open windows the higher they climbed. Eventually, they made it to the top floor.

Steve followed Sir Lambert onto a strip of red carpet that led to a pair of golden doors. A guard stood to the side of each door. One wore a full suit of red armor, the other, a full suit of blue. Both bowed in unison at the sight of the Supreme Commander. The two warriors turned and walked towards each other and then grabbed the golden door handles at exactly the same time. Their movements mirrored each other perfectly.

Steve smiled in impression, but the smile was more for what he anticipated to see once the two veterans opened the doors. Beyond them was the only room in the entire tower: The King's Throne Room. At exactly the same speed the two warriors opened the doors and the room was revealed.

60

"Sir Brightflame, welcome to the top of the King's Tower, the King's Throne Room," Sir Lambert said with a hint of pride.

They entered into a huge circular room. Inside the throne room stood eleven of the Guardian Knights. That number became the full twelve now that the Supreme Commander joined them. These respected men were the sworn protectors of the royalty. It was the highest rank a warrior could achieve. They all had moments of heroicness that were told throughout the kingdom to warriors and to children as bedtime stories. None of the stories were so impactful that they would become legends, but they were stories that would orally live on for the next couple of generations before eventually being forgotten; either that or they were reduced to outlandish tales that only children would believe plausible.

These were the most honorable, trustworthy, and morally good men in all of Element. Two thirds of them had risen through the warrior ranks in Celestial itself. The rest had come as warriors from other cities, after their stories had reached the ears of the king, and he wanted to meet them face to face.

Twelve knights and one honorable mention. Steve felt completely inadequate among these men and knew his small action to save the Giant and the Dwarf could not even begin to compare to the sacrifices and decisions these men had made in their moments of glory.

The king's Guardian Knights were all standing around in their full sets of armor featuring red, blue, and some gold pieces. Some were talking amongst themselves in small groups, similar to how Steve saw the warriors talking in the castle lobby.

This attack has shocked them as much as everyone else. Four of the knights stood around a miniature replica model of Celestial. It was a perfectly accurate representation of Celestial on a smaller scale. Each one was pointing at different sections

61

of the city with the tiny sticks they held in their hands. *No doubt they are in the middle of planning strategies.*

Steve's eyes went to the center of the room. A magnificent tall and golden chair sat in the center of the room facing away from him. *The King's Throne! There it is!* Steve had seen paintings of it, but not even the finest color could match the perfect gold it was made out of. In the back of it, he could see a warped reflection of himself standing next to the Supreme Commander in the doorway.

In front of the throne a man stood looking out an enormously wide observatory window. His back was to Steve, but Steve saw that he wore golden armor from neck to boot. He also wore a long red cape, the same color as Steve's armor. Just as Steve knew he was entering the King's Tower, and then the King's Throne Room, he also knew right away who this man was.

The window was the widest and largest Steve had ever seen. It took up more than half the circumference of the circular tower. The view to the north was amazing. He could see miles and miles away. *Whitebark Woods. Evergreen Forest. I can even see the beginning of Lake Azure.*

Even though he didn't want to, Steve could also see the entire north side of the city. Sadly, it was just as destroyed as the south side of Celestial, if not more. He could partially see the east and west sides as well. The fires and plumes of smoke looked like a ring around the outer part of the city. This was because cheaper houses made of straw and wood were farthest away from the castle and closest to the inner wall. They burned more easily than the stone buildings towards the middle of the city. Also, most of the flaming projectiles from monster catapults in the fields could not fly far enough to hit most of the stone buildings.

The last of the monsters were climbing over the inner wall with their ladders or entering through breaches. Most of the attacking army was in the streets. All looked tiny specs flowing through the city from so high up.

A hand lightly tugged Steve's tunic sticking out of the plate of armor at his waist, bringing Steve back to reality. The Supreme Commander was already on the ground kneeling, trying to get Steve to do the same by pulling him down. Steve went down on one knee and stared down into the royal red carpet.

How could I forget to kneel in the presence of this man? He felt like a low class slave with no manners. *Everyone knows you're supposed to kneel at first sight of the king.*

"What is your report?" The golden armored man asked, still looking out the window. He had known his Supreme Commander would be the next one that walked into his throne room.

Steve remained kneeled as Sir Lambert rose and gave his answer, "Your honor, this is the largest attack we have ever witnessed. We've never had so many causalities in one day. Seventy-five warriors have made it back to provide additional support in the guarding of the castle. As you know, multiplying that number by five would still not be enough men to cover all our stations."

"Any word on Prince Silas's location?"

"We have searched everywhere, but he is nowhere to be found, your majesty. He ditched his guard and disappeared this morning." The Supreme Commander cut an angry look at two guards who stood talking to each other. Steve assumed they had been the ones who lost track of the prince.

The man breathed a deep sigh of frustration. After weighing the possible meaning of his missing prince, he asked, "Who did you bring with you?"

Steve was amazed that the king knew he was in the room, especially since the king's back was to them the entire time since they had entered. *He must have seen our reflection in the window.*

Steve continued to kneel with his head lowered. He heard the sound of clinking armor and footsteps as the man turned and began to walk towards him. Steve's heart was beating faster than the times when Ty convinced him to talk to a pretty girl.

"For his heroic sacrifices on the battlefield, that I observed firsthand, I present to you an honorary Guardian Knight," Sir Lambert announced.

Steve saw golden boots enter at the top of his view of the floor. *He* was standing before Steve.

"Rise." The man's powerful voice boomed as he commanded such a simple word. Steve obeyed and stood up, meeting King Oliver Zoran face to face.

Chapter 8

As Steve stood up, his eyes went from the golden boots, upward to the weapon the king kept in the sheath at his side. *There it is.* Steve thought. *The Aurelian Sword! The very sword Oliver Zoran used to kill the five-headed dragon, Draviakhan.* Steve stared at the long, double-edged weapon. The Aurelian Sword (also known as Aurelia [meaning golden] or the King's Sword) had a curved golden blade, classifying the weapon as a scimitar. The hilt was beautifully decorated in jewels. Five stones representing the elements were attached above the sword's optional one or two handed handle. There was a red ruby for fire, a green emerald for wind, a blue sapphire for water, a yellow topaz for electricity, and a brown jasper for earth. In the center of the circle of jewels was a large diamond. The diamond symbolized that there was strength in bringing the five elements together. The diamond was a rare jewel. It was a perfect, flawless gem, incapable of being scratched, thus making it highly sought after.

For someone like Steve, who had spent many years of his life designing swords and weapons for warriors, Aurelia was an amazing sight to behold. Steve stared in awe at the beautifully crafted weapon of the king. He finished standing up, realizing he was as excited to meet the sword as he had been to meet the king himself.

King Zoran wore a golden crown. The piece was related to his impressive sword. It also featured the five elemental gemstones equally spaced around the circular crown. A diamond just as large as the one on the Aurelian Sword was front and center. The crown had twelve spires. Twelve was an important number in the Celestial City. There were twelve Guardian Knights, twelve warriors' watchtowers, twelve catapults, and twelve cesspools.

Steve realized he had been staring at the impressive sword and crown instead of meeting the king eye to eye. He quickly lowered his gaze. Now he was looking into the king's blue eyes.

Steve heard Sir Lambert clear his throat. Once again, he was trying to quietly warn the new Guardian Knight of something he was not doing right.

I'm still holding Brightflame! Steve realized. In the same instant it crossed his mind, Steve dropped his sword. It loudly clattered on the marble floor, making all of the other knights turn and look at him. *I am royally embarrassing myself.*

Steve's face grew as red as his armor. It was considered disrespectful to hold an unsheathed weapon in front of the king. Steve had been carrying Brightflame since he left the arena because his sheath had been burned along with the squire.

King Zoran smiled at the young warrior to help relax and calm him. He could see Steve was nervous. "What is your name?" he asked.

"Stephen Brightflame, your majesty," Steve said with as much confidence as he could muster.

The king was a burly man with a black bushy beard and a full head of slicked back hair, exposing his forehead. Strands of gray lined the black hair on both his head and beard, and there were dark shadows under his eyes. These features were acquired from the stress of ruling his kingdom for the past forty years.

"Sir Stephen, I thank you for your bravery on this unfortunate day. Since you are the only one here that has been on ground level, we will need to hear your firsthand account of what you saw. But as of right now, we have hours of planning to do." The king began to turn around and walk towards the model of Celestial when he stopped and turned back to Steve.

Zoran waved his pointer finger at Steve with a puzzled look on his face. "You look familiar to me. Have we met before?"

"No, your highness, this is the first time I've ever met you," Steve said, equally confused.

"I have seen you before, but I can't remember where. Don't worry, it will come to me."

Steve wondered about how the king might have recognized him. *Maybe he saw me in a promotional advertisement from the Jousting Tournament. Why didn't I realize that's probably what he knows me from? I should have said something.*

Zoran was conferring with four of the Guardian Knights at the strategic planning table. Three of the knights stood by the large window and called out destroyed parts of the city to the king and the men around the model of Celestial, who made markings on the three-dimensional map. They marked fallen warriors' watchtowers, breached sections of the wall, and large buildings that had been demolished. The damage done by monsters was being accounted for. After it was all tallied up, the king and his advisors would be able to see where their strengths and weaknesses were.

Since Celestial had never been in this stage of an attack before, Steve wasn't exactly sure what the next step would be. According to Sir Lambert's plan, the castle would become a central hub for strategy. Doves carrying messages would be sent to the warrior occupied watchtowers, detailing what the status of the rest of the city was, as well as of any plans for counterattacks that their specific tower would be ordered to carry out. Warriors would be sent into the city on missions to battle monsters and then retreat back to their watchtower, where they would await further orders.

Our counterstrikes might begin as soon as tonight. They might ask me to lead a group of warriors in an attack, Steve hoped.

The last time monsters attacked (unsuccessfully) Celestial that Steve could remember had happened when he was a child of only six years. Steve, Ty, Darren, and Warrior Thatcher were all sitting at the kitchen table eating lunch when watchtower horns interrupted their conversation.

Thatcher immediately got up, grabbed his gear, and commanded, "Stay here until I come back." Then his voice grew ever more commanding as he spoke to the three young boys, "Do not move from your seats until I get back. Do you hear me?"

Thatcher was already locking the door behind him by the time they all mumbled out a timid, "Yes."

Thatcher fought on the inner wall, kicking off ladders and killing any monsters that made it to the top. Meanwhile, Steve and his two adopted brothers sat at the kitchen table, watching the door for nine hours, unmoving from their chairs. The next creation that came through the door would either be their adopted father or a monster. Steve had never felt such relief when Thatcher came in through that door. He, Ty, and Darren, all got up and ran to hug him.

I wonder how many children and how many wives are sitting in their homes, watching their doors right now?

In the attack where Thatcher defended the walls, the warriors had defeated the small monster army that attacked Celestial. Today's defense of the Circle City was not as fortunate. The warriors failed. For the first time monsters had won. Steve took the blame personally as part of the failure. He was a warrior. It was his job to aid in the defense of the city during an attack.

As Steve reflected the past attack and the current one, a voice caught him off guard.

"How have you been son?"

Steve turned and almost became emotional at the sight of the man standing before him.

Sir Titus Thatcher.

Chapter 9

Steve cleared all of the emotions from his throat. "The armor of a knight suits you, Commander Thatcher."

"You can still call me father, you know," Sir Thatcher said before he embraced Steve in a tight hug.

He must have felt the same way I did when I sat in that kitchen chair. He watched the attack from this tower, worrying about me as I tried to survive down there.

Titus Thatcher was the third oldest man in the throne room. The Supreme Commander was the oldest, at seventy. King Zoran was just under sixty name days. Sir Thatcher was around fifty years old. Even though he was younger than the king, he had twice as many gray hairs.

Probably from having to raise both Ty and I.

Other than Sir Lambert, he was the oldest of Zoran's Guardian Knights, but the newest addition. Sir Thatcher was by far the most honorable and wisest man that Steve had ever known.

Steve had been abandoned as a two-year-old at a watchtower by his parents. Most orphans were taken to orphanages, but for some reason Steve was left with the warriors. At the time, Titus Thatcher had just recently lost his wife. She had died in child birth of what was to be their first child. The baby died before being born. It had been early in their marriage, only three years in, but she was already gone forever. What he thought would be a relationship until he was old and gray, ended far sooner.

70

Three days after his wife died, a woman came to the warriors looking for someone to adopt her two-year-old baby boy. Warrior Thatcher accepted the opportunity, knowing it was what his wife would have wanted. He hoped that she was looking down from heaven, proud of him for taking in the child.

The warrior treated Stephen like the child he never had the chance to know. Every night Titus read Steve bedtime stories of heroes of the legends. The stories taught Steve the important characteristics a man needed to exemplify to be a hero: faith, selflessness, courage, bravery, friendship, and kindness.

He was a strict father and instilled in Steve the importance of hard work and never becoming lazy. Steve served the warriors in every capacity imaginable. He fed and groomed horses, saddled flying monsters, helped with cooking and cleaning, and sharpened weapons. At times he felt so sore, he wanted to give up, but Thatcher would never allow it.

When Steve was older, Thatcher began to teach him the art of swordsmanship. In all of those lessons, in all of Steve's childish murmurings and complaining, not once did Titus raise his voice in anger. He raised his voice many times to make sure Steve took in the point he was trying to make, but never was it harshly directed at the boy. Even as a child, Steve knew that someday his father would become a great leader in the warriors. He had a certain swagger that commanded obedience and respect from everyone he fought alongside.

The day after Steve and Ty passed their masters' tests and officially became warriors, Thatcher, who was a Watchtower Commander at the time, told them that King Zoran had personally asked him to enter into his service as a Guardian Knight. He said he had accepted Zoran's offer and was to become a knight and officially dubbed "Sir Thatcher" the next morning.

Steve believed that his father had been asked years before, but politely declined until Steve and Ty became official warriors and could financially provide for themselves.

Titus Thatcher developed Steve into the person he was, and Steve was forever grateful for him. Steve wished that he could become a man of character like Sir Titus Thatcher and teach his own future children the same values. The knight may not have been one of the legends of heroes painted on the walls in the tower staircase far below them, but to Steve he was more of a hero than any of the men or women in the stories he was told as a child.

"I've heard of your success in the joust," Sir Thatcher said as he held Steve's elbows after they pulled out of a hug. "Sorry I wasn't able to make it there to watch you today."

"Don't worry about it. I know your duties require you here most of the time. It's probably better that you weren't in the stadium anyway. I barely made it out alive. Did you have any knowledge of this attack?" Steve asked.

"No, none at all. They took us completely by surprise. It's too organized. There has never been an attack with so many monsters."

"I was thinking the same thing. There wasn't even an alarm horn from any of the outer towers."

"We have no idea how all four of them were taken," Sir Thatcher said. "There are many questions we are trying to figure out right now."

There was a moment of delay in their conversation (as well as everyone else's in the room) when two flying monsters engaged in battle outside the wide tower window; a friendly warbird vs. a green and brown feathered phoenix. The warrior and his warbird were outmatched and killed easily.

Warbirds were monsters that looked like giant-sized birds with razor sharp beaks and talons. They were unique because their feathers were one of the colors of the elements, but they could not attack with any element. Normally monsters that did not have elemental powers had gray skin, feathers, or fur. But the warbirds were somewhat of an anomaly. They did not have long lives like dragons, gryphons, and phoenixes, and were considered a lower tiered monster. Because they had no elemental abilities and could not easily be taught to obey the commands of a rider, warriors did not utilize them. The few that were used were ridden by a warrior archer, just like the one who died outside the King's Tower. They would shoot arrows at enemies while their warbird attacked whatever it felt like.

The flying monster warbird brought another one of Sir Thatcher's adopted sons to mind.

"Tyrus said he managed to switch his schedule around so he could watch your match earlier. Did you see if he made it out of the arena?"

"Yes, he did, right after he saved my life." Steve didn't want to tell him that Ty had gone up to battle in the air, where Steve saw no survivors.

"You can't let him pull away from you in this game of saving each other's lives that you two play. Is it still tied up 4-4?"

"It's four to five now," Steve corrected him with the tiniest feeling of jealousy. Ty was now leading by a point because he had saved Steve from being killed by the minotaur.

"I see he is up to his usual mischief," the knight chuckled.

Steve laughed, "You saw what he did with the horses?"

"Yes, as soon as I saw Celestial at the front of the parade, I knew something was amiss. And when something is out of the ordinary, you can be sure Tyrus is behind it." Sir Thatcher looked at the sword Steve had picked up from the floor. "You still carry Brightflame I see."

Steve saw the slight smile in Thatcher's face as he asked the question. It would probably not be the last time he made an indirect jest at the fact that Steve had been tightly clinging to his sword the first time he met the King. *Somehow Ty will find out about this and I will never live it down.*

"I haven't found a better sword yet," was all Steve could say as he purposely chose not to acknowledge one of the many nervous mistakes he had made in front of the king.

The Guardian Knight nodded in agreement, "I doubt you ever will. We all saw how much time you spent forging that blade."

As a child, Steve had been fascinated with how swords and armor were created by blacksmiths. He spent a lot of time just watching and learning the sword making process. Once Steve was old enough to lift a hammer, Thatcher encouraged him to experiment in the art. He caught on to the trade fast. Some days, he lost track of time and was punished for not showing up for his other chores.

Steve could always be found with the blacksmiths. He not only enjoyed their work, he enjoyed their company. They, in turn, thought Steve was mature for his young age and appreciated the free and uncomplaining help he supplied. The men even began to see he had a knack for the trade.

The older and stronger he got, the more Steve was allowed to experiment. Soon he was designing and creating his own styles of weapons and armor for the warriors. Steve felt a sense of pride knowing that the metal he forged was protecting the lives of warriors and in turn, protecting the lives of the people of Celestial. He felt like he was contributing his part to the brotherhood and to the city.

Steve advanced through Warrior Training and his apprenticeship very quickly. He was the second person in the history of the warriors to graduate early at age seventeen (this was a fact that Ty was jealous of). Steve had tried to find out who the other one had been, but no one he asked would tell him the man's name. The most Steve was told was that the man "should have never been allowed to become a warrior."

Knowing that he was going to become a warrior himself, Steve wanted to make his own sword. He needed a weapon he could trust to aide him in his battles against monsters. Hardness, strength, balance, and sharpness were the requirements needed in a sword. Most swords had only one or two of these characteristics. Some swords were hard and strong, which meant they lasted for a long time, but were difficult to wield and didn't stay sharp.

Over time he had written down all of his ideas and methods; what worked and what didn't. Steve believed he had created a recipe that combined all of the strengths of the swords he had made without any of their weaknesses. This new sword would not be strong in just one or two of the needed characteristics, but it would be the perfect blend of everything: hardness, strength, balance, and sharpness.

Using his own gold that he had saved up for ten fortnights, he purchased the best materials he could buy. He bought Dwarven steel, known for the strong iron and carbon it was made from. There was no finer basic metal. Steve heated up the steel until it was red hot. Now he could begin adding his own alloys, the ingredients to the recipe he had concocted.

Steve used chromium to make the metal into stainless steel that wouldn't rust. Nickel and vanadium added strength while tungsten would help provide a sharp and long lasting edge. Silicon gave the steel a rough hardness.

Each of the alloys was added in layers, upon which Steve folded over and over each other eighteen times, one for each of his name days. His special recipe of alloys mixed in with the molten Dwarven steel, creating the perfect combination of what would become the blade of his sword.

Steve poured the molten mixture onto a table and began to use his anvil and hammer to draw it into shape. Heat then hammer, heat then hammer; before it became too cool and inflexible. For sixteen straight hours, Steve hammered out the steel. With each strike it looked more and more like the sword he envisioned. Many warriors heard of what Steve was creating and stopped by the blacksmith's tent just to watch him work.

Somewhere in those sixteen hours, Steve was dubbed his last name. After so many warriors had stopped, watched, and chatted about this young, talented blacksmith, they soon found out he had been abandoned and adopted by Commander Titus Thatcher. All that anyone had ever known about him was that his name was Stephen and his friends called him Steve. Most people didn't even know that much.

When people found out Steve didn't have a last name, one of the watching blacksmiths said, "We should call him Brightflame, because even in his youth he has a knowledge of blacksmithing I haven't seen in men who have been doing this for forty years. The kid is full of potential."

An older warrior watching also favored the name, "No one spends this much time on one sword. The boy's an unending fire of perseverance. Brightflame is the perfect name."

And so the name stuck to Steve, like a fly sticks to honey. Stephen Brightflame.

After the sixteenth hour, Steve had finally reached the point where he could take a break while the metal cooled. He ate a breakfast meant for three, slept for fourteen hours straight, and ate breakfast again. It was his favorite meal of the day.

"Special days deserve more than one breakfast," was something Steve had always said. He had no idea where or who he heard it from, but to him, it was truth. After the second breakfast, he took Clyx out for a long, enjoyable ride through his hometown near the arena, around the castle, and through his favorite sections of Celestial. *May this sword be used to protect the people of this city*, he prayed. Then he returned Clyx to the stables. It was time to finish his work.

From here on out he worked behind closed curtains. The sword would be unveiled to everyone when it was fully completed. Steve used a grinder to work out the edge and point of the sword. After grinding, he stuck it in boiling water to heat it quickly, and then plunged it into the cold waters of the Fluorite River. The steel cooled fast and hardened completely into solid metal for the first time.

Steve tempered the blade by lightly heating the sword. At the same time, he coated the middle of the blade in wet clay, leaving only the edges exposed. The wet clay made the metal center of the sword stay flexible, so it could be a better absorber when clashing against other steel. The edges were unprotected by the clay, thus heating into a harder state for penetration through enemy armor in battle.

After removing the clay, Steve spent twelve hours finalizing the grinding and then using rocks to sharpen the double-edged sword. He could not touch its sides in the slightest, lest he prick his finger. Then he polished the blade. It was such shiny silver; he could clearly see his reflection in it.

The last part was the hilt of the sword. He used the long bone tooth of the first monster he had ever fought, a rare monster named Sabertooth. He wrapped it in coils and then red dyed leather to provide absorption to his hand from the impact of blows. The tooth gave the handle a slight curve at the end, making it unique. Steve felt it was surprisingly comfortable to hold.

The finishing touch was a perfect red ruby. It was the second most expensive part of the sword. The first was the Dwarven steel, but the cost of the ruby was almost equal in price. A gemstone of the ruby's size was rare. He used it as the pommel, fashioning it to the bottom of the handle of the sword.

It was wider than the handle, so it helped him keep ahold of the sword if his hand slid down too far during battle.

Steve's sword was finished. Just like the King's Sword Aurelia, it was able to be used one handed or two. Steve preferred to fight with a shield in his left hand, so his new sword would have to be equipped in only his right. The great sword had the hardness, strength, balance, and sharpness he set out for. It was by far the best piece of metal Steve had ever created. In fact, it was the best sword he had ever seen. His opinion was biased, of course, but in truth, it was one of the best weapons in the entire world. Steve never bragged about the sword he created, only gave thanks to the good god for blessing him with the ability to blacksmith.

Steve called Commander Thatcher into the closed curtained part of the tent. Steve was very proud of his work, and he wanted his father to be the first one to see it. Thatcher himself believed it was the best sword he had ever seen in his life. He gave Steve a sheath he had purchased as a present for the accomplishment (the same sheath that was burned while being worn by the squire).

Steve brought his sword out to a large crowd of warriors who had heard the work was finally complete and gathered around to see the finished result. They passed it around to a chorus of "oohs," and "ahhs." Many warriors cut it through the air, surprised by the lightweight feel of the larger bodied weapon.

"What are you going to name it?" one warrior asked. "Every special sword deserves a great name."

"I will name it after my own name. Warriors, meet my sword, Brightflame."

There were no cheers, only scattered clapping from the crowd when he announced the name of his sword, but whenever Steve thought back to this proud moment, he liked to imagine that everyone cheered.

More than once after its creation, warriors, and even townspeople, had come up and offered him vast amounts of gold for Brightflame, but Steve always declined their offers. People had even requested he make a personal replica for them. But Steve declined those as well. He could have died a rich man with some of the offers he received, but gold did not matter to the Steve. Some things couldn't be bought, and Brightflame was one of them.

Steve was enjoying catching up and reminiscing with Sir Thatcher when he heard a familiar sound of air being sucked in from behind him on the windowless side of the tower. Instantly Steve recognized it as the same sound he had heard before the dragon had blasted its element into Ostravaski's watchtower, causing it to collapse.

A monster is attacking.

A loud thump on the tower roof made thirteen out of the fourteen men in the throne room jump at the unexpected noise. The only one who didn't flinch was King Zoran. The twelve Guardian Knights drew their weapons out of their sheaths. Steve readied Brightflame. He planned to use what little energy he had left to battle whatever was above the throne room. *It's time to live up to the title of Guardian Knight.*

Immediately following a second thump, a chunk of the pyramid shaped ceiling crashed down onto Steve, Sir Thatcher, and a group of knights Sir Lambert had gone over to talk to. As Steve looked up and saw debris coming down, he pushed Sir Thatcher away with both hands, sending him falling to the floor on his butt. Steve had pushed him out of the path of the falling stones, but within the blink of an eye Steve was crushed by the tower's debris.

He was extremely dizzy from getting hit in the head and had to concentrate to fight off losing consciousness. This was the second time today he had taken a hard hit to the skull; however, neither was bad enough to completely knock him out.

Steve couldn't breathe. The wind had been knocked out of him when a huge stone piece of the broken tower fell across his chest and pinned his back to the floor.

He hated the feeling of not being able to breathe in. His face grew pale as he tried to gasp for air under the tremendous weight pinning him down. For a second, he thought he was paralyzed, but he noticed he could move his arms which were outstretched in front of him. And he could feel the weight of broken parts of the conical tower roof on his lower legs.

As he stared up through the gaping hole in the ceiling, he caught his first glimpse of the greatest living monster known to man: Nightstrike - son of the Imperial Dragon, Draviakhan. Nightstrike was the strongest and largest living dragon. His dragon's scales were the same as his father's: the darkest shade of black, mirroring the evil that was inside him. With the thickness of thirty pieces of armor stacked on top of each other, weapons and arrows were useless in damaging his body. He had horns coming out of his head and spikes on his back that were meant to ward off any aerial assaults. Nightstrike's name came from the fact that he was so large and black, that when he attacked a city, it appeared as if darkness had come early. Just like how Draviakhan was also called the Imperial Dragon, Nightstrike had a secondary name as well; he was sometimes called the Dark Dragon.

The Dark Dragon controlled four of the five elements: wind, water, electricity, and earth. He looked down into the throne room with a menacing stare followed by an ear-piercing screech. Steve watched a man with a black hooded cloak slide down part of Nightstrike's neck and then jump off, falling down through the hole in the ceiling. He landed right next to the king.

Who is that? Nightstrike has never had a rider before. No one has ever been evil enough to be worthy of calling the Dark Dragon their own.

The squared marble floor chipped into pieces underneath where the figure landed hard on his feet. The front part of his cloak was open, revealing a metal plate of silver armor. The man wore silver gauntlets which covered each of his fingers individually as well as most of his hands and forearms.

Under the gauntlets, he wore black leather gloves. He must have had shoulder spaulders on, because Steve could see the risen lump underneath the hooded cloak. Steve heard a slight jingle emit from the man. *He must be wearing chainmail underneath.* All of his armor looked like Dwarven-made steel, some of the strongest and most expensive. The man was prepared for battle.

From the waist up, he was armored like a warrior, but his legs and feet were not armored at all. He wore black pants and black leather boots (instead of steel boots). He also did not have on cuisses, which was armor that protected the thighs.

He's forgoing the protection of lower armor so that he can keep his speed. Steve realized it was similar to the strategy he had used when he took of his leg armor to run to the castle faster.

In his right hand, he held a large silver, doubled-edged sword. Its hilt was a custom-made miniature sculpture of the figure of Nightstrike. The tail of the dragon hung down and formed the handle of the weapon. The blade gleamed, having been cleanly polished. It looked sharp enough to cut through diamonds.

The man looks even more dark and evil than the dragon he rides. Steve felt the hair on the back of his neck rise at the sight of the villain. He tried to look at the man's face, but it was hidden under the darkness of the hood. *He looks like death personified. A Hooded Phantom.*

Even though Steve couldn't see him, he could tell the figure was real. It was not a skeleton or a ghoul. He moved like a person and his chest moved up and down as he breathed. Steve wondered why any person would voluntarily fight against the twelve Guardian Knights all by himself. In addition to the knights, the Hooded Phantom would also have to battle the element wielding king.

The twelve Guardian Knights started to run at the man with their weapons drawn. They abruptly stopped when the king yelled, "HALT!"

The Hooded Phantom stood tall and looked directly at the king. He took his left hand and reached underneath the hood, pulling a black leather mask off his head.

Steve saw the king's shocked face as he pulled his sword out in a golden flash and took a couple steps back.

"You! How are you still alive? I thought I killed you long ago!" Zoran's surprise was apparent in his shaking voice.

The man put the mask back on and then spoke in the most unique voice Steve had ever heard. The angry deep voice had the bass of a Giant's, the rasp of the Supreme Commander's, but also King Zoran's confidence and authority.

"I am back to fulfill my destiny. It's time for you to die," the man in black commanded.

The king roared in anger and turned his golden sword into fire.

Chapter 10

King Zoran brought his fire sword crashing down on the Hooded Phantom, who blocked it with his own two handed sword which was suddenly made out of blue water. This man had control over the elements as well. A couple minutes ago, it was believed that Oliver Zoran was the only one in the world who could say that about himself.

The Hooded Phantom crouched down and caused the king to go down on one knee by kicking him hard in the knee cap. Four of the knights were already sprinting at the figure dressed in black and silver when he stood up. His dragon hilted sword turned from blue to bright yellow, making a crackling sound. The Hooded Phantom did a 180 degree spin as an arc of lightning shot out of his weapon and blasted two of the knights hard into the tower wall. They hit the floor convulsing. The other two crashed through the large window. Whether that impact was the wall or the ground far below, the results were the same. All four of them were dead within seconds.

The king was back up and angrily swinging a brown sword made of rock at the enemy. The Hooded Phantom simply ducked and drove his foot into the king's side. The king's armor protected him from most of the blow, but it still wobbled him off balance momentarily.

Nightstrike clung to the top of the tower with his razor sharp talons and used the horns on top of its head to smash through the remaining part of the tower top. The stone debris rained down and crushed three of the knights. A bunch of the debris headed right for where King Zoran and the hooded assailant were battling. Before it hit them, it stopped in midair, right above their heads, as both men held brown colored weapons.

The Hooded Phantom nodded at the wreckage and sent the stone pieces flying away from above him. They all shot out in a circle. Some punctured through the windows, leaving tiny holes that began cracking and spider-webbing. The rest of the debris crashed into the thick stone walls of the tower, leaving large dents. Two knights were hit in the stomach by the high speed stones being mentally controlled by the Hooded Phantom. Both knights were killed as their body armor wrinkled like paper when the stones hit.

The red and blue warriors that had been standing outside the throne room doors came in to join the battle once the tower ceiling began to crumble. They, along with a knight, bull rushed the hooded assailant. They swung their weapons violently, risking leaving themselves open in exchange for hoping to land a critical hit on the excellent swordsman. Three highly skilled warriors were all attacking this man at the same time, and he killed each of them without taking a scratch.

Steve had never seen a man move so fast while delivering such precise and accurate strikes with a sword. He noticed how fluid and agile the man's attacks were. One attack flowed into another with expert speed. His instincts and awareness were incredible too. He never left himself open to be hit.

Steve was struggling to get free when he heard the groaning of someone trying to lift the heavy rock off his chest. It was Sir Thatcher. Even when lifting from the top and having Steve use all his strength to push from the bottom, the large piece of debris remained in place. Sir Thatcher tried lifting from the side to give Steve enough room to squeeze out, but this technique didn't work either.

He looked up past the face of his adopted father to the black scaled dragon above in the giant hole where it had demolished the whole ceiling of the tower. The dragon sucked in its breath and sent a chilling vapor of frost down that spread through the entire room.

Steve instantly felt colder than standing naked in a winter blizzard. He could see the clouds of his breath when he exhaled. The blood in his right ear and on his forehead froze solid. Every surface in the room was covered in a thick frost. The coldness became even more unbearable with each passing second. Steve struggled to keep his eyes open as his eyelashes were coated in frost. The cold called for him to allow his eyes to close and rest in the warmth of darkness.

Steve was about to give in to the temptation when Sir Thatcher crouched over Steve and covered him with his body to prevent Steve from freezing. Sir Thatcher's skin and armor began to frost over and he turned a shade of blue. Unlike the other knights in the room, Sir Thatcher was not screaming. He showed his strength in front of Steve.

Sir Titus Thatcher looked down at the boy he had adopted, the one he had raised, and with a shivering jaw, managed to say, "I love you, son," before ice covered his body and Titus Thatcher was frozen solid.

Steve screamed, "Nooo!" but the word froze in his throat.

If it wasn't for debris covering him, and Thatcher shielding him from the freezing vapor, Steve would have died. Four of the other remaining knights froze like ice statues where they stood. All were dead. Usually if a monster attacked with frost, the effect would only result in frostbite, but Nightstrike was no ordinary monster. His elemental attacks were incredibly strong.

The other guardians who survived the attack were moving slowly, half frozen. Crouching down into balls and covering their bodies with their shields had saved their lives.

The Hooded Phantom had turned his armor on fire, saving himself from the attack. King Zoran had been attacking with a sword of hot, sizzling water, but now it was frozen. Sir Lambert, the Supreme Commander, must have dove through the golden doors, out of the room, because he was not in Steve's field of vision.

Nightstrike screeched as he was hit in the back by a blast of electricity. A group of five warriors on flying monsters had come to battle the black monster.

Steve had thought all the aerial warriors were dead, but apparently some had survived. *Maybe Ty is still alive too.* Steve hoped he wasn't on one of the monsters that had just attacked the giant dragon. Although they had successfully lured Nightstrike away from the throne room, he could hear each one of them being easily killed by the Dark Dragon's rage.

Steve knew the two fierce fighters in the center of the throne room recognized what was happening at the same moment he did, but they were too focused on each other to do anything to stop it. The large observatory window that supported two thirds of the tower had started to crack badly from holes in it. The frost only furthered the glass splintering.

The Hooded Phantom backed away from the king, who was outmatched in the sword duel and was breathing heavily from defending himself against the vicious blows. The villain's sword was covered in hard stone. He waved it in a horizontal arc towards the golden doors and the tower wall on both sides of them. Stones emerged and ejected from the sword and pelted the wall, furthering the damage that had already been made.

If the attack was any lower, it would have hit Steve and killed him. The stones flew over Steve and through the lower part of the curved wall, badly damaging the entire length of it.

The Hooded Phantom parried a wild strike of attacks from the king before once again backing away from his enemy, who was even more winded from exerting so much energy. The Hooded Phantom raised his brown glowing sword made of stone and stuck it down into the marble floor. The throne room began to shake violently. Steve felt some of the debris shake off him. A couple loose stones from the destroyed top of the tower fell down from the quake. One smashed through a frozen knight encased in ice.

The breaking glass window spider-webbed faster and faster until the tiny lines of cracks met each other and the entire window shattered into a million pieces. On the opposite side of the tower, the wall near Steve had a horizontal crack from the stones that had hit it. The shaking of the floor further damaged the weakened wall. There was an awful creaking sound as the wall began to pull apart at the crack. The low creaking turned into a grumbling ripping as the wall broke and separated into two parts.

Since the observatory window was two thirds of the room, it had been supporting the majority of the tower above it. With the window gone and the wall disconnected, there was absolutely nothing supporting the top part of the tower.

At first, Steve thought he was moving as he lay helplessly, looking up at the white, cotton ball clouds through the hole in the top of the tower that Nightstrike had created. Then he realized it was not him that was moving, but that the tower above was tilting. It fell down on the heavier window side. The wall above where the window had been, crashed down to the floor. On the other side, the broken upper wall was lifted up and away from the floor.

Steve heard an even more awful noise than the creaking and ripping he had just heard. As the tower began to slide down, it made a bone jarring screech of stone on stone. Steve realized he was in a giant, hollow tube that had been diagonally cut in two and the top part of the cylinder was sliding down the incline.

A jagged piece of the tower wall caught the huge stone pinning Steve to the floor and knocked it off. Steve watched as the wall slid over top of him and then crashed into the ice sculpture of Sir Titus Thatcher, breaking him in two and then carrying the pieces along. The other frozen knights also broke when they were hit by the inside wall of the descending tower. The king and the Hooded Phantom both dropped to the marble floor and lay as flat as they could on their bellies. The wall came narrowly close to squeezing them both to death.

The top of the tower disappeared, falling over the edge of the floor and crashing through part of the castle roof far below. Steve heard part of it fall into the moat because there was a slight splashing sound.

Hopefully it crushed some monsters waiting outside the castle, he thought. Steve looked around and saw that there were no more Guardian Knights. If the men hadn't been hit by electricity, crushed by debris, impaled by the Hooded Phantom's blade, or frozen by Nightstrike's freezing vapor, they were killed when the falling tower took them down with it.

Only the Hooded Phantom, the king, and the Supreme Commander had ducked and dropped flat to the floor in time. In addition to Steve, these were the only four men that had survived. The golden throne and the model of Celestial were still in the room, but they were knocked over.

Those things are worthless compared to the lives that were just lost, especially my father's life. Steve knew it was not time to get emotional over the loss he had just suffered. All he could do in the moment was vow that he would kill both

Nightstrike and his rider for killing the man who taught Steve everything he knew and made him into the man he was.

Steve wiggled his way out of the smaller and lighter debris, now that he had been cleared of the main weight holding him down. He stood up, but was almost knocked back down to the marble floor. There was a strong wind whipping over the open circle platform high in the sky with no walls or windows to block it. Steve got on his hands and knees and frantically searched for Brightflame in the rubble. He had dropped it when he was crushed. *It has to be around here somewhere.*

Meanwhile, the king and the Hooded Phantom fought back and forth, swinging their swords at each other, while their weapons kept turning different colors. They were both fighting with all five of the elements, fire, wind, water, electricity, and earth. Flashes of elements filled the air. The king's red cape and the hooded man's black cloak flapped behind them as they fought in the high winds.

King Zoran's attacks and defenses were getting slower with each deepening breath. The Hooded Phantom rained down an array of blows which the king defended, but it backed him up dangerously close to the edge of the floor. Falling off the side would mean falling to death. The king rolled out of the way, dodging an attack. The genius move positioned the Hooded Phantom in between the king and the drop off to death.

But it was the Hooded Phantom who got the upper hand after he dodged Zoran's aggressive attack meant to send him flying off the edge. The Hooded Phantom stabbed the off-balanced king straight through his right pectoral. If it had been the left side of his chest, the sword would have pierced his heart.

Zoran loudly grimaced in pain when the Hooded Phantom pulled the sword back out, covered in blood. The Hooded Phantom then capitalized on the king's blinding pain and swung his sword in a downwards arc. It went through the king's golden armor and more than halfway through his thigh. There was a loud snap as the force dislocated his femur from his pelvis.

King Zoran fell to the marble floor, writhing in pain. He suppressed his screams with a grimace. The Hooded Phantom stood over him, peering down at the king through his leather mask.

"Why don't you kill me already?" Zoran asked, trying not to sound like he was begging for a favor.

"I already have." The Hooded Phantom had barely finished the sentence when the Supreme Commander almost impaled him through the back. The Hooded Phantom turned around just in time to block the attack. Steve found Brightflame and quickly ran to the king's side and crouched down next to him. Behind him he heard the clanging of steel on steel as the Supreme Commander used all his energy to battle the villain.

Seventy name days. Steve, as well as Sir Lambert, knew he wouldn't reach seventy-one the moment he picked a fight with the leader of the monster army. At some point earlier in his life, he might have been a worthy challenge, but all he could do now was grant the king an extra minute of life.

Kneeling down beside King Zoran, Steve looked at the man sitting with a pale and blank look on his face. Blood ran down his golden armor from where he had been stabbed through the chest. One leg was straightened out, the other lay crooked and broken. Steve examined the wounds and gulped.

There is no way he will be able to survive. Steve wished there was something he could do to heal the king so that this great man could live to fight another day, but his life was quickly ending.

King Zoran turned to look at Steve. With his uninjured left arm, he grabbed the warrior by the armor and pulled him close. The king squinted, trying to get a closer look at the young man.

"You have the same blue eyes. I remember now...I remember who you are," Zoran said with the brightest of smiles. The expression was uncharacteristic for a man who had just been mortally wounded.

Steve was confused by the king's revelation. Before he could ask, "What?" the king said, "We have met before, but you don't remember."

Chapter 11

A puzzled Steve turned around when he heard the metal clanging stop and a man yell out in pain. The Supreme Commander's sword arm lay on the marble floor, disembodied, with his weapon still gripped in the fingers of the hand. The Hooded Phantom savagely grabbed him by the throat and held him up into the air with one hand. Supreme Commander Lambert hit the Hooded Phantom repeatedly with his left hand, trying to break the hold. Sir Lambert twisted, turned, and kicked, but could not escape the death grip. The Hooded Phantom wasn't trying to slowly choke him to death; he was trying to crush the man's throat with his hand.

And he succeeded.

Steve saw Sir Lambert's eyes bulge out of his head and his throat cave inwards and collapse under the pressure. The Hooded Phantom tossed the dead Commander over the floor ledge. In less than five minutes, the twelve famous Guardian Knights had all been killed.

The Hooded Phantom casually walked over towards Steve and the king. Steve stood up to meet him in attack stance. With Brightflame out in front of him, he looked at the Hooded Phantom. From where Steve stood, it looked like there was nothing but shadows and darkness under the hood. He could see no face. It was concealed by the creepy black leather mask. Steve couldn't imagine what was behind it. The only thing he saw was moving, piercing eyes behind the slits in the mask. One was brown; the other was a milky white. Steve could only see a little of what was below the mask. There was some viewable flesh on his neck. He had white skin, like Steve, but it was bruised and damaged in ugly purple and red.

Steve was afraid for his life, but he did not let an ounce of fear show in his face. He tried not to cringe at the hauntingly deep and chillingly slow, raspy voice.

"You've seen what I've done to your warrior brothers. Yet you would stand against me? You would die for this king?"

"I would die for this kingdom," Steve said, surprising himself by the power in his own voice. Without thought, he swung Brightflame. It reached dangerously close to slitting open the throat of the Hooded Phantom. The enemy did not flinch in the slightest.

"Then die you shall," he said coldly while his sword turned to fire. Steve felt the heat of the blade on his face as he deflected blow after blow. The speed of the enemy's attack seemed unreal. Steve felt like every swing of his opponent's blade was going to cut him. He didn't know how he blocked the attacks, but he knew if he was even a tenth of a second slower at any moment, he would be dead. He also knew to watch out for the man's kicks with his black leather boots. The Hooded Phantom had caught the king off guard with some of those powerful kicks.

Where did he acquire these skills? At some point he must have been a warrior, but his skills are much more advanced than what we are taught.

The Hooded Phantom switched over to green, and the already strong wind picked up around Steve. He swore that when he fought, there were times he felt his feet begin to leave the floor. But Steve held his own, blocking attacks while digging his foot under some of the debris to keep himself grounded.

The man's hits were so hard that each one sent a jolt through the ringing steel of Brightflame and pained Steve's arms. There were times he didn't even feel like he was gripping

93

the red leather handle as his fingers and forearms were turning numb. *I'm surprised one of these hits hasn't knocked Brightflame out of my hands.*

Steve managed to surprise himself by parrying a couple attacks. The opening allowed him to swing his sword at the Hooded Phantom, but the elusive man easily ducked and dodged out of the way.

Steve was hoping to land a lucky deathblow. He needed to kill this expert swordsman sooner rather than later. Steve was confident in the swordsmanship skills he had learned in Warrior Training, as well as what Titus Thatcher had taught him, but he knew he was no match for the skill of this enemy. He would not survive a technical duel. His chances of landing a killing blow were a long shot, but he would not give up.

Steve tried everything he could. He threw rocks and debris. He bull rushed, trying to get the Hooded Phantom to take a misstep and fall off the edge. The last tactic he tried seemed to work the best, but it didn't help in the attack at all. He picked up a fallen Guardian Knight's shield to help defend against attacks while he swung Brightflame with one hand instead of two as he had been. The sword and shield was his most comfortable set of weapons in battle.

Nothing was working for the young warrior. All he could do was prolong the battle and hope for a misstep by the Hooded Phantom. Even that was a bad strategy because Steve would probably make fifty mistakes for every one that his talented opponent made. The odds were stacked against him as the Hooded Phantom remained in complete control and composure.

Steve reached a point when he could not physically take anymore. His attacks and defenses were slow. His arms, legs, and torso ached, and he could not catch his breath. Luckily, a man walked up onto the circular floor from the tower stairs.

King Zoran called out the name before Steve broke concentration to see who it was.

"Prince Silas."

Silvanus (Silas) Zoran was the son of the king's late daughter. He was the one and only heir to the throne since the king's only daughter had been murdered. The prince looked similar to his grandfather but better in every way. King Zoran was known as a big, strong, and good looking man, but his grandson took those three characteristics to a new level. If anyone had what was considered a man's body, it was Prince Silvanus. His body was immense. He was not fat; he just had a huge frame. He was stocky with broad shoulders and wide hips. The prince was taller than even Sir Lambert, a mighty tower at 6'8". Muscles naturally rippled his body without the need to work out to maintain them, but he lifted weights anyway, making himself even stronger.

Few men were as physically blessed as he was. Also similar to King Zoran, was his hair. They both had dark black hair. His however, was wavy instead of straight and slick. He wore it at a medium length. He parted his hair down the middle of his head, having it fall to the sides over his ears and away from his brown eyes. It stopped at the line of his wide and strong jaw. The prince had a wide face and a large, strong chin. He grew out a goatee which gave him a sense of attitude and superiority, further adding to his already enhanced ego.

Prince Silas's ego was his main attitude problem (out of many). Silas Zoran was physically similar to King Zoran, but morally and as a person, he was the complete opposite. It was a running joke that the prince was so wondrously gifted physically that the good god must have forgotten to give him an attractive personality or discernment in making morally good choices. He was an absolutely horrible person. He was selfish and impatient. The smallest inconvenience would awaken his wild and violent temper.

Steve never cared for the prince. He had met him a couple of times before in his life. Most recently, the prince had come to meet Steve after he won the Celestial Qualifiers. The meeting was not pleasant.

It happened just a week and a half ago; on the same day Steve had had his party after winning the Celestial Qualifiers. The prince always jousted against Celestial's winner in a friendly exhibition match the weekend before the tournaments began. Everyone knew the match was fixed. Since Prince Silas started the tradition at the age of twelve, he had not lost once. Steve had not accepted the castle's invitation to hold his celebration there, so the Prince had to come and find Steve to schedule the match.

That night, after the community celebration, Prince Silas came to Steve. The warrior was putting Clyx to bed in the stables, who had just spent the whole day giving rides to children. Steve knew the prince had not come to politely introduce himself and meet Celestial's winner. He came so he could set a time to joust and command Steve to take a dive, as he had told every warrior prior. Prince Silas wanted this year's exhibition to have the same outcome as the past seven.

Steve could tell how strong the prince was from his size. Silas probably could have defeated Steve without needing him to purposely lose. But the fact that Silas had to ask Steve to lose meant he had no confidence in himself. All he cared about was how he appeared to the civilians of Celestial. Silas thought he always needed to appear strong and powerful since he would be king someday.

"Is this the famous Clyx?" the prince asked Steve as he walked over to the horse. When he went to feed Clyx a carrot, Clyx bucked and smashed his front legs into the prince's chest, causing him to stumble backwards and fall into a huge pile of horse droppings.

Clyx always acted mischievous around people that he sensed were evil. He strongly felt this way towards Prince Silvanus. The prince angrily pulled himself out of the pile of feces. His white cloak and tunic were covered in the stinky brown mess. He swiftly walked over and punched Clyx in the jaw and then drew his sword to kill the horse. Steve quickly reached for Brightflame, but realized if he did draw it, he would be cut down by the five Guardian Knights protecting the heir to the throne.

As the prince brought his sword down, Steve jumped in front of Clyx with his arms outstretched, guarding his horse. The prince stopped his downward swing just before hitting Celestial's jouster. He spat in Steve's face and yelled as he hurriedly walked away, "I hope that horse receives a sharp lance through its head during the tournament."

Before that incident, Steve had heard many stories of the careless prince. He was always drinking, gambling, and sleeping with loose women (and it was rumored men as well). The spoiled child, who was exactly the same age as Steve, had no respect for authority and acted as if he were entitled to anything and everything. He treated all of the civilians as if they were below him and did not deserve to be in his immaculate presence.

Steve didn't like the prince because of the things he had heard, but the moment Silas pulled his sword out to kill Clyx, Steve hated the man. It was time someone taught him a lesson. Before the prince walked out of the stables, Steve yelled out, "If you want to joust, we do it tonight!"

When the Hooded Phantom saw Prince Silas come up the stairs in his full suit of shining white armor, he swung his rock encased sword upwards at Steve. Steve blocked the attack, but the force was so hard that it sent him flying backwards, airborne through the air. He dropped Brightflame as he painfully crashed down on his butt and back. The marble floor didn't stop his movement. He continued to slide. There was nothing to catch on to, nothing to stop him from sliding off the edge of the platform. Steve's eyes widened as he began to fall.

He reached up his hand and caught onto the ledge before he fell. His feet were dangling and the wind felt like hands wrapping around his legs, trying to pull him down to death.

The whole time he was testing me, playing around. He wasn't even using the full extent of his powers. Steve felt like a fool for even briefly believing that he was actually holding his own in the fight. He tried to lift himself up, but could not find the strength to pull his body all the way back up onto the ledge.

Steve looked down from where he hung and saw where the broken tower had smashed into the castle ceiling below. His hands almost slipped as he felt dizzy from the height. He quickly took his eyes off the ground and stared straight ahead.

"I shouldn't have done that. I shouldn't have done that," he said repeatedly, vowing to himself never to look down again.

The strong wind picked up and began whipping his body around like a flag. *I can't hold on much longer.*

Prince Silas walked over to his grandfather, the king, who looked even more ghostly pale, sitting in a pool of his own blood. The prince removed the king's two-piece plate armor as well as his chainmail. His white undershirt was drenched in blood, making it stick to his chest. The prince smiled as he examined the wound.

"Get out of here, Silvanus! This enemy is too powerful."

"I know, old man. I know of his power and I know his identity. I found out everything. Why did you never tell me? Did you think I wouldn't eventually find out?"

The prince's deep and manly voice had an annoying quality to Steve. Steve hadn't thought about whether or not he realized the voice was annoying until before or after he had decided he disliked the prince after he attempted to kill Clyx. The voice was a mixture of the prince trying to sound authoritative, while also having a bit of cockiness.

Silas picked up the king's Aurelian Sword that was lying on the floor next to where King Zoran sat. Steve pulled himself up just enough from the ledge so he could see eye level with the marble floor.

"You told me as a child that you believed I would be the one who would eventually fulfill the prophecy hidden in this sword," Silas Zoran said as he looked up and down the sword, admiring the beautiful golden design. "After all these years, I finally get to see what it says."

Silas stared at the blade of the sword and looked closely to see what the prophecy said. The prophecy could only be seen by someone who was a bloodline heir to the throne or the king himself. Silas and King Zoran were the only two people in the world that fit those qualifications. Zoran had decided never to allow the prince to see the prophecy until the boy took the throne and became king. Prince Silas was frustrated and annoyed every day that the secret was kept for him. He didn't have to be kept in the dark any longer.

After the prophecy appeared to him sentence by sentence, the prince finished reading, and a look of disappointment filled his face.

"This can't be true! THIS CAN'T BE TRUE!" he yelled.

"It is," was the only two words the king said back.

"You've known this all along! Tell me who he is," Silas commanded of the king.

The king offered no answer in response. The ends of his mouth turned upwards in the faintest of smiles.

"TELL ME WHO HE IS!" Silvanus screamed at his grandfather, hating to see that the king knew a part of the prophecy that remained a mystery to him.

Zoran shook his head sideways. "Never," he defied, putting an abrupt end to the requests. "I will never give away his identity."

Steve could have sworn that for the briefest of seconds, King Zoran's eyes flashed over and looked at him.

"It doesn't matter. The prophecy still speaks of me. I will find him, and I will kill him. It is my destiny to lead the monsters to victory. Nothing can stop me," Prince Silas declared, sounding as if he was trying to convince himself as much as he was his grandfather.

"That may be..," Zoran said grabbing Silas and pulling himself close to the prince so that he could whisper in his ear. He wanted his grandson to be the only one to hear what he had to say. "But you and I both know what the prophecy says: whatever happens, you are going to die."

"Then...at least...I will die as the king," the prince stuttered. The shock of the prophecy's revelation of his death was written all over his face.

He reached up and took the crown off Zoran's head. Prince Silas had dreamt of this moment since he was a boy. Becoming the king was going to be the happiest moment of his life, but he had no joy as he placed the crown on his head. He couldn't stop thinking about the prophecy. Its revelation robbed him of his happiness.

Silvanus glared at the king, making sure that his dying breath would be knowing his grandson betrayed him to become the new king. Silas turned the Aurelia into ice and went to stab it through his grandfather, but for a brief moment, he hesitated. He looked back at the Hooded Phantom who stood and watched him. The mask showed no emotion except for the sparkle of anticipation in his only working eye.

"Kill him," the Hooded Phantom said impatiently. The command came from years of pent up anger towards Oliver Zoran.

The realization that his grandson, the heir to the throne had turned evil was hard to bear for the dying king. He felt more pain from the weight of that fact than from the pain he was feeling from battle damage. Zoran then said something aloud which no one in the room fully understood except for himself.

"I chose the wrong one."

"Kill him," the Hooded Phantom commanded again before Silas could question what the king had said.

When the prince continued to hesitate, the Hooded Phantom began to walk forward to finish off the king himself. He had already inflicted enough damage to Zoran that he would die before the day ended, but he didn't want to give him the luxury of extra hours of life.

Prince Silas turned from the Hooded Phantom and back to Zoran. Silas had requested that he be the one to deliver the killing blow. The Hooded Phantom couldn't have made the killing any easier for the prince; Zoran was about as dead as any live man could be.

The prince placed his ice sword onto the king's injured and unarmored chest. Instead of stabbing him straight through, the prince pushed the blade downward at an angle. The blade went ever so slowly into the king, ripping open his internal organs and cementing his already inevitable death. His grandson was torturing him in his final moments, but King Zoran was already beyond the point of feeling any pain. To him, his body felt numb. If his eyes hadn't been open, he wouldn't have even known he was being stabbed again.

Zoran reached up and knocked the prince's hands off his sword, the one that he used to win the most important battle in known history. King Zoran put his own hands on the hilt and pulled the sword the rest of the way into himself.

As he did, he spoke with strength and confidence, "If you want to kill me, do it quickly. The sooner I die, the sooner someone will rise to defeat you."

This time there was no denying that the king looked directly at Steve as he spoke. Then the king said one more thing that Steve would never forget.

"As long as there is darkness, there will be light to fight it."

Those were the last words that King Oliver Zoran ever spoke.

Steve watched as the king's eyes closed and his head and shoulders slumped forward. The king was dead with his own sword punctured through his front and out his back.

"Well done, prince. Well done," the Hooded Phantom rasped. The prince grabbed the handle of the Aurelia and pulled it out of the dead body. The sword, the crown, and the throne now all belonged to him.

A rage filled Steve like none he had ever felt before. Adrenaline gave him the strength to pull himself up and over the edge of the platform. He stood up and sprinted straight for the prince, not slowing down as he bent down to pick up Brightflame.

"BETRAYER!" Steve screamed in anger as he jumped through the air with his sword held over his head. He forcefully swung it in a downward arc in an attempt to cut the prince into two halves from skull to crotch.

The prince never saw the attack coming.

In midair, a second before Steve brought the blade down, a blast of electricity shot the warrior in his red armored chest. The force threw him sideways through the air, and he crashed onto the top of the tower stairs. For a second, he felt the same nauseous feeling he had after being launched through the air from the boulder that killed Clyx.

Steve lay paralyzed. He couldn't move his arms or legs. It was a disturbing feeling, being able to think about moving his arms and legs, but being physically unable to do so. The more he wanted to lash out in anger at the inability to move, the angrier he became. After a minute, he realized that all he could do was be patient. As he lay uncomfortably contorted on the stairs, he heard the Hooded Phantom speaking to Prince Silas.

"I have dreamt of this day for over twenty years. All the time I spent planning and preparing has paid off. Zoran is finally dead and Celestial belongs to us," The Hooded Phantom declared. Even though the words he spoke were of accomplishment, there was no tone of happiness or satisfaction in his shallow voice. He did not even bear a smile, let alone a grin underneath his leather mask.

"There is no one to stop us now," the prince agreed. Unlike the Hooded Phantom, the prince was smiling as he repositioned his new crown atop his head and admired his new golden weapon.

The Hooded Phantom found fault in what the prince had just said. "There was never anyone who could stop us. And there never will be anyone or anything. It is impossible to stop destiny."

"You got what you wanted. Zoran is dead and Celestial is defeated." The prince thought that summarizing the outcome of the siege would brighten the Hooded Phantom's spirits. At the very least, maybe he wouldn't always sound so angry when he spoke.

"Yes, but it is only the beginning. We have a lot of work to do," The Hooded Phantom responded. "Misengard awaits."

"When should we order the army to start marching north?" Silas wondered.

The Hooded Phantom answered somewhat annoyed, "Why are you asking me that? You were the only heir. The king is now dead. Are you not the ruler of the kingdom now? Are you not holding the King's Sword in your hand and wearing his crown on your head? You are the king. You make the commands."

"They will leave in the morning," the large-muscled and white-armored prince said meekly.

"When tomorrow?" The prince's answer had not been sufficient enough for the Hooded Phantom.

Silas gulped in nervousness. "In the morning."

The Hooded Phantom cocked his head. Again he wanted a more precise answer. Prince Silvanus knew it was impossible to appease the man standing before him. He could never read the emotions of the man behind the mask. He was the only living man that the prince feared now that King Zoran was dead.

"At the break of dawn. At the break of the dawn," he stuttered. "That is when they will go to Misengard. Every town and village along the way will be attacked and taken over."

Now that the Hooded Phantom had received his answer and was no longer annoyed, he spoke more plainly to the new king. "Our god believes you will be the one to fulfill the prophecy hidden inside that sword you carry. You are the catalyst. He has given the both of us the power of the elements to use against the good god's creations to end this war with victory in his favor. No matter what happens, we cannot be defeated." The Hooded Phantom repeated something he had said just minutes before. "It is impossible to stop destiny."

"Destiny," Silas said aloud in a depressed chuckle. For him it was both a gift and a curse. The prince looked down at Aurelia and found a small glimmer of hope among its foreboding secret words. Based on what the prophecy said, his destiny was that he would lead monsters to worldwide victory, but it would only be achieved through the sacrifice of his life. The Hooded Phantom did not know the prophecy's words and Silas wanted to keep it that way. He didn't want anyone to know about his upcoming death. He would die as a king and as a hero of legends (among monsters). Both were titles he had lusted after since his youth. They would grant him the respect that he always wanted in his life, but never felt he had received.

"What do you say we introduce Celestial's civilians to the wonderful 'destiny' we have for them?" the prince asked without lacking sarcasm.

"It's time they learn what they were created for," the Hooded Phantom agreed.

"Indeed it is," Prince Silvanus said with an even brighter smile. He repositioned the crown on his head and gestured his arm towards the tower stairs.

"Lead the way, father."

Chapter 12

Steve heard the sound of boots crunching debris getting louder as the men got closer to him. The two villains stood above Steve and looked down at the helpless warrior. They looked like complete opposites since the Hooded Phantom was dressed in all blacks and silvers, while the prince stood in all white.

"He's still alive," the Hooded Phantom blatantly stated. Steve wasn't sure if it was a question or a statement, but there was an ounce of surprise in his raspy, angry voice.

The prince's face got red and scrunched in anger as he looked down at the paralyzed warrior. The prince recognized the man in the full suit of red armor.

"It's him! This is the jouster that made me look like a fool!"

It was true. Steve had been furious at Prince Silas after he attempted to kill Clyx. Most people had gone home after Steve's day of celebration had ended, but then news of what had happened in the stables started to be spread from door to door. Someone mounted a horse and rode down the streets yelling, "Prince Silas versus Stephen Brightflame in the arena tonight!"

Three hours after the incident in the stables, the match started. Everyone who had been at the day of celebration walked to the arena, since Steve's community was less than five minutes away. It had been such a fun day of celebration that Steve's neighborhood had never experienced before. He was the first jouster from the arena district to win the Qualifiers. Everyone was disappointed when the day of celebration ended, but now the excitement would continue.

People dropped what they were doing and ran to the arena. Even from their homes miles away, people ran or took horses to make sure they didn't miss the event. Parents brought their children with them despite the fact that on an ordinary night they would be getting them ready for bed at this time. But this was no ordinary night. Unexpected, exciting events rarely happened in Celestial. No one wanted to miss out on what was about to go down in the arena. It was sure to be the talk of the city for the next week.

It was a beautiful fall night. It had just turned dark, and the blue and red moons (which were the origination for the colors of Celestial) both shined gorgeously in the sky. The night air was the perfect temperature.

Thousands of people piled into the torch lit stadium. The stands were completely full. People were pressed together with no space in between them. A large portion of the crowd stood on the sand floor of the stadium because there were no seats left to sit in.

Prince Silas versus Celestial's Qualifiers winner had attracted less and less of an audience with each passing year because people always knew the prince would win. Based on the rumors of what had happened, everybody in the arena knew Prince Silas was not guaranteed victory like he always had been in the past. They all wanted to see him defeated; now more than ever, since they had heard that he tried to kill the fans' favorite horse, Clyx. There were more people for this exhibition than for some of the Qualifier's matches.

The crowd was going absolutely crazy.

In his Celestial red armor, Steve hit the prince as hard as possible with every pass, powering his lance into the prince's shoulder, stomach, and head.

Some civilians had been hesitant to come to the arena, figuring the incident in the stables and the abrupt setting of the jousting match was just a ruse Prince Silas used to try to get people to come watch him. Once they heard that Steve was purposely trying to not only defeat the prince, but also trying to hurt him, they too ran into the arena and added their cheers to the record breaking crowd.

The prince felt the painful hits from Steve's lance, but felt even more pain from the cheers of the audience enjoying seeing their warrior hit him. His temper hit a boiling point and his anger cost Steve. The prince turned out to be an exceptional jouster when he was mad. Steve figured that Silas's large build and strong muscles would aid him in jousting, but he didn't think they would be enough to compensate for his inexperience.

Steve was wrong.

The white-armored prince scored three consecutive major hits that gave Steve bruises that he could still feel.

Back and forth the two jousters battled. Steve would get the upper hand, but then the prince would steal the momentum. It all came down to the last pass.

Steve had never heard a crowd so riotously loud. It brought a smile to his face as everyone chanted his name. His armor was damaged, and he was hurting; but the cheering sent rushes of adrenaline through his body, and he forgot all about the pain.

Clyx and the favored warrior charged forward at the rising of the flag. The prince did the same on his huge white destrier from the opposite direction. The crowd went completely silent as the two men raced towards each other. A blur of red and a blur of white were about to collide. Not a sound could be heard other than the horses' gallops.

Steve aimed his lance and smashed it straight into the helmed face of the prince. The powerful blow to the head knocked Silas unconscious. He fell hard to the ground, unhorsed.

The massive crowd erupted in cheers and ran from the stands and into the center of the arena, surrounding Clyx and Steve. Two Giants lifted Steve up, between their shoulders, as everyone stood around cheering the awesome outcome of the exhibition. The Giants carried him all around the stadium so that everyone got a chance to congratulate their champion and see him up close. It was a classic tradition in jousting that was rarely done.

Steve had already had a large fan base from winning the Qualifiers, but it grew exponentially because of his gutsy rebellion against the unpopular member of the royal family. When Steve advanced far in the jousting tournament, it was hard to find a Celestial civilian who didn't want to cheer for the warrior. Some visitors from other cities even preferred Stephen Brightflame over their own jouster.

"This boy beat you?" the Hooded Phantom asked in surprise. He glanced down at the size of Steve compared to the size of his massive muscled son.

The prince's temper flared at the tone of mockery in his father's voice. He lifted the King's Sword to end the life of Steve. Before he brought it down, the Hooded Phantom stopped him.

"No. He has a lot of fight in him. People like this are better to be made examples out of. Tonight during our address, we will hang him. Let him be a lesson that anyone who tries to leave the city, fights back in any way, or disobeys our orders will die like this boy."

The prince motioned to a monster that had come up the stairs to greet his leaders. "Visuvis, take this warrior to the prison cells. Keep him alive. Prepare the gallows. I will be the one to hang this warrior."

"Yes, master," Visuvis said, bowing to his new king before looking down at Steve.

"And I don't care if he comes to me covered in scratches and bruises. Just keep him alive," the prince said as he followed his father down the circling tower stairs.

Steve could tell this monster was of high rank based on the amount of armor he wore which fit well on his body. *Monsters don't spare highly valuable armor on anyone.* The large, dark brown furred minotaur reached down and tried to take Steve's sword. Steve gripped it firmly in his hand. It wasn't until the monster painfully stepped on Steve's forearm, that he involuntarily released Brightflame.

Visuvis held Brightflame up to the bright yellow sun and examined it. He saw how well-crafted the warrior's sword was. He took an old silver mallet out of his sheath and replaced it with Steve's sword. The smiling minotaur looked down at Steve and watched as the injured warrior began to move his hand towards the sword as it was taken away from him.

His paralysis was wearing off. Visuvis reckoned that an unmoving prisoner was easier to transport than a flailing one. He lifted his metal boot, covered it in hard rock using his element of earth, and brought it down hard on Steve's face.

Steve spent a couple of hours locked in a dark cell in the underground castle dungeon, passing in and out of consciousness. Visuvis would come in sporadically and beat him senseless. After taking a solid punch on the jaw, Steve felt his right ear pop and his hearing come back. He wished it hadn't. All he could hear from his cell was yelling and screaming from people somewhere in the castle.

After a while, Visuvis forcefully lifted Steve up and pushed him out of the cell. They made their way out of the dungeon and back up into the castle. The two stopped before a giant set of wooden doors. Steve realized he was standing where he had already stood today. It was the doors he had come through earlier, leading into the castle lobby, where Sir Lambert had stood and called out orders to the seventy-five warriors.

Steve could hear someone giving a speech from the other side of the doors, but he could not hear what was being said. He heard the muffled sound of someone yelling out, but could not make out any of the words. There was a crackle of thunder followed by a flash of lightning that Steve saw from between the seam of the two doors. He heard cries from children, screams from women, and yelling from men in the crowd.

After a minute of more mumbling from the other side of the door, it opened. The yellow and orange sunset blinded Steve's eyes. The change from the darkness of the dungeon cell to the bright light was painful. He couldn't block his eyes with his hands because they were tied together behind his back. When he squinted to block out the sun, he saw tens of thousands of people standing before him. He was on the large platform in the huge castle courtyard. Hours before it had been a medical attention site for wounded civilians and warriors.

It seemed like every person in Celestial had been gathered here. Smoke pillars from fires rose to the sky from all over the city beyond the castle wall. There had to be hundreds of fires. After the sun went down, the entire city would still be lit as if the sun hadn't left for the night.

The monsters had made a bonfire from the dead bodies of civilians that had been killed in the siege. The smell was sickening to Steve as he was pushed past it. Monsters were in the crowd keeping order, and there were monster guards with bows and arrows lined all along the top of the circular castle wall. There were many monsters, but there were so many more people. The dirt and soot stained faces of the civilians Steve looked down at were full of fear, tears, and anger.

111

As Steve was led forward onto the wooden gallows on the platform, he listened to the end of Prince Silas's speech.

"It would be most profitable for you to you obey me and follow my commands to avoid these worries. I know that when you do, you will begin to feel an inner peace as you realize you are fulfilling your true purpose. However, if anyone should feel the need to fight back, flee the city, or disobey any of my or your superior's orders, you will be forced to watch your entire family be tortured. Then you will be killed and end up just like your precious King Zoran and the many others who have died today. To show you what I mean, we have our first victim of insubordination. This warrior will be hanged for trying to assassinate me in my throne room."

Steve was led up the wooden stairs of the gallows. The prince was already standing on them, smiling as he looked down on the defeated warrior. Steve was smiling too, but on the inside. He knew he was going to pass right by the prince. *What do I have to lose?*

Even though his hands were tied, Steve lunged forward and head butted the prince in the chest. Silas stumbled backwards, saving himself right before he fell off the back of the gallows. Visuvis struck Steve in the back with the large ruby on the end of Brightflame. Steve fell to his knees from the blow. The prince came forward and swiftly brought his armored knee up. It hit Steve right under the chin. Steve was almost knocked out, but he refused to give any satisfaction to the betrayer of the kingdom. Steve simply looked up at the prince and smiled as a waterfall of blood came out of his mouth.

Prince Silvanus was furious that Steve was seemingly unaffected. He struck Steve across the face with the back of his gauntleted hand.

"What's one more bruise after a hundred?" Steve laughed, even though his entire body was in terrible pain.

"What's one more death after ten thousand?" Silas answered in a cocky response. He motioned for Visuvis to lead the rebellious warrior to the center of the gallows, onto a piece of wood that would soon fall away underneath Steve's feet.

Everyone could see him from the high stage he was on. Steve had no sackcloth over his head, which was one of the universal unwritten requirements of a hanging. No covering showed a lack of respect for order from the monsters and their two Human leaders.

The prince wants people to see my face contort as I struggle to hold onto my waning life. Steve also took note that the rope was not very long. A long rope meant a long drop, which meant a quick death because of a snapped neck. The short rope meant this hanging would be prolonged by possibly a couple minutes, until his lungs ran out of air. It was yet another subliminal message from the Hooded Phantom and the prince, telling the civilians that this new change of order would not be quickly ended, but prolonged and painful.

Steve still wore his red armor. He shifted uncomfortably as some of the dents in the armor pressed hard into his body. Steve thought the monsters would take the armor from him in the cell, but they hadn't. Prince Silas must have felt that people needed to know a warrior was being hung and not just some random civilian. And not just any warrior either, but the one who defeated him in the exhibition joust.

Steve felt the worst he had ever felt in his life. Between the jousting in the morning, the battles since the jousting ended, and the recent beatings by Visuvis, he had cuts and bruises all over his face and body. Even worse than that was the pain of knowing that in a few moments he would be dead.

The feeling of not being in control was one of Steve's worst fears. As he stood on the trapdoor, he felt alone, powerless, and defeated. *There is no escape from this.* He would soon be dead, just like the three great role models of his life,

King Zoran, the Supreme Commander, and Sir Thatcher. All were great men of character who were brutally murdered. Great legacies of wisdom and valiance had been ended in an instant.

The prince himself tied the noose around Steve's neck. He tied it so tightly that Steve wondered if he would die from asphyxiation before he was hanged. At least he was able to partially breathe the smoky air into his lungs. Steve looked over at the prince, who walked to the lever that would drop the trapdoor beneath his feet. He was playing with the suspense of the crowd, who nervously watched.

Steve looked up and saw a bright red object hovering in the sky. He thought he heard a deep roar come from it, but wasn't quite sure. Steve looked around, but no one in the crowd was looking up. Neither was Visuvis or Prince Silas who were both standing near him.

The only one that did notice was Nightstrike, who was perched on the tip of one of the front castle towers. The enormous black scaled dragon looked up, as Steve had, and was squinting, trying to make out the object. His nose was quickly inhaling, trying to use the dragon's ability of heightened senses to catch a scent of the creature. He must have smelled something because the Dark Dragon screeched, abandoned the tower top he was perched on, and chased after the flying object.

The Hooded Phantom, standing on a castle balcony behind Steve also noticed the hovering red object among the clouds, but only after he watched his dragon take off after it.

Was that who I think it was? Even though it was far away, Steve thought it looked like the great fire red dragon that King Zoran supposedly rode in his victorious battle against Draviakhan.

Crimson Singe?

The legend of Oliver Zoran versus Draviakhan was one Steve had seen depicted through many artistic mediums from plays to paintings. It was the last painting in the staircase of the King's Tower before the walls went blank. Steve had heard the story countless times among the warriors. Everyone had imagined themselves as the triumphant young man singlehandedly killing the greatest monster to ever walk on Element. The story had so many incarnations that no one knew what had really happened. But every story contained Crimson Singe aiding the king in his quest of vengeance against Draviakhan.

It can't be him. It must be flashes of a story from my childhood manifesting itself before my eyes, so close to my impending death. Steve convinced himself that what he saw could not have been the mythological beast. It was rumored that the dragon had died from injuries it had sustained in the battle against the Imperial Dragon.

Steve looked up again. The red shape was zipping across the sky like a comet. Nightstrike was unsuccessfully trying to catch up to it. The Dark Dragon wanted to confirm who he thought it was as much as Steve did.

Steve gazed at the pink sky, the scattered vanilla clouds, and the bright yellow-orange sun which had all but disappeared from the horizon. It was a beautiful sight to behold. He wasn't looking at the crumpled buildings, the burning fires and smoke in the distance, or the monsters that were seemingly everywhere. Steve stared at the beauty and serenity of the sunset as it cast an orange sparkling reflection over the water. Soon he would disappear as well, just like how the deep blue Darien Sea was swallowing up the giant sunset fireball.

Steve thought about the good and blessed life he had been given. He looked out into the crowd. He lived for all of these faces as a warrior. He was their friend, their protector. He enjoyed waking up in the morning and was excited to go to work.

How has it all come to this? I just had the greatest month of my entire life. It started with earning the honor to represent Celestial by winning the Qualifiers, then the celebration with my neighborhood the following day. That night I defeated the prince in the exhibition joust. The outpouring of support was amazing. Yesterday began with the parade, followed by advancing through the tournament. Today I made it all the way to the semifinals match, and was appointed a Guardian Knight (albeit temporary) but now...

Steve noticed someone in the crowd raise up their arm and put two fingers into the air. Another person on the other side of the courtyard copied the gesture. More arms started going up faster and faster; until soon every single person in the courtyard was holding up two fingers in the air.

They all saw his red armor. The majority of the people knew the man about to be hung was Celestial's jouster, but even if they didn't, they joined in with everyone else on this amazing gesture. Tears welled in Steve's eyes as this was one of the most moving sights he had ever seen.

The people of Celestial were united as one. No matter what was going to happen in the upcoming reign of evil, Steve knew that they would all stick together. That's was just how the people of this city were. They were strong and good-hearted - just like the one who created them.

The beauty of the sunset was stunning, but the sight of the people of Celestial united as one was absolutely breathtaking. Steve allowed it to be the last sight he ever saw as he closed his eyes and said a quick prayer.

God, you give every life, and you allow it to be taken away. I thank you for giving me life and for the time on Element you have blessed me with. Thank you for the good memories I take with me. I made many friends and few enemies. But the enemies I have made have defeated me as I stand here now. I am just one of many people who died today, God, but together we all cry out to you that the innocent lives still alive in this plaza would be protected from evil. I ask that a hero would rise and defeat the men and monsters that caused so much pain to your creations today.

As Steve ended his prayer, he kept his eyes closed. All he could see was the darkness of the back of his eyelids.

He heard a slight creak as Prince Silvanus pulled the lever and the trapdoor dropped.

Then Steve fell. If it wasn't for the rope tied around his neck, Steve's feet would have touched the ground.

But they never did.

Chapter 13

Tyrus Canard sat alone in a sea of red and blue banners. The majority of the crowd was wildly waving Celestial's colors, drowning out the few people who wore yellow as they cheered for Cyrus from Casanovia.

It was one of the most beautiful days of the year. The sun was peeking in and out of the fluffy white clouds. The air was a comfortable temperature with a slight breeze. The smell of various animal meats drenched in different barbecue sauces filled the stands as people ate them on sticks.

As Ty looked around, he couldn't find anyone who wasn't smiling. Maybe it was the jousting; maybe it was the beautiful weather; or maybe it was just the peaceful state of the kingdom, but everyone was happy. Ty leaned back in his seat and smiled to himself. This was one of the times in his life where he realized that he was in a moment of complete happiness.

Ty heard the voice of a small boy in front of him.

"Mom, can I get some cotton clouds, please?"

A pot-bellied Dwarven vendor in a greasy apron walked up the bleachers, getting closer and closer to the little boy's row. The halfman sang out the names of the foods he was selling to all of the spectators. He loudly and emphatically stressed the last syllable of each item, making it seem like his list of food was a song.

"Turkey Legs...Sausage...Rainbow Lollipops...Meat or Fruit Skewers...Cotton Clouds."

The Dwarf vendor stopped and looked down the row the seven-year-old boy sat in. Sam could have sworn the man looked right at him, and yelled out "Cotton Clouds" while holding up a bag for him to see. Sam had asked his mom, but she hadn't answered. He started to ask again, assuming she hadn't heard because of the noisy arena. As soon as he opened his mouth, she gave him the answer he didn't want to hear.

"No. Samuel, we spent enough gold so we could watch from these seats. You'll have to wait until we get back home to eat."

"But mom, this is the only place where we can get cotton clouds," Sam said, dragging out the word mom.

In a stern voice, his mother put an end to the begging. "I told you, we do not have the gold for that right now. Stop whining and watch the joust. We may not be able to afford to see this again until you are a teenager.

After Ty heard the conversation in front of him between the mother and son, he motioned to the vendor as he shuffled up the bleacher stairs. The Dwarf stopped and held out the tray of delicious choices for Ty to see. "What can I get for you, warrior?"

"One bag of cotton clouds and a meat on a stick," Ty selected.

"That'll be twenty bronze, ten silver, or one gold. All are one in the same."

Ty reached into his pocket and pulled out some loose coins. Each one featured the faces of heroes and legends imprinted on them. As he was sorting through them, the Dwarf interrupted him.

"Since you're a warrior, and this is your special day of honor and celebration, I'll give these to you buy one, get one free."

Ty handed the cheerful vendor five silver and five bronze coins. "The extra is for your generosity, kind sir," he

119

smiled. In return, he was handed a stick of pink and blue cotton clouds and meat on a skewer.

Sam turned around, having overheard the warrior's order. His eyes widened when he saw the fluffy candy. His expression was a mixture of happiness that he was so close to his favorite treat and sadness that he was still so far from allowing it to melt in his mouth. The young boy turned back around to watch the joust.

A minute later, Ty dropped the cotton clouds into Sam's lap. When Sam turned around, the warrior was frantically looking all around, side to side and under his seat.

"I...I was just holding cotton clouds in my hand, but I can't find them anywhere," Ty said, shrugging his shoulders. "I must have dropped them."

Sam meekly held the uneaten snack up to show the warrior sitting behind him. "Is this it?" he asked.

Ty scratched the blonde stubble on his chin. "No, I think mine looked different. That one must be yours."

The boy smiled, realizing the gift he had just been given. He erased the smile and looked directly into Ty's green eyes as he extended his hand, trying to show this warrior he was polite and respectful.

"Thank you, sir", he said.

"You're very welcome," Ty said as he shook Sam's hand, impressed by his manners. "You've got a firm grip, lad. Maybe someday, you'll be the one jousting for Celestial in front of all these people."

That made Sam's smile return, larger than when he realized the cotton clouds belonged to him.

His mother turned around to see the face of the warrior that had been so nice to her son. The man was holding out his meat skewer for her.

"Here you go, ma'am," he offered.

She returned his warm smile and mimicked her son's appreciation. "Thank you," she said as she began reaching into her purse for what little coin she had to pay the warrior.

Ty shook his head. "You don't have to pay me. It's my treat to both you and your son for supporting us warriors by buying tickets to the joust."

The three spectators returned to watching the joust as Celestial's own Stephen Brightflame landed a devastating blow onto his opponent's chest. Sam stood up and cheered, arching blue and pink colors back and forth through the air. After sitting back down, the boy pulled off a large piece of the cotton clouds and held it behind him for the warrior, all while keeping his eyes glued to the jouster in front of him.

"Thank you," Ty said, placing the fluffy treat on his tongue and feeling it melt away. "Do you know the name of Celestial's jouster this year?" he asked the boy.

Sam turned around to face Ty and looked at him as if he had been living under a rock for the past month.

"Of course, I know his name! He's Steve Brightflame, the hope of Celestial! He rides his carrot-crunching warhorse Clyx."

Ty loved the child's enthusiasm and just like the cotton clouds, he had one more surprise for the well-mannered child sitting in front of him.

"That's right. And it just so happens that he and I are very good friends. How would you like to go out and meet him after this match?"

The mother turned around again. She was as surprised as her son. "That would be...just magnificent for him. Stephen is all he talks about. Sam is always running around the house with a wooden stick as a lance, pretending to be Stephen Brightflame."

Ty turned to Sam and awaited his response. At first the boy was too excited to answer. "How about it, Sam? I'm sure he'll let you pet Clyx. If you're lucky, he might even let you ride him. Then you can see how fast he really is."

"Yes! Oh, wow...yes, that would be amazing!" Sam bounced up and down in his seat.

"May I have your name, warrior?" Sam's mother asked. If he wouldn't accept her money, the least she could do was remember his name.

The warrior extended his hand. "Ty Canard. Pleased to meet you."

Ty belonged to the Elven race. He was slender and of average height, if not a couple hairs shorter. Elves tended to live long lives at around 150 years. Ty was only twenty-two. In a way, he was very young, but at the same time he felt like he was in the prime of his life. Like his foster brother Stephen Brightflame, he had a warrior's muscular body and was incredibly fit and healthy.

Ty had dirty blond hair that grew straight. He kept the length fairly long. It stopped at the middle of his neck. He obsessively ran his fingers through his hair to put it behind his head. He would often hold it behind his pointed ears, to show his pride in his Elven heritage. Sometimes he would tie it in a ponytail when riding horses or in battle, so he wouldn't have to adjust it or bother with it. Ty had bright green eyes and a pure white smile full of straight teeth.

He was a naturally attractive person, a heartthrob for the ladies. The Elf was a person you would glance twice at in a crowd. For the ladies, it was almost always more than twice and longer than just a quick glance.

He was not married; in fact, marriage to Ty was still a far way off. The unbreakable bond of marriage only seemed like a way to tie him down and force him to commit to something long term. It was the exact opposite of his personality. That is not to say that Ty didn't care about being in the company of women. He had many beautiful girls interested in his appealing

122

lifestyle and sharp looks. Just because he was not ready to get married, didn't mean that he couldn't encourage the many girls who found him charming to spend their time with him.

Other than his obligation to serve and protect civilians as a warrior, Ty did not allow anything to hold him down. He enjoyed waking up in the morning and not knowing what would happen to him that day. "Every day is a mystery to be explored," was something Ty constantly said. Instead of looking backwards or forwards, he always lived in the moment. Ty loved taking on new obstacles and trying new experiences. A day where he went to sleep without a good or funny story was a wasted day.

He was very content and happy with who he was and the life he lived. The happiness inside him was easy to notice from the outside. He was one of the most easy-going people a person could know. Being around Ty was sure to be a time full of laughter, due to his never-ending jokes and humor. He was the kind of person people easily gravitated towards because of his attractive personality. Ty was always the life of the party.

It seemed like the only thing he wasn't blessed with was gold. Perhaps that was because he spent it all on his girlfriends, but Ty didn't mind a lack of coin. He had learned that charisma was sometimes just as valuable as gold. *Be a friend to them and they'll be a friend to you. Friendships are easier forged with smiles and laughter than with gold.* No matter where he went or what he did, he had no worries about anything because he could always use his charm to get someone to help him out.

What made Ty happy most of all was that he was a warrior. Like all other children at the age of sixteen, Ty had learned the basic fundamentals in school and was ready to choose a profession. His class learned about the highlights of every career before they chose which one they wanted to work at for the rest of their lives. Some of the common professions were merchant, messenger, banker, librarian, writer, teacher, pastor, blacksmith, innkeeper, inventor, tailor/seamstress, carpenter, farmer, baker, and a representative to mayor/politics, among many, many others.

Ty didn't need to know anything about these trades. He already knew what he wanted to be - a warrior, just like his father and grandfather before him. As a boy, Ty looked up to warriors as his role models. It was no surprise that he wanted to emulate them when he became a man. In fact, most young boys wanted to become warriors. They all wanted to create their own legacy, similar to the many tales of warrior legends they were told by their parents before going to bed; or maybe they just wanted people to respect them for being in a position of power and authority. Whatever the reason, many young boys dreamed of becoming a warrior. Unfortunately, the road to becoming a warrior was not an easy one.

Only a certain amount of warrior trainees were accepted each year. Hopefuls had to pass certain mental and physical tests to be admitted into the warriors, which most young men could not pass. Even for those who did pass the test, they still had to score in the highest percentile compared to the other boys who also took the admittance test.

There were five main ranks of warrior: training, apprentice, warrior, captain/commander, and knight. In training, the trainee would practice with different weapons until he found one he was most comfortable with. After three years of extensive physical and mental training and being taught how to react in scenarios of complex moral choice, the trainee would then become an apprentice. The apprentice would train with a master of the same weapon. The master taught his apprentice everything he needed to know about the responsibilities of a warrior. After two years of being an apprentice, the master would concoct a challenge to see if his pupil had acquired the mental and physical skills required to succeed as a warrior. When the apprentice passed his master's test, they became eligible for the warrior draft. All of the apprentice graduates were ranked and then drafted by the commanders of the watchtowers. Once they were selected, they were officially deemed a warrior. The majority of warriors never got promoted any higher than this basic rank.

In Celestial, the warriors were divided into groups called clans. There were three clans in each of the twelve warriors' watchtowers. Each warrior could choose which one of the three he wanted to be in: Land, Air, or Naval. Land warriors covered street patrols and the guarding of the inner and outer walls. Aerial warriors flew on friendly monsters and battled enemy monsters. They were also used to pour pesticides on the fields in between the inner and outer walls. Water element friendly flying monsters were used to put out fires in the city. Naval warriors worked on battleships and fought against sea monsters.

The clans became tight knit groups of men who were like brothers to each other. Each clan was led by its captain. There was a Land Captain, Squadron Captain (for the Aerial Clan), and Fleet Captain (for the Naval Clan). The three captains all answered to the commander of their watchtower, of which there was only one. Each tower was named after its commander. Upon retiring, captains had the option to become teachers of the trainees. Retiring commanders could choose whether or not to become masters.

The only warriors who ranked above each of the Watchtower Commanders were the twelve Guardian Knights of the royal family. These men were handpicked by the king, and they served as his personal advisors and security guards. Anyone of them would sacrifice his life to save the king's in a heartbeat. The Guardian Knights were led by the Supreme Commander. Warriors, captains, commanders, knights, and the Supreme Commander all answered to the king, who commanded all Land, Aerial, and Naval forces.

Ty had been a trainee and then an apprentice. Then he passed his master's test to become a warrior. He graduated one year early at the age of twenty. He had been a warrior for two years now, and he was having the best time of his life. The fact that he was so young and healthy and had such a bright future only made him happier.

Everything in Ty's life was great, except for one flaw that always lingered in the back of his mind: none of his male ancestors (who were all warriors) lived to 150 name days. His grandfather, Jackson Canard, was killed in action in his mid-thirties. Ty's father, Caesar Canard, along with Ty's mother, were murdered when Ty was only five years old.

Death haunted Ty. It followed his family closely. Ty had already had many close encounters with death, but always seemed to barely escape. He didn't know if that meant he was lucky or not, but he figured with all of the early deaths his forefathers had had in previous generations, he and his brother Darren were due for a prolonged life. This was part of the reason Ty lived life in a happy-go-lucky way and as freely as he did. He didn't know when his time on Element would come to an end. So until he found himself in an encounter that he could not escape from and death finally defeated him for good, he planned to live every day of his life full of smiles, laughter, and love.

Chapter 14

After buying Sam and his mother food, Ty went back to watching his friend compete. The Elven warrior was an avid fan of the joust. He had made it far into the Celestial Qualifiers himself, but ended up losing to Steve in one of the final matches. It had been one of the most exciting jousts of the Qualifiers. Ty took an early lead but got cocky and began pandering and playing to the crowd. Steve capitalized on Ty's loss of focus and won the match.

Even though Ty wished he could have been in the saddle Steve was currently sitting in, he didn't allow it to bother him or put a damper on his excitement for the Annual Warriors' Tournaments. He lost the battle fair and square to his best friend. Now he could allow himself to relax, enjoy the festivities of the weekend, and support his friend in the Warriors' Joust. No one was more proud of how far Steve had come than Ty. Ty was the only one who truly believed that Steve could make it as far as he had.

Ty had actually made it far in one of the tournaments: Warriors' Combat. He had made it into the top five of qualifying warriors for Celestial, which meant he could participate in the official tournament. The Joust was the only competition limited to one person from each city. Warriors' Combat was a single, one on one battle with blunted weapons, rather than the Warriors' Melee, which was hundreds of warriors in a field in an epic last man standing match. Ty would have chosen Melee over Combat. The Melee was an adrenaline rush, amidst the madness of the action. But Ty had missed the Melee Qualifiers because he had advanced so far in the Jousting Qualifiers.

He wasn't too upset though. Ty's brother Darren had made it into the Melee. Ty wasn't sure how he would react if he came across his brother in the chaos. Darren was three years older than Ty, but he graduated from the warriors at the average graduation age – twenty-one. He had two more years of battlefield experience than Ty had. *But I was always better than him with my swords.* Ty didn't know who would win if they were forced to battle each other. It would be a battle of talent versus experience. *If I was in the Melee, Darren and I could have teamed up and been the last two men standing.*

At least Ty had made it into the Warriors' Combat Tournament. Many warriors didn't even get to participate in one event. Warriors were allowed to enter the Celestial Qualifier's for any two competitions of their choice, but they were only allowed to participate in one of the tournaments (if they had won both of their Qualifiers). Since winning in a tournament was so prestigious and it was only held annually, some warriors trained year-round for one specific event. Ty was not that dedicated. Once he had told a warrior, "There's too much in life to be explored. If I train for a year and lose, then all that time I would have spent would be a waste."

Ty wanted to do the best that he could in Warriors' Combat. His father had won the event the year before he died. Caesar Canard's name was etched on the golden trophy cup. Ty wanted to honor his father's memory by winning and getting his own name added to the ongoing list of champions. Any weapon other than the bow and arrow was permitted for Warriors' Combat (the bow and arrow were used in the Archery tournament). A variety of weapons were used: swords, shields, axes, hammers, spears, and maces. Some weapons were one handed, while others required two. Ty equipped what he felt most comfortable with: double swords (one in each hand).

128

The competition was much harder than the Melee free for all. Ty had to come into each new match and consider the strengths and weaknesses of his double swords against whatever weapon his opponent was using. Ty ended up coming in a respectable sixth place out of the sixty-four that competed.

He beat himself up for not getting first. Even if he had gotten a medal for third or second place, he still would have been frustrated. That was his way. He was only completely satisfied when he was the best. If someone was better than Ty at something, he would freely admit that, but it would bug him so much that he would practice endlessly. Entering the tournament next year and not placing any higher would not be acceptable to him. Steve had encouraged Ty after his loss and told him that at next year's event, he would get first place.

During the current Annual Warriors' Tournaments, Ty had enjoyed one thing almost as much as he enjoyed seeing Steve winning every joust. Each year, a parade was held for the cities that had come to Celestial to participate in the events of the special weekend. The parade was held the morning before the tournaments began. It started by going in a full circle around the castle, and then it turned down the south main road and carried on until it reached the arena. Civilians had lined up alongside the sides of the streets for the entire route to cheer on their favorite competitors. Non-competing warriors who had traveled to Celestial to support their city's participants were also allowed to walk in the parade.

Since Steve was Celestial's Jousting Qualifier's winner (and jousting was the main tournament), he was allowed to pick a group of warriors to walk beside him with their armor and weapons. He asked every jouster he had defeated in the Qualifiers to do him the honor of walking by his side. Steve wanted to give them one of the highlights of the weekend's festivities that they would have missed out on by losing to him. He also let his four squires walk alongside him as well.

The Celestial warriors usually pulled a prank on the visiting cities that marched in the parade. One year, they had paid some of the civilians to reroute the path and then snuck away from the back of the line, so that when the other cities' warriors made it to the arena, the Celestial warriors had magically arrived there before them. Another year, they had civilians run frantically through the middle of the main road, right into the parade, yelling and screaming. They were being followed by some of Celestial's warriors, who came chasing after the civilians dressed up as fake monsters. That prank was not as well-received.

This year, Ty was a part of the parade. Since he was the funniest person Steve knew, Steve asked him to be the one to come up with the prank. The night before the parade, Ty tasked Steve's four young squires with sneaking into the stables and feeding laxatives to the visiting warriors' horses. Instead of having Celestial's competitors and company walk in the back of the pack, as was the annual custom, Ty had them walk in the front. At first, the cities behind them couldn't figure out why Celestial had volunteered to walk in front of the parade. Usually Celestial was last, to build up the suspense for the host city. Once they smelled what their horses were leaving behind on the trail, they understood.

All of the excitement and fun of the weekend came to an abrupt end the minute the man ran into the middle of the arena yelling, "We're under attack!"

Ty forced his way through the panicking crowd, trying to get to his jousting friend in the center of it. After pushing and squeezing his way through people, he realized he was not making any progress.

A spray of tiny rocks and small boulders sprayed down on Ty's side of the arena. People in the crowd ducked down and covered their heads from the barrage, but Ty saw his opportunity. Unlike the rest of the spectators, he had on most of his warrior's armor. All warriors had been commanded to wear the top half of their armor out in public for the weekend. It gave civilians the opportunity to recognize them and give special thanks to the men that protected them and the city.

All warriors started out with a full set of silver armor. Once they did something heroic on the battlefield or in the city, they would be allowed to paint their armor. Each city had one or two colors they were known by. Celestial was the red and blue city. Casanovia was the city of blue and yellow. The purple city was called Almiria.

Warriors could choose any piece of their armor to be painted one of the colors of their city. Some veteran Celestial warriors had suits of armor in all red, all blue, or a mixture of both. You gained a lot of respect from fellow warriors and civilians alike for having earned the colors of the city. If a warrior achieved the rank of a Guardian Knight, they could start to earn pieces of rare golden armor to replace their red and blue painted armor made of silver.

Ty was somewhat jealous of Steve, seeing him in all red armor. Even though it was just a special suit only to be worn for the Warriors' Joust, it made him look like a warrior veteran. Steve and Ty wouldn't reach that level for at least another twenty years. All Ty had earned up until now was two blue gauntlets.

Because of his armor, Ty was able to vault and hop through the ducked crowd. He still would die if he was hit by a boulder, but unlike the civilians, he was protected from ricocheting debris. Since he wasn't wearing a helm, Ty held his blue armored forearms up to the sides of his head for protection.

He could see over the entire cowering crowd, but unfortunately that meant he was watching as a flaming boulder crashed down and rolled over a section of people on the arena floor. One of them was one of Steve's squires. He had been so close to escaping the boulder's path.

Ty made his way onto the floor and ran in the trail of the boulder's wreckage. He saw Brightflame next to the boy's body and picked it up. It was hot to touch, but manageable to hold.

The crowd was back up and running again, making it hard for Ty to see where Steve was. Suddenly, the red armored warrior appeared in a blur. He was still mounted on top of the charging blue armored Clyx. Steve lowered his lance and aimed it at a group of minotaurs.

Ty pushed through the crowd, only to see Clyx running around without a rider. "Steve!" he called out, not seeing his brother. It wasn't like Steve to abandon Clyx in the midst of battle. For a second, Ty feared the worst.

But then he saw Steve on the ground, with a black minotaur about to bring its electrical axe down on him. Ty reached the monster just in time to stab Brightflame through its back. "And with that I take the lead! Five points to four," Ty yelled, pulling a blood-dripping Brightflame out of the minotaur's back. He reached down and grabbed the arm of his best friend Steve and pulled him up off the ground.

"Cutting it close that time, huh?" Steve yelled over the sounds of destruction.

"I wanted you to see how helpless and vulnerable you are without me around."

"What would I do without you?" Steve sarcastically smiled.

"I don't know. I wouldn't want to live in a world without me." Ty flipped the sword and grabbed the blade, holding it hilt out towards Steve.

"Brightflame!" Steve said as he grabbed it from the Elf excitedly.

"I know how much that sword means to you." Ty said, happy he was able to retrieve the weapon for his friend.

"Why is this hot?" Steve asked, as he looked up to Ty.

Ty didn't want to tell Steve about the grotesque sight he saw when Steve's squire was trying to run out of the way to avoid getting crushed by a rolling, flaming boulder barreling down his path. Unfortunately, the poor boy had no chance to escape. The boulder rolled over top of him and stopped, crushing him partially underneath. Trapped, the child burned to death.

Ty could already see Steve mentally reaching the answer for the question he had just asked. Ty didn't need to give him the details, so he saw no point in giving an answer at all.

"You didn't hear any warning horns from the outer watchtowers did you?" Steve asked.

"No, there was no alarm. I have no idea how the catapults got close enough to launch into the city without being noticed by the patrolling warriors."

"I've got a bad feeling about this, Ty."

"As do I. Where are you headed?" he asked Steve.

"To protect the castle," Steve said as he nodded in the direction he would be heading. "What about you?"

Ty pointed up to the sky, to the monsters flying overhead.

"Be safe, brother." Steve told Ty before they hugged.

"What's the fun in being safe?" Ty said before running off into the dense smoke, leaving his friend behind. He hoped the next time they saw each other that they would both still be on Element, alive.

As Ty ran out of the stadium his eye caught the colors of pink and blue lying on the ground. The stick of cotton clouds had been half eaten. Next to the candy, Sam and his mother were lying dead on the arena floor. One of the minotaurs had

133

killed them. Ty continued running out of the arena while trying to mentally erase the images from his mind and focus on the battle above him that he would soon be joining.

That was the last day Tyrus Canard ever ate cotton clouds.

Chapter 15

Ty headed for the warrior barracks, where his gryphon Wildwing would be waiting for him. Ty was an aerial warrior. It was a very dangerous role, but one of the most important.

Enemy flying monsters were some of the most powerful. They were not held back by fortifying walls and could easily do major damage to a city. Aerial warriors flew one of three types of monsters: phoenixes, giant hawk-like feathered birds; gryphons, winged lion's bodies with the oversized head of an eagle; and dragons, the main and most vicious flying monster. All of them could attack with the element or elements they were born with.

Warriors had some phoenixes, gryphons, and dragons of their own. They were monsters who had converted from their evil ways and decided to serve the good god instead of the evil god. Once a monster turned good and decided not to harm people, they often sought out shelter in a city, to avoid being persecuted by monsters in the wild. The warriors gave them this protection, but requested use of the monster's elemental abilities to aid them in battle.

Female friendly monsters were mainly used to produce eggs. Since larger monsters had longer lives, their time from conception to birth was prolonged. Phoenixes, gryphons, and dragons spent almost a full year in their egg.

Warriors who were interested in becoming an aerial warrior could obtain a monster by finding an egg in the wild or by having a monster "choose them." Young monsters sometimes sought out the person who they believed was meant to be their rider. It was said that there was a mental connection between a monster and its true rider. When the two met for the first time, both would feel an immediate bond.

Another way a warrior was able to obtain a monster was if he saved one from being killed by another monster. He could also get one by defeating a flying monster in battle, if the monster chose to surrender its life to serve rather than die.

Ty had saved the life of Wildwing with the help of Steve when they were in Warrior Training. Ty convinced Steve he had felt the strong connection, and together they rescued the monster. Ever since that day, the gryphon and Ty had grown to become great friends. Both Ty and Wildwing loved to fly and fight.

Looks like there's more than enough fun to be had today, Ty thought as he looked up.

The agile Elf took shortcuts through back alleyways and secrets paths that few people knew of. The only reason he knew about them was because he and Darren had grown up in this section of Celestial. As children, they had explored everywhere they were allowed to go, and even more so where they were not.

As he ran, Ty heard screaming, yelling, and heavy impacts coming from every direction around him. People were being injured as flaming boulders crashed down and demolished buildings and streets. Ty continuously glanced into the sky, keeping a look out for any boulders coming down in his direction. He was also trying to see how many flying monsters were in the air and if any warriors had already engaged them in battle.

Ty turned a corner and collided with a Dwarven man, almost knocking them both down. But both the Elf and the Dwarf were able to keep their balance.

"Ty!" the Dwarf said, surprised. Ty could hear the quiver of nervousness in his tone. The voice of the halfman belonged to Klar, a fellow warrior brother of his same aerial clan. Like the Elf, he was also headed to mount his ride.

"Pushing me down so you can get to the barracks first and steal Wildwing for battle?" Ty joked. "I know you've always admired his speed."

Klar was too nervous to see humor in anything. "Sorry," the Dwarf said, taking the blame for bumping into Ty even though they both knew it was Ty's fault for not looking where he was going. "We have to hurry. I was on the wall. I saw a large horde of flyers headed in from the west."

"How large?" Ty asked, somewhat scared of what the answer would be.

"Too many to count." It was Klar's best estimate.

Ty and Klar started running side by side down the narrow street, side stepping and dodging their shoulders out of the way of civilians running in the opposite direction as they all headed toward their homes. The faster the two warriors could get onto their monsters and into the air, the more innocent lives would be spared. It was their job to attract the monsters' attention away from destroying buildings and hurting people by engaging the monsters in battle high in the skies.

Ty and Klar were running when they heard the screams of women and children coming from somewhere on the adjacent side of the buildings next to them. The screams were followed by the angry growls of monsters.

"Monsters have advanced this far into the city already?" Klar doubted.

"This fast? Impossible," Ty agreed. He looked up and down the street for a way to cross to where the screams and growls were coming from. *There aren't any alleys to cut across.* Klar, who was jiggling door handles, was trying in vain to find one that was unlocked. Most of them were probably full of families cowering under their kitchen tables or in their basements in fear.

"There's no time for that!" Ty yelled, backing away to the opposite side of the road. He ran forward towards the door next to where Klar was standing. He shouldered into it with all his weight, breaking the lock and cracking the wooden door. After a powerful kick, the door flew open. Ty entered into the building as Klar followed behind.

They had come through the back door of a fur merchant's shop by the looks of it. Decorative pelts of animal furs hung for sale on clothing racks. Winter was coming, so they were a popular item. No one was in the store on the first floor, and they didn't hear any sounds from the merchant's home on the second story. Either the merchant thought Ty and Klar were monsters breaking in and tried to remain quiet, or he was not in his shop when the attack commenced. Ty and Klar dodged around circular racks of pelts placed throughout the store and then crashed through the front door and out into a small open plaza.

The first image Ty saw was a Human female. She was only a few years older than him, lying dead on the ground in a pool of her own blood. Behind the body stood two young children, girls no more than four years old. The moment Ty came through the front door of the merchant's shop, a blue ogre, standing in front of the girls, killed both of them with a single mighty swing from the rusty bronze swords he had equipped in each of his giant hands.

Ty had seen dead monsters, dead animals, and dead people, but he had never seen sweet, innocent children brutally murdered in front of him. His jaw tightened and his teeth clenched together in anger as his heart expanded in sorrow.

The woman had sacrificially given her life to buy the two girls at least a few extra seconds of life on Element. Had those seconds been even slightly longer, the two warriors might have been able to save the two girls, and that woman's final life choice of sacrifice would not have been in vain. Unfortunately, time is time, no one can add to it, and no one can take it away.

Ty wished with all his heart that he could have heard the screams a little earlier or wished he had run a little faster through the shop. He tried to think of any one thing he could have done differently that would have saved their lives, but it didn't matter. He was too late. The woman and the two children lay in pieces of mutilated body parts. Death cannot be undone.

The blue ogre's swords dripped with the red blood of innocence. Ty was lost in the gruesome images of the moment until he heard the screams of more children. Three girls and their pregnant mother stood huddled together. They were surrounded in a wide circle by five monsters, including the murderous blue-skinned ogre. The circle pressed tighter and tighter together as the five walked toward the helpless unprotected family.

Monsters enjoyed watching their prey cower in fear. The mother was crouched down with her back to the monsters. Her arms were outstretched over the three girls, using her body as a covering shield. All of their eyes were closed, but they were all screaming, waiting to be impaled by the monsters' weapons.

Ty realized the woman who had been killed looked similar to the cowering one, except for the fact that the live one was pregnant and the other was not. *They must have been sisters.* The woman's scream had more emotion in it than just the terror of the impending death of her, her daughters, and her unborn child. Her cry was also lamenting over the fact that she had just watched her sister and two nieces murdered in front of her.

Ty shouted out and gained the attention of the five monsters. They all looked up at him and Klar and welcomed the tougher challenge. Although five on two odds was still an easy fight in favor of the monsters, anything would be considered a harder challenge when being compared to women and children without weapons or armor. Monsters often sought out the tougher battle. It proved their own power to themselves, the monsters they traveled with, and the people they were killing.

Knowing the grim chances of survival, the warriors of Elven and Dwarven descent gladly accepted the battle as they stole the monsters' attention. The five monsters spread out into a horizontal line, smiling and walking towards the two brave warriors. Ty looked past them and saw that the pregnant mother was able to lead her daughters out of the plaza. *Hopefully they get to safety*.

Klar unsheathed his two handed sword. Ty crossed his arms over each other and reached behind his shoulders. He simultaneously pulled his two swords out of the cross sheaths on his back.

The strength of Klar's two handed sword was that it was designed for power, but its weakness was that it left him unprotected after attacking. Ty's double swords were the exact opposite. They may have lacked power, but they were exceptionally fast and accurate; perfect for fatal counterstrikes. Steve's Brightflame was a sword that combined both of those strengths, but had neither of their weaknesses. Brightflame had the power of a two handed sword, but was very lightweight and fast. Ty wished he could use Brightflame for himself, but his double sword style suited him, and it hadn't failed him yet.

One of Ty's swords was bigger than the other. He consistently found victory in battle with his two swords by using the larger one to knock the enemy off balance and by using the speed of the smaller and lighter one to deliver a fast strike into monster flesh.

He began to analyze the enemy, a conscious priority that had been engrained into the minds of all warriors from their training. He knew that Klar, standing next to him, was going through the same mental process.

Two ogres, two orcs, and a minotaur.

The minotaur looked similar to the one Ty had stabbed in the back earlier, but the ogres and orcs provided a different type of challenge. Ogres and orcs were Anthropomorphic Monsters: vile and twisted forms of the good god's creations.

Ogres were comparable to Giants. They were about the same height, but far more bulky and fat. Their arms and legs were as round as tree trunks. Because of their size, they were very strong. They usually carried heavier weapons because they had no problem swinging them. Like minotaurs, ogres were not skilled in the nuances of weapon fighting technique. Rather than focusing on one enemy at a time, they would swing aimlessly all around their general vicinity, attempting to keep enemies from getting close.

Ogres did not have necks. Their heads stuck out near the top of their chest from between their massive shoulders. They had ears that were short, but floppy. Their noses rivaled the large size of a Dwarf's nose. Their teeth looked exactly like horse's teeth. Two short fangs rose up from the bottom of their oversized jaws. Their appearance as a whole was very frightful and intimidating.

Orcs were the opposite of the ogres' immense size. They were around the size as Humans and Elves and physically looked exactly like the two races. The only real difference was in their facial features. Orcs had long, skinny ears that horizontally stuck out from the sides of their heads. Their jaws were like a bear trap with their yellow teeth all coming to sharp points. Their noses were short and wide, and had big nostrils.

Orcs, while not as intelligent as people, were considered smart among Anthropomorphic Monsters. They had impressive instincts and could react quickly in a fight. This made it easier for them to defend against warriors and counterattack. They also knew how to formulate basic battle strategies, but getting the other monsters in their party to follow orders was the real

141

challenge. Some of the stronger orcs had the ability to speak, but only knew the basic words of the language used by the four races.

Ty knew this would be a difficult battle. He needed to beware of the orcs' combat skills and avoid their counterattacks, while also dodging the ogres' wild swings. The good thing about the ogres was that if he could get past the range of their wild swings, he could get in close enough to attack. *I have to make sure that they miss.* Ty knew getting hit with a weapon by an ogre would mortally wound him if it didn't kill him upon impact.

Ty continued his analysis by observing the color of the enemy's skin. Unlike the minotaurs, who had horse-like fur, ogres and orcs were hairless. Their skin was basically the same as Ty's skin, except it featured the color of whatever element the monster had.

Every warrior knew the shades of color and which element they stood for: red for fire, green for wind, blue for water, yellow for electricity, and brown for earth.

Ty could see one orc was a shade of red, and one ogre was orange. This meant both could control the element of fire with the speared staff and the double-edged, two handed axe they were respectively wielding.

The other ogre was a pale shade of blue. His bronze swords both turned the color of her skin. He had the ability to fight with the element of water/ice.

Ty set a special mental marker on the blue ogre. He had been the one that murdered the mother and her two daughters. *I will be the one to kill him.*

Looking closer, Ty realized it was not a male as he had thought. It was a female ogre. He couldn't blame himself for getting it wrong. Some monsters did not have viewable distinguishing features to recognize their gender from (such as minotaurs' horns). Underneath their ragged clothes was where the difference could be found, but those were body parts Ty did not care to see.

Ty also analyzed the shade of the colored skin of the monsters. There were many shades of the five elemental colors. The paler the monster's color was, the lesser their ability with their element. A monster of a brighter shade of color was stronger.

Aerial battles between friendly and enemy monsters were amazing to watch from the ground because the dragons, gryphons, and phoenixes were monsters with some of the brightest shades you could find. The colors of their large bodies and the elements they attacked with painted the sky.

The monsters Ty and Klar were about to battle were a mixture of average and pale shades. It was trickier to tell how powerful the minotaur was with his element, or even what element he had. Unlike the colored skin of ogres and orcs, a minotaur's skin was covered in fur. There was no distinguishing color. What little skin showed was the same color as its fur. The only way to tell what element it possessed was to see what color its weapon turned.

The element of wind, Ty diagnosed as the minotaur's mallet turned green. The glow of the weapon was faint, meaning he was not very powerful.

The remaining orc was gray. This monster was the weakest of the five and must not have been birthed with control over an element. That was common. Not all monsters were born with an element, but he still held a sword of his own, making him just as capable of causing death.

He is wearing armor. Monsters don't waste armor on powerless monsters. He must make up for his lack of an element with skill in using that sword.

It was easier to obtain armor for a smaller bodied orc than an ogre because orcs were around the same size as people. Ogres could only fit into armor that belonged to a Giant, and even then the Giant would have to be overweight and oddly proportioned.

Ty knew his plan of attack and called out to Klar, knowing the monsters wouldn't be able to understand what they were saying unless he slowly annunciated each word. Even if he did that, only a word or two would be comprehended, probably by the orcs. Monsters and language were two things that were not compatible. They mostly used gestures, motions, and frustrated grunts to communicate.

"You kill the armored orc and then the fire ogre. I'll take the blue ogre followed by the minotaur."

The Dwarf grunted in agreement, "Whoever gets done first can have the fun of killing the last orc." He grunted again after he spoke, this time in excitement to battle the monsters. The two warriors ran away from each other, separating the monsters. The red orc in the middle would have to choose which warrior he wanted to fight. He decided on Klar.

Ty turned to the blue skinned ogre and waited for her to strike first, which she did. The monster fiercely arched both of her swords sideways, parallel to each other, in the same direction. Ty ducked and rolled out of the way in a fluid motion. As the weapons passed closely across his back, he felt the heat of the blades and heard them sizzling. The she-ogre was using scalding hot water. Even though it was in liquid form, it held steady around the shape of the metal blade it encased. The Elven warrior came out of the roll and kicked the approaching minotaur hard in the stomach, launching him backwards. The minotaur fell to the plaza floor on his butt.

Ty turned back to the blue female ogre whose wild swing had thrown her weight off balance. Ty had already turned back towards her before she got her large, clumsy feet squared back to him. He inserted his larger sword into her exposed ribcage. The savage monster yelped out in pain and turned away from Ty. Then Ty stabbed her in the top of the back with both blades and brought them down. A cut like the one to the ribs would quickly kill a monster the size of an orc, but with the ogre being larger, he felt safer to do more damage by slicing her entire back open.

He glanced over at the minotaur he had kicked. It was still sitting in the spot where it had skidded to a stop, just eerily watching him. Ty had felt the stomach give in from the powerful kick, but did not hear any of the monster's ribs break. It must not have wanted to get up and fight after seeing how quickly the ogre had been killed. Ty looked over to Klar just in time to see him cut off the armored gray orc's arm from the elbow down.

"Look out!" Ty yelled, but it was too late. The orange ogre swung his great axe of fire and cut cleanly through both of Klar's thighs, right below the waist. His legs were separated from the rest of his body. Klar never saw the attack coming since he was outnumbered three to one.

Ty knew that Klar's chances of survival had dramatically dropped the second the red orc chose to join the orange ogre and gray orc in the fight against the Dwarf. Ty had hoped that the middle monster would have come to him. The speed of his double swords would have been more effective, when surrounded by multiple enemies, than Klar's slow, powerful, two handed long sword was. Those types of weapons were most effective in one on one battles.

Ty had tried to defeat his enemies as quickly as he could, so he could provide aid to his warrior brother. Once again, having a few more seconds could have changed the fate of yet another life gone too soon.

The warrior's torso and legs fell to the plaza floor. For a second, the top stump of the halfman who had been cut in half was still alive and twitching as he looked right at Ty with a face full of shock and surprise. Then Klar's eyes closed.

The orange ogre and the red orc turned to Ty. The one armed gray orc followed behind the two fire monsters, not letting a missing limb stop him from continuing the battle. The coward minotaur that had been sitting and watching stood up to join the fight.

What? Not afraid to fight me now that you aren't as likely to die? Ty backed away from the line of monsters advancing on him.

I have pressed my luck too many times. I've always managed to escape death, but now it's time I pay for the good fortune I've always had in battle.

Ty joked with the monsters getting closer. His questions didn't stop them, but he continued with them nonetheless. "Four on one? Well...three and a half if you count you there with the missing arm."

Ty kept backing up until his back was pressed up against the window of the fur shop. He had nowhere to run.

"I tell you what; maybe we can work something out. I have some warm furs behind me here that you can have for free. Warmth for the upcoming winter?" He gestured to the large fire ogre. "I doubt we have anything in your size, but we'll put you on a diet and see if you can slim down a little."

The monsters were all smiling, but not at Ty's humor. They were smiling just as they had been when they closed in on the pregnant woman shielding her daughters. Their prey was helpless, with no chance to escape. Monsters didn't care if their enemy was crying like the woman or joking like the Elf. They only saw what was similar in the disappointed eyes of their victims: a look of defeat, knowing their death was imminent.

Ty knew it wasn't his words that supplied their amusement. *I wonder if monsters get more pleasure from knowing that their enemy knows that they have been defeated or from doing the actual killing by hacking the life out of their victim's body.*

146

Before the grinning monsters savagely brought their weapons down on Ty, there was a loud thud on the stone floor of the plaza behind them. The thud was followed by an ear piercing scream causing the monsters to cover their ears. It was a roaring scream Ty had heard many times before.

The four monsters turned away from the warrior to look and see what monster had made that sound. The last question they heard before they were torn to pieces by sharp talons from a lion's body, chewed apart by an eagle's beak, and blasted with the element of wind was Ty asking, "Have you met my friend Wildwing?"

Chapter 16

Again, precious seconds cost a life. *If Klar could have survived for a little bit longer; if I had killed my enemies faster; if Wildwing had arrived sooner, then...*

But Klar was dead, just like the two girls and their mother. *At least Wildwing came when he did, or else my seconds would have run out too,* Ty realized.

He walked over to his gryphon and greeted him by rubbing the top of his eagle's head as the monster kneeled down. The Elf tied his shoulder length blonde hair in a quick knot behind his head. He didn't want the wind to whip it around in front of his eyes and obstruct his vision in the middle of battle. Elements were shooting around everywhere. If he missed out on seeing one headed for him and Wildwing, it would mean their death.

His giant monster lowered the rest of its body to the ground. Ty reached up and grabbed the side of the saddle. *One of the warrior trainees must have put this on Wildwing when the attack began.* Ty pulled himself up onto the enormous beast, put his foot in the stirrup, and vaulted his leg over Wildwing's back, sliding his other foot into the other stirrup. He sat down in his brown leather saddle. It always made a creaking noise when he climbed onto his dark and light green feathered friend. While buckling himself into the leather harness, Ty said, "Thanks for coming when you did, Wildwing," and then Ty grabbed the reins.

Flying a monster was similar to riding a horse, except that the average size of a gryphon was six to seven times larger than a steed. Phoenixes were the same size as gryphons, but dragons were far larger than both. Most flying monsters were taught and able to follow basic commands such as go faster, slow down, barrel roll, canopy roll, somersault, loop, dive, pounce attack, and element attack. Some did not have riders and were capable of fighting on their own, but a rider gave the monster an extra set of eyes. The rider could pull on the reins to give direction to his monster, which let it know if an enemy was in its blind spots or on its tail. The best monsters trusted in the more advanced and tactical minds of their riders and let them have total command over their movements and attacks.

Wildwing was fully submissive to Ty's direction. He even found that the warrior's decisions often paralleled the same choices he would have made in battle. Their camaraderie was the main reason both had survived so many aerial battles together.

Wildwing flapped his wings as the dust on the floor of the plaza was brushed away from the gust of wind underneath the gryphon. He launched off his muscular legs, straight up into the air and then used his wings to propel himself up toward the clouds. Ty looked down over Wildwing's feathery side to the ground. The mother, her two daughters, Klar, and five monsters were strewn dead around the bloody plaza. Wildwing flew higher and higher, until the shapes became only tiny dark specs in the plaza far below.

What had occurred below was happening in many other streets and plazas throughout the city. The higher Wildwing flew, the larger Ty's bird's eye view of Celestial became.

Monsters were everywhere. Most of them were running towards the castle. Ty watched as a brown dragon about a mile away shot a blast into a warriors' watchtower near the castle. It toppled over, tearing the aqueduct down with it as it crashed across the Big Square and partially into the Fluorite River.

Dense black smoke from fires rose in high pillars all the way up to where Ty was in the sky. Enemy monsters flew everywhere around him in the air. One pounced on the back of a friendly monster and tore off its warrior rider, throwing him to the ground far below. Others were in high speed chases, tailing an enemy and firing their element at them. The warriors did the best they could to swerve and dodge, trying to avoid being killed.

A female enemy gryphon screeched as it shot through a pillar of smoke right next to Ty. Wildwing dove down just in time as the yellow feathered gryphon shot a blast of electricity right over Ty's head. A second blast hit Wildwing's leg. Ty felt a brief jolt travel through his own legs and through the rest of his body, followed by a sense of numbness. Wildwing flew away, trying to avoid another direct hit as the yellow gryphon gave chase.

Ty pointed to the nearby smoke pillar. "Dive!" he yelled against the whipping winds. Wildwing shot down through the center of the smoke column. He used his element of wind to blow smoke out of his and Ty's eyes. The smoke flew up into the eyes of the gryphon chasing them, forcing her to slow down. The technique created distance between them and the enemy on their tail. Wildwing did a backflip loop once the gryphon had lost sight of him in the smoke.

Now it was the green gryphon's turn to follow the yellow one. The yellow gryphon didn't know Wildwing was above her. She slowed down and flew out of the blinding smoke to see how far down the column her target had gone. Wildwing took advantage of her moment of confusion and pounced on her from behind. She let out a wild screech of pain when he dug his sharp talons into her back, holding on. She had no way of defending herself, because he had dug so deep into her flesh that he could not be shaken off.

There was a loud inhaling of breath as a ball of green light gathered in Wildwing's mouth. He then blasted a beam of wind energy at point blank range down onto the enemy gryphon's head. The blast ripped through half of her skull as blood sprayed up and hit Ty in the face. As he wiped it off, Wildwing let go of the lifeless yellow gryphon, whose limp body fell down somewhere into Celestial.

Ty heard the whiz of an arrow. It landed with a thud as it struck Wildwing in the side and buried itself deep in his flesh. Ty reared the reins and turned Wildwing to the left, to face the next enemy. It was a phoenix with long white and blue feathers. On top of it was a saddled gray orc. It wasn't odd to see monsters ride some of the stronger flying monsters as long as they had obtained a saddle somehow. If there was a rider, it would probably be an expendable monster with no elemental powers, such as this gray orc.

The orc pulled back his bow string and launched another arrow at Ty and Wildwing. This time it almost hit Ty, whistling right past his pointed ear. The phoenix attacked by opening its mouth and launching hundreds of tiny frozen icicles at them. Wildwing sat back in the air and flapped his wings hard. He utilized his element of wind to send a huge gust into the icicle pack zipping at them. Most of the icicles slowed down and fell, but there were about thirty that lightly punctured Wildwing in his stomach, arms, and legs. Since Wildwing had been sitting back, Ty had avoided the strike.

Wilding had been hit by similar attacks in the past. It felt like getting stung by a swarm of bees all at once and then left an odd cooling sensation in each puncture wound. Ty's gryphon was briefly stunned as he felt the effect. The brief pause was all the enemy needed for his next attack.

151

The phoenix and its rider flew in close to Wildwing and shot out a freezing vapor all over Wildwing's exposed underbelly, arms, and wings. The gryphon's green feathers were frozen into solid ice where he had been hit. Ty felt his stomach twist as they rapidly began to fall down toward the earth. The phoenix flew down after them, waiting for its stamina to build back up, so it could produce its next attack. Ty knew the monster would try to frost the rest of Wildwing, so that he would have no chance of breaking free of the ice.

The orc fired a fleet of arrows down at Ty. They had all missed him, but each one painfully lodged into Wildwing's topside. Ty needed to do something to save his gryphon from the onslaught of attacks. He reached behind his shoulders and took out his two swords. He quickly brought them out and dangerously swung the tips towards himself, cutting the leather straps of the harness that attached him to Wildwing. Ty wasn't afraid of cutting himself; his accuracy with the two swords was beyond excellent. He always landed his attacks precisely where he wanted.

The tension of the straps released, and they flew behind Ty, flapping in the wind. The Elf removed his feet from the stirrups and let himself fall off his monster. He felt like he hovered in the air for a brief moment as he saw Wildwing plummet down towards the Circle City without him. Ty turned in the air, facing towards the white and blue phoenix flying down at him.

The phoenix tried to bite him in the air, but Ty bent out of the way as the phoenix's large jaws snapped just inches from his face. The Elf stabbed his swords into the side of the enemy monster. Ty almost lost his grip when it felt like his shoulders were going to be ripped out of their sockets from the change of direction, but he had successfully transferred monsters in a death defying move.

With no holds for his feet, Ty used every ounce of muscle in his arms to pull out each sword and then plant it higher than the previous impalement. The phoenix stopped giving chase and leveled out in the air, unsuccessfully trying to reach his neck around to bite off Ty, who was in his blind spot. Since the beast was at the same horizontal level as the ground, the orc got out of his saddle and began walking towards Ty, who had been able to pull himself up onto the phoenix. Ty was lying on his back on the phoenix's back, exhausted from the physical toll climbing the monster had taken on his biceps and shoulders.

He rolled out of the way to avoid the orc stomping down in an attempt to crush his face. Ty created space by spinning on his butt and somersaulting towards the phoenix's saddle, rolling past the orc. He stood up and turned around to face his enemy.

The orc had already drawn an arrow from his quiver and was pulling it back in his bowstring. There was no way Ty could kill the monster before he released, so Ty ran at the gray orc with his bloodied swords. The moment Ty saw the orc's bicep twitch, he ducked, and the arrow sailed over his back, grazing his cross diagonal sheaths.

Ty stood back up to a full upright position and continued charging towards the orc. He swung both swords down onto the enemy. The orc dropped his bow and caught both of Ty's wrists in his hands. The two struggled. Neither had an advantage in leverage. The savage monster reached his head down and bit his sharp teeth into Ty's right forearm. Ty yelled in pain and reeled backwards from the unexpected attack. He accidently let go of his primary sword as it bounced off the phoenix and fell down to Element.

The orc bent down and picked up his steel bow. He brought it up in defense to block the warrior's downward strike with the secondary sword in his left hand. Sparks flew as steel hit steel. With the sword being the more balanced weapon, the orc needed to use both of his hands to hold up the bow.

Ty used his free right hand (covered in blood from the deep bite) to reach down into the small sheath on the right side of his thigh to pick up the only other weapon he carried – a dagger. Every warrior, no matter what, carried their main weapon, and then somewhere on their person had a secondary backup weapon. Ty had his attached to his leg.

The orc saw him pull it out, but there was nothing he could do to stop Ty. He could not let either hand off the bow which defended him from Ty's sword. He would not have the strength in one hand to hold up the skinny bow against the power of the heavier sword pushing down in the center of it.

Ty watched the orc's already ugly and disfigured face become even more twisted in anger. Usually in the moment when a person or monster knows that they are about to be killed, they will either choose to surrender or die.

The gray orc did not surrender.

Ty drove his dagger three quick times upward into the orc's unarmored stomach. The orc stumbled backwards, and backwards, and right off the back of the phoenix. Out of the corner of Ty's eye he saw a green beam shoot through the air. He jumped off the back of the phoenix and into the air. The powerful blast of wind energy smashed into the face of the phoenix he had been on, knocking it unconscious.

Ty began spinning and twisting towards Celestial. He knew his gryphon was alive and was the one who had just shot the phoenix. Wildwing would have easily been able to shake free of the ice before he hit the ground.

In the air, Ty put his dagger away and sheathed his only sword across his back. He enjoyed a minute of free falling until Wildwing flew over to him. The gryphon came in next to Ty so that they were falling together. Ty easily grabbed onto Wildwing's green feathers and pulled himself into the saddle.

The two continued fighting, killing monsters from behind who were trailing warrior friends. Overall, the warriors were vastly outnumbered. Friendly monsters were dying fast. They might have been able to take out two or three enemy monsters before ending up plummeting down soon after them.

Ty and Wildwing had lasted for a while when a huge black dragon being ridden by a hooded man cloaked in black joined the fight. He and his dragon took total control over the battle. The dragon was by far the largest Ty had ever seen. He had heard about this beast. Its reputation was notorious. Ty had never seen him before, but he knew who it was the moment he saw the size of the obsidian-scaled dragon. *We as people of the four races have our heroes of legend. Among the monsters, Nightstrike is considered a monster of legend and he hasn't even been alive for fifty years.*

As he moved through the center of the aerial battlefield, Nightstrike blasted water, wind, electricity, and earth elements into every warrior's monster. He had an amazingly high level of stamina. Nightstrike didn't need to wait to recover energy before using his next elemental attack. Right and left, Ty watched dragons, gryphons, and phoenixes ridden by warrior friends be brutally defeated. They were encased in ice, paralyzed, and suffered broken limbs. If the first impact didn't instantly kill them, it hurt them enough that the remaining enemy monsters quickly finished them off.

Ty watched all of the warriors' monsters die: *Lavaflame. Rip Claw. Whirlwind, and two of his three sons: Whirlwind Brother 1 and Whirlwind Brother 2. Flashbolt. Stonescorch. Starfire. Aftershock. Pyrosurge.*

He knew all of them. His father had introduced him to most of these friendly monsters. These monsters had known Ty for his whole life. Pyrosurge, Father Whirlwind, and a couple of others had known Ty's grandfather Jackson Canard and even Ty's great grandfather before him. The large monsters had been through many generations of people's lives since they lived for hundreds and hundreds of years. Their lifespan was far greater than even the 150 year lifespan of Elves. Each one of the ancient monsters had scars, acquired from countless battles from wars of the past.

Ty could not believe what he was seeing. It was hard to say goodbye to friends who had been so stable and dependable for so long. Ty always thought they would still be alive in his children's lives and their children's lives as well. These monsters had helped build Celestial. They had helped the civilians of Celestial and saved the Circle City from fires and other natural disasters.

It was not only the monsters Ty was saying goodbye to, it was their riders as well. Some of them were veteran warriors that had grown up with Caesar Canard. After his father's death, when Ty passed his test and was accepted into the warriors, these men took the young warrior under their wing in memory of his father. The veterans taught Ty the strategy and tactics he frequently used in battle. These men were like uncles to Ty. He watched in horror as each one died in pain.

Ty was the last one to be attacked by Nightstrike and its hooded rider. Wildwing was zapped with a huge blast of lighting from the giant black scaled dragon. It was much more powerful than the blast they had gotten hit with from the yellow gryphon earlier. Ty felt the breath leave Wildwing as the electrical surge passed through the gryphon's body.

Wildwing was killed on impact.

The gryphon's large body absorbed most of the surge, sparing Ty. But the Elf was still electrocuted. He felt numbness move through his entire body. The feeling would not go away. He could not move his legs at all, which were tightly hugged to the gryphon's body since he had cut his harness earlier. Ty struggled to move his arms. He could only move them slowly and restrictedly.

He used his bodyweight to lean back with the reins he held, hoping to steer Wildwing. He didn't want to believe his best monster friend was dead. He wanted to take him into future battles, to play around with him in the barracks, and to tell him his problems and worries. Ty would always voice and vent his issues aloud when he was with Wildwing. Wildwing always listened to Ty. Even though he couldn't understand Ty's words, he always cared about his rider. Everyone needed someone they could talk to freely without having to feel like they were being judged. Wildwing was that to Ty.

Ty let go of the reins and laid his head down on Wildwing's soft, feathery neck. He slid his fingers deep into the green feathers and grabbed on for support as they spiraled down toward Celestial. The Elf spoke to his monster even though he knew his words went unheard.

"We began this fight together, so we'll end this fight together. I'll see you in a minute, Wildwing."

It seemed like slow motion as Wildwing fell, with Ty saddled on his back. Ty's heart beat faster as the buildings got closer. Celestial was quickly growing in size below him.

The Elf feared he would end up just like so many people whose lives were lost on this terrible day. Each one of the deaths played out in his mind. *The people in the stands of the joust, the burned squire, the mother and her girls, Klar, the veteran riders I fought alongside, Wildwing. I am going to end up just like my father and grandfather. Continuing the legacy they left: warriors who die in their youth, before we ever really have the chance to live. At least the cursed legacy will end with me since I left no child.*

Deep down, Ty rescinded his last thought. He had always wanted a child. Every man wants to leave a legacy, for his surname to live on. Unlike Ty, his child might have finally been the one to break the curse.

Ty thought about all of the girls he dated in his life. He had always had some girl he took around wherever he went, but he never met that one girl that stood apart from the rest. That was completely his fault though. He had always been interested in quantity over quality. As soon as he went out on a date, he purposely found a flaw with the girl so he could be with someone different the following week. Finding flaws in others was easier than confronting his personal flaw: the fear of commitment.

Ty somewhat regretted not taking the time to get to know the girls he dated on the inside, rather than just on the outside. Maybe if he would have changed his perspective and given more of himself, he might have found someone he wanted to spend the rest of his life with. Maybe he would be married already. Maybe he would have already had a kid by now.

Would'ves, could'ves, and maybes. There is so much more in life I haven't experienced yet.

Ty closed his eyes to avoid the sickening pit in his stomach as his worst fear came to mind. *I've done nothing in my life to be remembered by. I've lived a wasted life. And now it's too late to change that fact.*

Precious seconds. If only I could have had more precious seconds.

Chapter 17

The wood splinters filled the air after Celestial's hometown jouster landed a devastating blow on his yellow armored opponent. The red armored warrior removed his helm and trotted in front of the stands on his way back to his side of the arena. Kari Quinn felt like there was something wrong with her for not being able to take her eyes off him. He was such an attractive man. It wasn't his physical looks that captured her gaze. What caught her eye was the warrior's huge smile and the fact that he was having fun. He wasn't nervous about the match, (from what she could tell) he was simply enjoying his life in that moment, smiling, and playing to the crowd who loved him.

When he looked directly at her, she quickly darted her eyes to the side, pretending like she hadn't been staring even though he was the center of the entertainment. When she looked back, his horse was riding back to its side, but the warrior had turned in his saddle and craned his neck, still fixated on her.

Kari couldn't help but smile back. She didn't even realize she was holding up two fingers towards him, showing him how many points he needed to advance to the championship match.

What are you doing, Kari? She lowered her arm and blushed as she thought about how stupid she must have looked to the jouster she had a crush on. *Of course he knows how many points he needs. He doesn't need me to tell him.* She saw that everyone in the crowd was starting to copy her gesture and raise their arms to put two fingers up. Kari put her two fingers up for the second time, to join in with the rest of the audience; this time higher than before.

She had overheard a group of women talking about this Stephen Brightflame a couple weeks ago when he was progressing through the Celestial Qualifiers. They spoke of his kindness from when he helped them as a warrior during his daily patrol. Whether it was carrying their groceries or walking alongside them with an umbrella, whatever the warrior did, he was always a gentleman, and he always treated the ladies with respect. The girls blushed when they discussed his attractive features. Rumor had it that Stephen Brightflame was single.

Kari hadn't ever met him before. Last night, she had a dream that she was the one he was helping out. She had been out in the woods, hunting for animals with her bow and arrows when she was attacked by a huge phoenix. Stephen came charging into the clearing on his large brown warhorse and ran his lance right through the monster. Then he protectively sat her in front of him on his horse. He grabbed the reins, enclosed his arms around her, and safely returned her to Celestial.

Kari smiled as she was reminded of the dream. Stephen looked like the perfect man. She didn't see any flaws in his physical person and more importantly no flaws in his character. Maybe Kari thought of him this way because that's how Celestial's propaganda wanted him to be perceived, as their flawless hero. Still, she allowed herself to believe what she had heard and read and couldn't help but have feelings for this seemingly perfect gentleman of a warrior.

Kari had always come to the Warriors' Joust with her father. It was tradition that he would take her every year as a father and daughter weekend of fun and activities. There was nothing like sitting next to her dad as they both cheered along together in favor of Celestial's jouster. Her father had been a warrior and a gentleman, just like this Brightflame character seemed to be.

But then the incident happened.

Even though he was no longer around, Kari continued on with the tradition. She had not missed one tournament since her father was murdered.

Like the warrior she was watching, Kari herself was quite the sight for sore eyes. She was twenty-three years old. She was half-Human and half-Elf. Her father was a Human and her mother was an Elf. She had an unblemished, light skinned face underneath straight, black hair. Usually she just let her hair flow straight down to the middle of her back and over her slightly pointed ears. She never allowed her hair to cover up her pretty face. Kari hated having her bangs distract her view and other's view of her. When she did allow her bangs in front of her face, they wouldn't go below her perfectly thin eyebrows.

Her eyes were the most captivating thing about her. They were large and round and a rare deep blue. If you looked very closely, you could see a black sunburst-like effect. Similar to the spokes of a wheel, a dozen thin black streaks cut through the amazing blue color. They were eyes you could stare at for days and get lost in.

Her teeth were as white as ivory. The bicuspids on the top row of her teeth were more prominent than the rest. It made her smile look better than if her teeth were perfectly straight. It was a cute, attractive smile surrounded by luscious full lips. Men and women in conversation with her spent half as much time speaking to her mouth as they did looking into her eyes. Either place of focus was captivating, just like she was.

Her figure was thin and muscular. Her body was well toned. She had large curves in areas that men spent too much time looking at. Even women sneaked a jealous glance wishing they could look like she did.

Kari's voice was like no other. The sound that came out of her 5'10" 160 pound frame was nothing short of angelic. Pure and clean voices like that were a gift from the good god. It was a shame the talent disappeared the same day her father died.

People used to be able to hear her lovely voice from blocks away, cascading through the air along with the birds that glided past and chimed in their own choruses. No one had any idea how she was able to pull off the notes she could; notes that were high and long and beautiful.

Everything about her was attractive. But despite her deadly gorgeous looks, she was equally dangerous. She always carried her father's bow and quiver behind her shoulders. It was a steel bow painted green, his favorite color. His father, who was a blacksmith, had worked on crafting it while Kari's father was in Warrior Training. Kari's grandfather gave it to his son the day he was drafted and officially became a warrior. Her father loved the bow second only to his wife and daughter. With its professional and intricate design, he felt like he could take down anything he aimed at. Kari's father used that bow and became one of Celestial's most notorious archers because of his accuracy.

Carrying the green bow around with her was a way to carry around her memories of him as well. Her father won many archery tournaments with his accuracy. He never bragged about his skill, because others did the bragging for him. His warrior friends would tell Kari, "You're father is the best shot I've ever seen."

Kari found that she inherited her father's accuracy. One morning, when Kari was only six years old, her father took her hunting in Whitebark Woods. He was going to teach her how to shoot. As she sat with him in the saddle, he talked about the importance of hunting.

"I don't know when my time will come, and hopefully it is not until I'm old and gray and you have a family of your own, but until then, I will not leave my family unprepared if something happens to me. You are a smart, beautiful girl, and most fathers wouldn't teach their daughters to hunt. To them it is improper, but I believe if you have a talent, then who is to say you can't use it whether or not you're a boy or girl? Kari, I have seen you with the toy bow and arrow I gave you for your birthday last year. You are only six, yet you hit your targets with better accuracy than I. We were given a gift from the good god that we can use to help provide for our family. I want to make a habit of this, you and I hunting together in the woods. Now that you are old enough to remember, I can begin to teach you the techniques I have learned. And someday, I will pass on to you, the bow that my father made for me."

While they were sitting in the quiet and stillness of the woods, Kari burst into tears. "Dad, I don't want to do this. I can't kill an innocent animal," she cried.

Her father let out a big sigh and set down his loaded bow. He put his arm around his daughter, wondering if he had brought her out here too soon. He had been only five when his father first took him out hunting. After a few minutes of letting her sob in his arms, he explained the purpose animals serve.

"The good god created people. The evil god created monsters. Both of them created animals. They are neither good nor evil. They are neutral in the ongoing war between both sides. They serve their created purpose of work, war, or food for both monsters and people. Some animals are better equipped to be put to work. Those, we can use to plow our fields and do other hard labor. We use others in war, like we do with horses and elephants. For food we domesticate animals. Luckily the monsters don't understand domestication, so that's why they fight over animals the way they do. Live animals are the only food that monsters know."

Kari eased her crying at the soothing sound of her father's calm voice. She pulled away and sat next to him, using her cotton sleeve to rub her nose and dry her eyes.

Her father continued. "Sometimes I sit out here and I don't see anything at all. Other times I see an animal and take the shot. I see it this way: I am here for a reason, to get food for my family. The animals were put here for a reason by the gods. Their purpose is to be the food that feeds us. So when I see an animal, I kill it, knowing there is a valid reason for its death, and it is serving its purpose in life."

"Do they hurt?" his daughter sniffled.

"If you hit them in the right spot they don't hurt at all. We want them to die quickly and painlessly. Over time I will show you, and you will learn the weak points for each animal. I want you to always aim for those spots, Kari. No person, animal, or monster deserves to be in pain more than they need to be if it has already been decided that they are going to be killed. And when we kill, it is never done for the fun of sport. Work, war, and food...other than those three, in addition to self-defense, there are no other reasons you should ever kill an animal. Do you understand?"

Kari nodded her head.

"You have to be careful out here, Kari. Even though animals serve their purpose as our food, they can be dangerous. They may not be able to talk or use elements like the monsters, but they can hurt us just as much. Usually animals won't bother us. Most of them are too small to hurt us: rabbits, squirrels, fish, birds, deer, and many others; but there are larger animals, like lions, wolves, bears, and wooly mammoths. They don't always feel like running away. If their space is aggravated or if they feel threatened, they will attack. So we always have to be careful. But I will be out here with you until you are old enough, so you don't have to worry about that. Does all of this make more sense to you now? Do you have any questions?"

"No, I understand," Kari said, no longer crying.

"Good," her father watched her for a minute as she contemplated everything he had told her. "I'm sorry I didn't discuss this with you before we left this morning. You know I'll never make you do something you don't want to do, Kari. You don't have to hunt if you don't want to. We can sit here for the rest of the day and talk if that's what you want. As long as we're together, I'll be happy."

As soon as he said that, a squirrel hopped across the ground and scurried up the front of a tree facing them. Kari reached down and picked up the bow and arrow in a flash. Her reaction speed had always been extraordinary. For fear of not scaring the prey, her father did not say a word. All he could do was watch as his daughter soundlessly lifted into a crouched position and aimed at the upwards moving squirrel.

She was too young to pull back the bowstring like he could, but she could pull it back far enough. She inhaled, held her breath, and released the arrow. He followed the arrow with his eyes, seeing that it had stuck into the tree. The squirrel's feet and arms let go of the bark and hung limp from its lifeless body. The arrow has gone right through its back.

"I've got my dinner for tonight," Kari said with dry eyes as she handed her father the bow back.

Chapter 18

That was the first and last time Kari hunted with her father. He was murdered on duty as a warrior shortly after Kari's first foray into hunting.

Kari never found out who the man was that murdered her father or what exactly happened on that dark night. All she knew was that many other warriors were killed by the same man. She didn't even know if the murderer was still alive, if he had been captured, or if he had been killed. Occasionally she would have nightmares that the faceless man was stalking her. Kari would dream that she was firing arrows at him, but even though the arrows entered into his body, none of them hurt him or slowed him down. The man kept coming after her, until she was cornered. He would then violently kill her, causing Kari to wake up in a cold sweat.

The questions in Kari's mind were never abandoned. It seemed that as time went on, the answers she desperately longed for slipped farther and farther away. She wanted nothing more than to put an end to the frustrating mystery surrounding her father's death. The one thing Kari did know was that if she found out the murderer was still alive, reality would be different from her nightmares. She would stop at nothing to exact vengeance against the murderer.

After her father's death, Kari's mother did not provide for herself or her daughter. She would stare absently at blank walls, had no appetite, and apparently did not think Kari had one either because she did not cook any meals. Kari took her father's bow and arrows and got her own food in the woods once their gold ran out.

Kari would sneak out of the city, usually by hiding in the backs of empty wagons, heading out to the farmlands to collect the harvest that would be brought back into the city. From the fields, she walked alone to the woods. She knew it was risky being alone, but she felt at peace in the Whitebark Woods. One of her final memories of her father had been him proudly looking down at her as he reached up and pulled the arrow out of the tree and handed her the squirrel.

Kari went hungry some days when she couldn't find any game, but when she did see an animal, she did not miss. Kari tried to feed her mother, but she did not eat anything. She had no motivation and barely said more than two words to Kari. It wasn't long before Kari knew she needed to seek out help for her mom.

One day instead of taking a right towards the forest, she took a left and headed further into the city. She had only been to her aunt and uncle's house a handful of times, but she remembered what it looked like. Who could forget such a magnificent place? Kari waited outside in the bitter cold of the winter until late at night, when her aunt and uncle finally came home. After sitting by the fireplace and warming up, she told them about her mother's depression.

Her mother's sister and brother-in-law decided to take Kari and her mother into their large house. They spent their own gold on the best doctors, trying to find someone who could heal Kari's mom, but nothing worked. She progressively deteriorated, which was something Kari thought had already happened so much that it was impossible to continue. Her once amazingly beautiful mother had grown into someone beyond recognition. Her mother's skin grew loose and her face grew small and skinny with her cheekbones pronounced.

Every time Kari hunted, she would come home and walk into her mother's bedroom. She knew her mother was looking at her, but her mother's emotion was no different than when she was staring at the blank wall of the bedroom. Kari would hold up her game in the air, hoping it might bring a smile to her mom's face, the same way her father had smiled down at her when he handed her that squirrel. But her mother's smile was gone.

Kari would cry herself to sleep at night, feeling like she was a failure as a daughter for not being able to nurse her mother back to health. She would have given anything for her mother to stop suffering. One night just past Kari's eighth name day, her mother's breathing was scarily shallow as Kari held her hand. She watched her mother, wondering whether or not each breath would be her last.

And then finally, one of them was. Her mother died as Kari held her hand. Kari climbed into the bed and lay next to her mother. She nestled her head in between the feather stuffed mattress and her mom's skinny stomach. Kari cried for the rest of the night.

In less than six months, she had lost her father and mother. Actually, she lost her mother the moment her father was killed.

Kari remembered what one of the many doctors had said. He had been the only one who had made the right diagnosis. "Husbands and wives are connected in marriage. Sometimes when one leaves and that connection is broken, the other loses his or herself because in truth, half of them is already gone." Kari found that was the easiest explanation to comprehend. Her mother's heart was irreparably broken. She was lost without her husband, and she fell into depression and gave up her motivation to live.

Kari wondered why she, as the daughter, wasn't enough to be her mom's motivation. *Maybe she knows I can take care of myself*, Kari always figured. Whatever the reason was, Kari always knew her mom loved her deeply.

The half-Human, half-Elf was like her warrior father, self-reliant and strong. Plus, she had her mother's beauty. She had inherited the best qualities of two great parents. Kari wanted to carry on those qualities in honor and memory of them.

She kept a silver locket around her neck with her mother's picture inside. On the inside was a small oval drawing of her parents holding her as a baby. A second picture was on the opposite side of the locket. It was a drawing of her mother early in her adult life, around the time her father fell in love with her, when she was at the peak of her beauty.

Kari wanted to remember her mother by that picture and the good memories she had of her, not by the way her mother looked lying sick and motionless in that bed. The locket became a part of Kari. She didn't even take it off when she went to sleep at night. Her father's bow and arrows were not so easily carried around. Her aunt and uncle didn't allow weapons in their home, and Kari feared they might ask her to abandon them along with the rest of her family's unwanted belongings. She begged and begged until her aunt and uncle finally gave in. They saw the importance of her father's bow in Kari's eyes. The locket, bow, quiver, and arrows were the only things Kari took from her old house.

Her aunt and uncle were wealthy and belonged to a higher social class of people. They lived in a tall stone house near the center of the city with decorative furnishings. They were both incredibly intelligent. Years ago, when they were first married, they pooled their money together and bought a high end tailor shop. They were very successful in inventing new types of expensive clothes. They provided the royalty with a lot of the clothes that were worn to public events. The business made an abundant return on their investment. The couple could have retired already, but they continued working in their shop because they took pride in the work that they loved.

Kari was taken along to all of their high class gatherings. She was obedient and spoke properly like a woman, as they had taught her too, while dressed in the beautiful attire they designed for her. Those things Kari didn't mind. It was fun when they let her pick out her own dresses and shoes. Like any girl, Kari enjoyed being treated like a princess. The actual party was what she despised.

She loved her aunt and uncle, but they were extremely boring. And so were all of their high class friends. They exchanged polite courtesies, but never talked about anything beyond the weather, their business plans, and fashion styles. Some stories Kari heard repeatedly at every gathering as if the person could not remember having told it before.

The whole night was nodding and smiling; so much so that after a couple hours, Kari's cheeks felt like they wanted to be fixed in that false happy position. She wondered how awkward and fake her smile must have looked.

The food was nothing she had ever eaten before. They ate foods like snails, sour grapes, fish eggs, and other things Kari couldn't even begin to guess what or who they came out of. All of the foods were an acquired taste that she could not acquire, no matter how often she tried them. She ate most of the foods she didn't like because otherwise she would go hungry. Her aunt and uncle did not cook much food at home. If they weren't at a party, they would go out to a fancy restaurant to eat, where the food was only slightly more palatable.

Kari thought these parties might be a good chance to meet other children since her aunt and uncle didn't have any, but the kids were just as boring as their parents. *Have they been brainwashed into only talking about the same topics as their parents?* Kari always wondered. Some of them were even spoiled and condescending towards her, since they knew her parents' story and felt she didn't belong in their social class.

One time Kari punched a boy in the nose when all evening he called her derogatory names, making her feel like the low class trash that he thought she was. She felt the nose give in and heard the snap as the boy cried out in pain. He ran to his mother and buried his face in her yellow dress, staining it with the blood gushing out of his nostrils.

Kari smiled until she looked up and saw her aunt briskly walking towards her, with a face full of horror and disgust. Kari had introduced two things to that party that these types of people rarely saw: bad manners and blood.

She knew her aunt would have ran at her and spanked her if it wasn't for trying to look proper in front of all of her high class friends. That was the only time Kari was thankful she was among them. However, the delay in consequence was only temporarily postponed. When she got home, she was punished. Her rear end was sore for three straight days. Kari complained to her aunt and uncle about how she was never again going to attend a party, but they refused that statement.

"A proper lady enjoys conversation."

"I don't want to be a proper lady. I hate these boring people, and I can tell they don't like me either." That is what Kari had wanted to say, but she didn't come up with those words until an hour after she argued with them. It seemed like that's how it always worked; she always thought of something intelligent to say after the argument ended.

Under the light of a full moon, Kari grabbed her bow and quiver, put the locket around her neck, and ran away into Whitebark. She was confident enough in her skills that she could hunt animals and survive on her own.

It wasn't two days before a party of hunters found her, told her it was no place for a little girl, and then brought her back into the city to the warriors. Kari wanted to become a warrior like her father, but they didn't allow girls into their ranks (which was something Kari thought was one of the stupidest rules ever created). Her aunt and uncle picked her up from the warriors and gave her another licking for worrying them. This spanking hurt ten times worse than the last.

Kari was forced to continue attending the parties, where she continued to hate the conversation, the company, the food, and the awkward forced smiles. She wished she could run away not just to a certain place, but to a certain time, when her father and mother were in their old house.

There, the conversation was interesting. The thought of the food she used to eat made her mouth water. There may not have been as many different tastes, but the taste of one good food was better than a hundred nasty ones. She missed chicken, fish, venison, steak, and her favorite – hamburgers. Those were the good foods.

In the social class she used to live in, stains from grease and barbeque dressings found their way onto people's shirts but the clothing could unashamedly be worn again later in the week, unlike one of her aunt and uncle's dresses. If that got a stain, it was deemed unworthy. It was given to a member of the "lower class," or it was given to a fire.

Kari longed to sit at the dinner table with her father again, to hear him tell stories from his day. Whenever he was called to go out of town on a mission, he would come back and tell tales of the monsters he fought, rare animals he saw, and the sights of nature that captivated him. His descriptions painted pictures in her head. Someday she would travel to those parts of Element like he did. She wanted to visit those beautiful places and experience everything for herself. He always brought back some sort of souvenir from each new location. She would carry it around for weeks on end and show it off to all her friends, repeating her father's stories of adventure.

Sometimes her mother and father would invite fellow warriors over to their house along with their wives and children. Kari loved playing with those kinds of kids, chasing each other, roughhousing, reenacting famous battles of legends, and dressing up as the heroes and villains to play the parts. That was the life she loved; the life that had been ripped away from her without any notice or warning.

Kari was twenty-three now. She moved out of her aunt and uncle's house as soon as she got her first job. She had been as happy to leave as they were to see her go. The two sides didn't hate each other, in fact deep down they respected each other, but they knew she was never truly happy with them as she was with her own parents. Her aunt and uncle used their connections to get her a job at a restaurant.

In the afternoons Kari was a waiter. She enjoyed serving people. But mornings were her favorite part of the job. She was paid to go to the woods and hunt game for dinners the following nights. *Getting paid to hunt. I love it!*

Kari didn't make much gold, but that was okay with her. Getting by on the basic essentials was all she needed. There was something liberating about living that way. People she met wondered why someone with such a beautiful face and perfectly shaped body spent her time getting dirt under her fingernails and sweating in the heat of a kitchen. She told them how happy she was with what she was doing.

The snotty boys she had grown up with at the high class parties saw how beautiful she had become and began to frequently visit the restaurant just to flirt with her. She thought some of them turned out pretty good looking as well (except for the one with the crooked nose), but she knew what they were like on the inside. *Looks change faster than personalities.*

Kari had dated a couple of nice boys her age, but she never fully gave herself into any of the relationships. She was doing everything she wanted to do in life, except for one thing:

she still wanted to travel and see the places her father told her stories about. All the boys she had been with wanted to settle down in Celestial and start a family. That would tie her down and keep her from what she really wanted to do.

Kari was not ready for marriage. She never allowed herself to fall head over heels in love with any of the boys because of that fact. She knew what she wanted and was patient and saved what little extra gold she made and stored it aside. She hoped she could find an honorable man who wanted to travel before children. That was all she needed to fulfill her dreams. It wasn't much to ask for, but why was it so hard to find that guy?

With her bow slung over her shoulder, a quiver full of arrows, and her silver locket attached to a necklace hidden away in the crevice between her breasts, Kari sat in the stands of the Warriors' Jousting Tournament. While thinking of what possibilities her future held, she was staring at the handsome Stephen Brightflame.

I can see him being the one I could travel the world with before settling down to start a family.

After the championship match ended, Kari was planning to go hunting in the woods. It was going to be a good day for remembering her father. She thought back to how they sat in these same stands years ago cheering for Celestial. Later Kari would reminisce about the happy memories with her father as she did what he loved to do - hunt in the woods.

When she looked up and saw the flaming boulder crash into the stands near her, Kari knew she wouldn't be firing arrows at animals today; she would be shooting monsters.

Chapter 19

The first flaming boulder looked like it was coming down in slow motion. Kari knew it was going to hit near her and that there was no way to stop it. All she could do was follow it with her eyes and hope it missed her. It smashed into the row of stands not more than twenty feet from where she was.

Bodies were sent flying on impact if they hadn't been crushed. The air was filled with horrified screams as people instantly caught on fire. Added to those screams were the cries from spectators who couldn't remove their eyes from the suffering people. Kari remembered screaming too, but she also remembered gasping and covering her mouth.

Everything seemed to be happening at an unreal high speed. The crowd simultaneously stood up and began moving away from the heat of the flames that were igniting the wooden bleachers. Kari was pushed and shoved from every direction by panicking people. Body masses slammed into her shoulders. She lost her balance and would have fallen and gotten trampled if it wasn't for being held up by slamming against someone next to her. The crowd was so tight it was impossible to fully fall down.

Kari began to hyperventilate. She did not care for tight spaces in which she had little control to escape from. She preferred the open air of the outdoors. Claustrophobia made it hard to breathe, and she began to panic as much as the people on fire.

Kari watched people on the opposite side of the arena in a column of rows in the bowl of the stadium. A huge boulder was coming down on them. They were all looking up at it while pushing into the backs of the people in front of them. They managed to create a small clearing where the boulder was going to crash down, but it wasn't large enough. The people closest to the clearing must have been pushing with all of their strength as the boulder got closer and when they realized they were directly in its path.

The crowd surged the opposite way from the eastern exit as a small group of minotaurs ran into the stadium. Luckily, Kari was heading to the only other exit; the western side of the arena. She was somewhat successful pushing and squeezing her way through people, headed down the wooden bleachers instead of to the side stair sets that paralleled each column like the majority of people were doing. She went to put her foot out on the seats below her when she received a slight accidental bump in the back from someone. She missed the step and fell hard into the wood. People began to step on her hands, knees, and feet as the screams from her section grew louder.

Everything got darker around her. A large boulder was casting its shadow as it came down on her column of rows. Kari felt someone grab her under both of her arms and lift her up like she weighed nothing. She didn't even get to see or thank the man that helped to pick her up because she was in the air a second after she was back on her own two feet. The flaming boulder smashed into the wooden rows just as she was hopping down. The top half of the column of rows caved in, which jutted everything below it outwards.

Everyone, including Kari, who was in the first fifteen rows closest to the stadium floor, was spilled out onto it. Kari picked herself up, choking and coughing on the sand she had inhaled. She stopped and looked herself over while dusting herself off, just to make sure she was still all attached. Sometimes it took a couple seconds for pain to register with the body. She realized that other than a couple bruises she was sure to have the next morning, she was fine.

Kari surveyed the possible exits. She was almost at the western exit, but it was incredibly smoky. The exit was narrowed because it was partially blocked by a tall building that had toppled and crashed through the side of the oval arena. The eastern exit looked to be void of the minotaurs now, but she would have to run across the arena to get to that side. She wanted to get out as soon as possible in order to avoid the falling boulders. Kari continued in the same direction figuring it was her safest bet out of two unsafe choices. The exit had already become bottlenecked, with so many people rushing out of the narrow escape.

A bright orange moving light stole her attention. It was a person, on fire, trying to roll in the sand to extinguish the torturing flames. Kari quickly unclasped the pin that held her blue cloak together and threw it over the man. The fire died as soon as the oxygen was cut off, but nothing was moving underneath the cloak. The putrid smell of burned flesh filled Kari's nostrils and made her gag. She was afraid to lift up her cloak, afraid of the grotesque sight she might see underneath; but she did.

It was worse than she possibly could have imagined. The man's hair was singed, along with his arms and legs. His clothes had been mostly burned through. What skin she could see was charred black and covered in disgusting red and pink blisters. A woman came over and collapsed to her knees in the sand next to the burned victim. She laid her body across his and was sobbing uncontrollably. "My Husband! Errol!" She screamed his name over and over again in agony.

Kari tried to grab at the widow and encourage her to leave and get to safety, but the woman swatted her gesture away. There was nothing Kari could say or do to fix the lady's broken heart.

Kari got up and pressed along with the funneling crowd out through the narrow exit, leaving the death filled arena behind her. She emerged out into the smoky air of the small plaza outside the arena. Abandoned carts with all sorts of fruits, vegetables, jewelry, and handmade products were scattered everywhere. Vendors always used the plazas nearby the stadium to sell their goods, especially when the stadium was in use, as it was today. A high amount of traffic guaranteed high sales.

The plaza also featured carved marble statues of Celestial champions from previous Warriors' Jousting Tournaments. They lined the curved wall of the entrance heading into the arena. There had only been six Celestial champions in the forty-five year history of the Warriors' Joust, but there were only four statues standing. A couple of them had been toppled over. One was broken by catapulted debris. The other was pushed over by a group of people onto a medium-sized black spider. The monster was about the length of Kari's shoulder to fingers. It was flattened under the heavy stone statute as a splatter of its dark yellow blood spilled out onto the plaza floor from both of its sides.

Kari saw two more spiders in the plaza. One was the same color black and the other one was a creamy white. The white one's focus was distracted while eating a half-alive Elf. Kari took her bow off her shoulder, drew an arrow from her quiver, and shot it into the monster's back. It crumpled up in pain and died within a minute. The half-alive Elf, lying on the ground with intestines spilling out of his open stomach turned to Kari. She saw the pleading look in his eyes and knew exactly what he wanted.

She shot an arrow through his skull so that he wouldn't have to endure excruciating pain in his final moments of life.

In less than a second, Kari had already notched another arrow and carefully shot it across the plaza, avoiding the running crowd, and into a black tarantula before it bit a child with its poisonous fangs. A couple other spiders that found their way into the plaza were being ganged up on and beaten to death by civilians with random objects. Broomsticks, chains, and canes can be just as deadly as a sword when they are swung in anger.

Kari notched another arrow even though no target was in sight. Expecting the unexpected never hurt anyone, and today was already a day full of surprises. Kari would not die on account of being unprepared.

She looked to the sky and saw something airborne that had also caught the attention of others. It wasn't a large boulder, but rather a collection of smaller objects that had been catapulted over the walls. Whatever they were crashed onto the stone floor and exploded like red paint with a horrific splattering sound.

Kari had a feeling she knew what had been launched from outside the inner wall. Looking closer, she realized in disgust that she had guessed correctly. Someone else in the plaza observed the catapulted ammunition being used by the monsters and yelled out what it was at the same time Kari did.

"Those are bodies!" The appendages of people were littered everywhere. Most of the people appeared to have been killed before they were launched. Based on the cheap clothing, the parts looked to belong to the farmers and field workers who worked in the miles and miles of farmlands between the outer and inner wall all around the city.

A little boy was crying as he kneeled over his dead mother, trying to shake her back to life. Kari saw white foam in the mother's mouth and what looked like a spider bite on her arm. The boy looked up at all the people frantically running past. One man stopped and picked him up into his arms. The kid started kicking and screaming as he was carried away from his unmoving mother.

That man just saved that boy's life.

Kari realized the child was too young to understand death and probably would have stayed by his mother until the monsters came through and killed him too. It wouldn't have been a quick kill either. Monsters enjoyed torturing people who could not defend themselves. Whatever the age, gender, or race was, it did not matter. Monsters would fill their prey with fear and pain before they violently killed them.

Kari noticed the boy was looking at her through tear drenched eyes as the man put him over his shoulder and carried the boy to safety. She mouthed the words, "It will be okay," as she nodded to the child. The man's selfless action of taking care of the boy reminded her of one of the greatest things about the people of Celestial: whenever you were in trouble, you could always count on the fact that someone would go out of their way to help you. Sometimes you might not even know who the person was.

Every week after Kari's father had left and her mother was in her eternal state of depression, someone left a basket of fruit and a case of milk on their doorstep once a week. Kari had always wanted to find out who that person was, but she never did. The anonymous donor was a hero to her.

In Celestial, people treated others as they wanted to be treated. Preparing meals for the sick, giving them some of their gold, and spending time with elderly to hear their stories was what the people of Celestial did. It was a city of good deeds. Celestial was like a brotherhood, just like the warriors were known to be. Everyone stuck up for one another and everyone loved each other. Being a part of the brotherhood was like an unbreakable bond.

The city wasn't perfect of course, nothing was. For every eight or nine people, there might be one person who wasn't a role model citizen, but even gruff people like that contributed in their own way. They may not have liked intimacy with people like everyone else, but they were the ones who hated monsters more than anything. If a monster was hurting a citizen of Celestial, they would be the ones brave enough to protect the person.

Kari shuffled through the loosening crowd, when a spider jumped at her from behind one of the large wooden vendor carts. She instinctively fell backwards to the stone plaza floor while pulling back the bowstring, releasing her notched arrow into the hairy gray and black spider's six-eyed face before her butt even hit the ground. Kari got up, loaded another arrow, and pressed on. She left the plaza and started to take the quickest route of roads that would lead to her apartment.

Down the road, about fifty meters from where she was, Kari saw a dog run out of a side alley with two of her litter wide-eyed and trailing behind her. An average litter usually consisted of six to eight puppies. Kari didn't want to think what had happened to the missing ones. The mother navigated aimlessly, lost in the confusion of the surrounding noise. It didn't matter where she ran, no place was safe.

A medium-sized boulder crashed through a nearby building. The poor dog was hit by one of the tumbling stones. Kari watched as it lay injured in the street, motionless, as her puppies nudged their mother with wet noses. Her breathing was shallow and her heavy eyelids blinked less and less until they didn't open anymore. The puppies looked at their mother's stomach, expecting to see it rise in inhalation of another breath, but it never did. One of the puppies lay down and curled up on the ground in between the mother's arms and legs. The other was not convinced she was gone and trotted around to her face. He lightly head-butted her muzzle, but there was still no movement. He, too, realized she was dead and snuggled up under her chin.

Didn't I just see the same thing happen with the little boy in disbelief at the death of his spider-bitten mother? How many innocent people have been killed? How many children have lost their parents? How many parents have lost their children? That is even worse. Parents should never have to watch their child die before them and in violent pain nonetheless. No one is exempt from monster attacks, person or animal alike.

Monsters are on a mission. A mission to breach the city, gain control, and keep control. They will kill every living, breathing, moving thing in the city, down to the last insect if that is what it takes for them to succeed in their goal.

Kari made a promise to herself that she would not become a victim like so many of the people (and animals) she had seen die today.

It would turn out that her promise would be upheld. She would be one of the few lucky ones to keep her life on this tragic day. But it wouldn't be easy. As if the past hour of Kari's day wasn't bad enough, things were about to take a turn for the worse.

Chapter 20

Kari's small apartment was not far from where she watched the dog die and the puppies mourn. She lived above the restaurant where she worked. The owner of the building was a friend of the family. He was a second cousin to her mother and aunt. He knew of Kari's rough life experience and allowed her to stay in the empty apartment for a generous rent.

Kari figured she would be safe at home. She would lock and bar the doors while she hoped and prayed the warriors could hold off the monster attack. She had to slightly change her path, since parts of a broken building blocked the street in front of her. At least she was close to home and knew this area well. Many people who had been visiting had no idea where to go. They were lost in a foreign city. Civilians were stopping and giving the visitors quick directions or leading them back to their own houses for shelter.

Kari ran down alleys, half spending her time nervously watching all around her. A fear had crept into her mind that a monster would come from around any one of the many corners she was passing.

She exited the alley and entered into the tiny, homey cul-de-sac her apartment was in. She gasped and immediately stopped in her tracks when she saw a huge red, orange, and gray feathered phoenix hovering in the middle of the half-circle of buildings. The monster was blowing flames everywhere, starting fires. Kari quickly darted behind the building she had just run past and then slowly snuck a peek around the corner.

The restaurant was already aflame. There was a sound of shattering glass as the intense heat broke the windows of the restaurant. The shattering was soon followed by a small explosion. *The fire must have ignited our cooking oil.*

Tears welled in Kari's eyes as she watched the flames rise within seconds and engulf her apartment above the restaurant. Everything she owned was in there save the bow, quiver, and the locket around her neck. The feeling in her legs gave out, and she sunk to a crouched position with her back against the building as she thought about everything she was losing.

She didn't have much in monetary value by the world's standards, but her belongings were special to her. Her favorite item in the house was likely one of the first to burn. An old friend of Kari's parents kept tabs on Kari unbeknownst to her. The lady knew Kari didn't have much financially. She had purchased Kari's parents' dinner table and chairs when their household items went up for auction after Kari's mother died. She gave Kari the kitchen furniture for free. Kari was moved by the act of kindness. It was the table she had sat at as a child with her father, listening to his incredible stories and tales of adventure.

The dinnerware that went on that table was the hardest earned item in the apartment. She wanted to have a fancy cutlery collection for when guests came over to eat, but she could only afford to buy a couple pieces at a time. Occasionally she would barter and trade to get parts of the complete set, but mostly she had to save up her money. One week, she only had enough to buy forks and spoons. The next week, she bought the knives. Two weeks later, she had saved up enough to buy the decorative plates and cups. Once Kari had dinnerware for three and felt that her home was adequately furnished, she invited her aunt and uncle to join her for supper.

Kari had been so upset when they had come in and ate with her, only to criticize the quality of the dinnerware. They then went around and critiqued all of her cheap paintings on the walls, along with the minor flaws they saw in the table, chairs, bed, and other furniture she had worked so hard to acquire.

All she wanted to do was make a good impression. She was so proud of what she had accomplished on her own, but it could never have been enough for them.

That was the last time she saw her aunt or uncle. She assumed if they were by her side right now, they would be happy to see the worthless junk burning. Although she didn't get along with them, she still loved them, and she would never forget how they lent a helping hand when she and her mother had nowhere else to go. *Wherever they are, I hope they are safe.*

Other than the family table, the thing that she was going to miss most of all was all of the gold that she had saved up for the trips she was planning. Sometimes it was just two or three gold coins a week, but it had been adding up for years. She had everything planned. Three weeks from today, she would have had enough gold to take a trip to Almiria.

Countless hours of hard work gone within minutes. Now I'm going to have to find a new job and a new place to live. Once again I will have to adapt in a new environment because things always seem to be taken from me unexpectedly.

She angrily stood up. The phoenix was setting fires at the other end of the small cul-de-sac. All of the buildings were connected side by side, with no space between them. No doubt every building would eventually catch the fire of its neighbor, but the phoenix was enjoying causing immediate destruction.

Kari sprinted behind the enormous beast and burst through the door of the unlocked building next to the restaurant. She could feel the heat already starting to come through the shared restaurant wall. The room Kari ran through was filled with smoke. She quickly took a flight of stairs two steps at a time and exited out onto the roof. In this less wealthy section of Celestial, roofs were considered another floor of the building. People often slept under the stars when the weather allowed for it. Cookouts and dinners were sometimes held on roofs as well. There was always a short barrier wall that surrounded the entire perimeter of the rooftop. It protected people from accidently falling off the side.

The barrier was tall enough to conceal Kari as she crouched behind it. She turned and slowly peeked over the short wall at the phoenix. *There he is.* The monster's entire focus was set on a house he was melting about four buildings to the left of the destroyed restaurant. There was screaming coming from inside the house. *The Gutlingers live there.*

The Gutlingers were a family of four, two parents and their two teenage boys. The boys were polite and well mannered. They frequented the restaurant Kari worked at and were always in good moods when Kari was their waitress. She knew they each had a crush on her, but she was too old for them.

Kari didn't know which one of the four Gutlingers was screaming, but she hated the thought of any of them experiencing pain. They were a giving family. Mr. Gutlinger was a farmer and didn't make a lot of money, but he gave what gold he could to help in the local community. He, his wife, and sons were always donating their time. Kari believed spending time doing volunteer work for charity was more beneficial than just giving money.

The side of the phoenix's face was exposed to Kari as he was burning the residence. Kari, still crouched down, moved along the wall to get a better angle. She notched an arrow, drew back her bowstring, and stood up. The phoenix noticed the tiny movement out of the corner of his right eye. But it was too late. The arrow flying into his eye was the last sight that eye ever saw.

It had only taken Kari a second to find her mark and release.

Bull's eye!

Kari was already off and running before the shot landed. She knew it would be accurate from the moment it left the bow. She hurdled over the roof's barrier and sprinted across the rooftops, away from the monster. Behind her, she heard the monster growl in pain as the center of his eye had been deeply impaled by the arrow.

The phoenix's powerful wings flapped up and down as he ascended high into the air. Since the phoenix had low energy from the amount of element he had expelled, he used his long, feathered tail to attack. The monster glided through the air, negating the distance Kari had created within seconds. The tail lashed down, smashing hard through the roof Kari had just jumped off of. The roof was nearly split in half from the impact. The next attack was horizontal instead of vertical. The phoenix smashed through the front of the next building, causing the roof Kari was on to sharply slant. Kari nearly lost her balance, but kept her footing and vaulted over the next barrier and onto the next rooftop.

The phoenix roared again partly because of the pain he was in, but mostly it was a roar of frustration. He wanted to quickly end the life of this halfling female that had blinded his right eye.

Kari jumped off a roof and over an alleyway gap before landing safely on another building top. She escaped her home plaza, which was now reduced to a giant ring of burning buildings. She ran over rooftops trying her best to create more distance between herself and the phoenix. Kari tried running to the right, on the phoenix's blindside. If he lost sight of her, she would have a chance to take cover and hide.

Another gap was jumped over, but the phoenix was still coming after her and getting closer. The beast was flying dangerously low, gliding over the rooftops she had already crossed. Kari landed on the inclined roof of a church. Shingles broke off underneath her, preventing her from finding stable footing. She started to slide down the roof, back in the direction of the phoenix.

This is it, was all she could think. *This is how I die.*

Luckily the angry phoenix was going so fast that he wasn't able to slow his massive weight. As Kari slid down, the monster flew right over her head. He crashed through the church's stone bell tower and spiraled down into the ground with the debris.

Kari realized nothing was going to stop her from falling off the roof as she skidded down the steep incline. There was nothing to grab onto for support.

A fall from this tall church roof will break both my legs, if it doesn't kill me.

Kari's only option was to jump for the stone balcony jutting out from the side of the building she had been running on before transitioning to the church's roof.

Her stomach landed right on the railing of the balcony, knocking the wind out of her. She fell backwards to the ground and smashed the back of her head on the street. She rolled around in pain on the ground trying to breathe air back into her lungs.

After recovering with deep breaths, she continued running without a specific destination. She didn't know where to go for safety now that her home was gone. *My aunt and uncle live too far away. I will have to head to the nearest watchtower.*

She turned the corner to run down the road and found herself staring into the eyes of three snarling dire wolves. Dire wolves were three times larger than regular wolves. Regular wolves were just animals, but dire wolves were monsters because they were created by the evil god. They were far more dangerous and vicious than regular wolves. One clean bite could tear off a person's limb.

The dire wolves' mouths were all dripping with red blood as they angrily bared their teeth and snarled at the sight of her, waiting for her to make a move. Two of them had their own blood on them, gushing out from deep cuts in their sides.

Kari knew she had no time to draw an arrow and loose it. Even if she had tried to shoot them, each dire wolf would require three or four shots to go down. There were only seven arrows left in her quiver. She turned and started sprinting back the way she came, knowing dire wolves ran five times as fast as people. The three, four legged monsters chased her down the road. Kari turned into an alley, hoping that the monsters would be too fast for their own good, like the phoenix, and not be able to stop and turn the corner as quickly as she could.

She underestimated the abilities of the muscle-bound beasts. The dire wolves could stop and accelerate very easily. Turning into the alley bought her no time. In fact, the dire wolves gained ground on her because of the move.

Kari kicked out the bottom of a stack of crates, sending them tumbling behind her. It took more time for her to do that than it took for the monsters to jump over them. She heard their growls getting closer and closer. There was nothing she could do to slow them down and nothing she could do to speed herself up.

The red, orange, and gray feathered phoenix had risen up out of the wreckage of the church's bell tower and roof. He had located Kari and saw her being chased by the three monsters. The alley was too narrow for him to fly into, so he soared above the rooftops.

Kari heard a snarled growl behind her and then the chomp of a jaw as the closest dire wolf, the leader of the pack,

189

took a bite out of the tunic she was wearing. The dire wolf lunged again. Kari knew this time it would bite more than just cloth.

Before she felt the pain, Kari felt the heat. The entire alley behind her was filled with a flaming inferno from the phoenix's element. All of the fire had nowhere to go except to quickly follow her down the narrow alley. It consumed the three dire wolves, killing them as soon as they were touched.

Kari burst out of the alley and into a tiny square plaza, as the flames exploded out after her. She fell to dirt floor and rolled around as her clothes caught on fire. The burning flames were suffocated, but they had not been extinguished fast enough. They had melted holes through the back of her shirt and burned her skin. It wasn't as bad as the man she had tried to save in the arena, but she still had suffered terrible second degree burns.

Kari cried out loud from the pain. There was nothing she could do to heal herself.

The only thing in the plaza other than buildings was an incredibly tall iron pole standing in the center of the square. On top of it was the statue of some famous warrior. Standing at the base and looking up, you could barely even see the statue. Kari hid behind the wide iron column as the phoenix descended into the plaza. The ground shook when he landed. The monster searched for her with his one good eye.

He hadn't seen where she went because his bright fireball blocked his view. As far as the phoenix knew, the woman could have been incinerated just like the three dire wolves. But he was not taking any chances that she might still be alive. Monsters always exacted revenge for pain caused to them.

Kari was breathing rapidly from all the sprinting she had done since she left the arena, but was trying as hard as she could to slow her breath and keep still and quiet. Her back was to the wide circular pole, and she took quiet sideways steps to keep out of the phoenix's sight as the monster prowled around the square. He was searching the vacant plaza and peering into the buildings that surrounded it in case Kari had escaped into one of them. He saw civilians in one and blasted fire into the building, killing the people inside and setting the home aflame.

Kari saw only two routes of escape from what she could see with her back to the tall cylinder. She could go back through the alley or sprint down the street that led into the warrior statues plaza. The third option she sarcastically refused, knowing it was a million to one shot. *Or I could shoot the phoenix in the left eye, and he will never be able to find me. Too bad I already used up all my luck hitting his right eye.*

Kari considered running into one of the houses, but decided not to take the chance that the phoenix would see her. If there were people in the building she ran into, they would be killed as collateral damage. *If it wasn't for me those people in that house wouldn't be burning alive right now,* Kari thought as she covered her ears from the sounds of crackling flames and the screams of people they were being cooked.

The back side of the plaza featured a high brick wall. *There must be some rich person's house on the other side. They always surround their magnificent houses, lawns, and gardens with high security walls for privacy.* Kari grew frustrated, just like the phoenix who was trying to kill her. Any choice she made would result in her death.

She continued to slowly step counterclockwise, keeping the phoenix on the opposite side of the statue as he searched for her. She took slow, cautious, quiet steps, trying to stay unnoticed. She hoped the monster would abandon his search and fly away. After a couple seconds, she didn't hear the monster's steps.

Kari turned her head to look to the right and screamed in terror. The phoenix's face was looking right at her; it was so close she could have reached out and touched him. The monster had been waiting for her to turn and notice that he had found her, so he could strike fear into her heart. Somehow, he had caught onto this game of hide-and-go seek they were playing.

The phoenix turned its feathery tail into fire and swung it into the warrior's memorial column. He hit the iron pole in the middle, causing it to snap into three pieces. Kari rolled out of the way as the heavy pieces came toppling down around her.

She sprinted the short distance in the direction she was facing, which happened to be the tall, bricked wall. She ran full speed at it and put her foot on the wall, trying to propel herself up enough that she could grab the top, but she was still four feet short. She jumped again, flat footed from the ground, but was two feet shorter than the last attempt. *Even a Giant would have trouble clearing this wall.*

Kari turned to the phoenix and put her back against the wall. The phoenix watched her (with his one eye). A hauntingly evil grin of crooked, razor sharp teeth spread across his face. He had won.

Kari drew her bow and reached for one of the seven arrows in her quiver, but stopped. Even if she multiplied her seven arrows times seventy, she would not have enough. There was an ancient legend told of a warrior who had battled a great phoenix with his bow and arrows. On the five-hundredth shot, the phoenix finally died. Kari didn't know if the story was true, but she knew nothing less than five hundred arrows would fall a great flying monster. The immense beasts were some of the strongest of the evil god's creations. Just to take one down, the warriors would need an equal amount of power to attack with.

Usually warriors used their flying monsters who had converted to serve the good god. If none of the friendly monsters were available, the warriors used all the powers they could summon: horses, catapults, and hundreds of armed men.

Sometimes all that was not even enough for them to leave the battlefield with their lives.

Kari realized there was nowhere she could go and nothing she could do, except to wait until the phoenix decided to kill her. The huge colorfully feathered monster flew up into the air, above the broken remnants of the statue. Now there was enough distance for him to use all of his stamina and energy to send his most powerful attack of fire to consume her. The phoenix was overcompensating of course. He could have simply killed her with one swing of his clawed hand or one chomp with his jaws. But this woman had hurt him. He would forever be blind in one eye.

Dragons, gryphons, and phoenixes lived for hundreds of years. This phoenix was fairly young, he had not even lived a full century. And now, for the remainder of his long life, he would be handicapped by this woman's incredibly lucky shot.

The woman had blinded him, annoyingly evaded him, and made him look like a fool when he crashed through the bell tower of the church. But he had her now, trapped. The phoenix saw her knees buckling in fear, but noticed she wasn't crying or curling up into a ball on the ground, hugging herself. For a woman, she had a strength he hadn't seen in most warrior men who he had cornered and killed. But he didn't care about her bravery. He was going to scorch in an inferno and char her to a crisp. This time, she would not escape.

Kari stood and awaited her imminent death. She was scared, but she tried not to show it in her final moments. She had lost all of her belongings today, her whole life. It was only fitting that she burn from the same flames.

The half-Human, half-Elf reached down and pulled out her locket. In one hand, she held her mother's memento and in the other, her father's bow. Kari looked up at the monster that was about to kill her. The phoenix opened his mouth and drew in a deep breath. The glow of a red and orange fireball glowed in its throat.

Kari closed her eyes, hoping that when she opened them again she would be staring into the faces of her mother and father.

Chapter 21

The pain she expected from being engulfed in an inferno of fire never came.

Kari opened her eyes and looked up just in time to see a lifeless green feathered gryphon come barreling down from the sky and crash hard into the body of the phoenix. The phoenix's head violently twisted as he was hit in the shoulder and wing from the unexpected falling object. The pyro attack meant to disintegrate Kari shot from the phoenix's mouth and up into the air. The impact drove the phoenix hard into the dirt floor of the plaza.

Kari covered her eyes to shield herself from the dust that was kicked up. When it settled, she saw the two flying monsters twisted together in a contorted pile of dirt and rubble. They were combined into one feathery ball of red, orange, gray, and green.

The gryphon's wing started lifting up from something moving underneath it. A bloodied, armored man was crawling out of the wreckage, grimacing in pain. He dragged himself from underneath the dead body of his gryphon, coughing terribly. Kari ran to the injured warrior.

The closer she got to the gryphon and phoenix, the more she realized how small she was compared to them. She had already seen the phoenix up close, but this was the first time she had seen a gryphon in her life, albeit a dead one. Kari knelt down next to the injured warrior of Elven descent. He didn't say anything as he sat up and looked around half stunned and half amazed.

"Where are you hurt?" she asked, looking over his body from top to bottom. Other than a plethora of scraps and cuts, it looked like nothing was broken. Some of the blood was his, from the crash-landing. The warrior had been thrown from the saddle of his gryphon and violently slammed into the hard ground. As far as the rest of the blood, she could not say where it came from. The gryphon? The phoenix? The monster? She was not sure.

The warrior checked himself over as she had just done, before saying, "I it my ung."

"What?" Kari said. Whatever he had said was incomprehensible to her, but then she saw the red in between his teeth and understood.

"I bit my tongue." He said more slowly and precisely, turning to his side and spitting out a mouthful of blood.

"Anywhere else hurt?" she asked.

The warrior thought for a moment then shook his head no and asked, "Ere em I?" as he began to look around. Before Kari had to ask for repetition of the question, he asked again, knowing he needed to focus on his words. "Where am I?"

Before she could answer, the warrior with blonde hair tied back behind his head was dragging himself away from her. His eyes were fixated on something on the other side of the plaza. He was using his arms to scoot himself across the ground on his butt.

The warrior started laughing quietly to himself, interrupted by bouts of coughing and spitting out blood. Kari figured he was crazy. He had slammed into the ground pretty hard. *He must have smashed his head, scrambling his brains. Either that or the Darien Sea is made of ale, and he just drank it in its entirety.*

The faster he scooted, the more he was coughing, but the louder he was laughing. Kari looked around the plaza, drawing and aiming her bow thinking his laughing would bring down the army of monsters on them. She looked back to the warrior who was holding up the head of the statue, which had broken off from the body when it was knocked down by the phoenix. He was playfully tossing it in the air back and forth between his hands. Kari couldn't hear what he was mumbling to the statue, but he kept smiling and laughing. She walked over to him, not knowing how to help the demented man.

He held the statue next to his head, both of the faces pointing at her. His speech was starting to become more understandable. "My grandfather," he said, laughing. "Of all the places to fall..." He took a moment to spit out more blood. "I land in the plaza of my grandfather's statue of honor."

Kari couldn't help but notice the resemblance between the face made of iron and the face of the warrior as he held it up next to his head. *Maybe he isn't crazy after all.*

"This is unbelievable," the Elf said. "It must be a sign...that my life will not end as early as his did."

Kari nodded, not knowing what she was agreeing to. "We have to get out of the open. Are you sure you're okay?" she asked. She didn't know what to do if he was immobile. She would not leave him here to be killed by monsters.

"I'm fine, just a little dizzy right now. My head is spinning." The warrior started to stand up, but immediately went as pale as a ghost and began slumping back down. Kari caught him under his armpit and helped him to stand, supporting his weight as he leaned on her.

The warrior took a good look at Kari and realized how beautiful she was; her face, her body, her smile. Those were always the first things he saw in girls his own age. But with her, he also noticed her confident walk and her caring tone of voice when she spoke to him. He had seen many beautiful women in his life, but this half-Elf stood out like no other.

"Usually I'm the one to rescue the pretty damsel in distress, not the other way around."

"You did rescue me. Although whether it was intentional or not, I'm not sure." She smiled, hoping the simple expression would relieve some of his pain.

"I'm just glad we both survived. I actually thought I did die, and you were the beautiful angel to greet me into heaven," the warrior said as the woman put on the necklace she was holding and dropped the attached locket down in the crevice of her chest.

"Me the angel? You were the one who came down from the skies to save me. If anyone is the angel here, it's you," she laughed.

The warrior loved her laugh as much as every other part of her. He took her response as a sign that she was somewhat interested in him. "A quick wit and attractive, topped off by a woman carrying a bow and quiver? You're my kind of lady: deadly attractive, but equally dangerous... depending on how good your aim is." The warrior had learned that complimenting a girl but also questioning her skill made her want to prove herself to him and seek out his approval. He was very skilled in the underlying technique of manipulating the thoughts and emotions of girls. Other than using his double swords and cracking funny jokes, it was the one thing he knew he was good at.

The answer she gave him was not what he was expecting. "My accuracy is excellent, warrior. You can be sure of that. It's a lot better than your weak flirting method. Do you go around telling all the girls they are pretty and funny angels?"

The Elf ignored the question and clutched at his heart in mock pain from this lady not accepting his advances. *It's not often I get shut down so quickly. She is different.* "There used to be a day when falling from the sky and saving a helpless woman's life automatically won you her heart," he said.

Kari let go of him, and the warrior was able to balance himself on his own. The dizziness of the spiraling fall and hard crash were fading away, but the pain in his mouth still throbbed. Kari could see it was bothering the warrior.

"Let me see inside your mouth. I can tell you how bad it is," she offered.

"You're a hard one to read. You didn't seem like the type of person that would want to progress a relationship so rapidly." The warrior said as he opened his mouth.

Kari could see the injury, but she said, "Wider," happily causing the warrior a little extra pain as a punishment for slightly insulting her. She stood on the tips of her toes to look in his mouth as she held his jaw. He was only a little bit taller than her at five and three quarter's feet.

"The cut is not bad, but it's not good either. You bit it pretty hard. The bleeding looks like it is starting to slow down though." Kari let go of his jaw. "At least you didn't bite it completely off. So you will be able to work on your pick up lines and maybe redeem yourself for the awful one you used on me."

"Does that mean you're giving me another chance?" he asked.

"Let's see if we can both survive this day and then maybe you'll find out."

"Sounds good to me. Where are you headed? I'll take you there."

Kari shook her head unknowingly. "Well, since my house is burning a couple of blocks over, I don't know where to go now. I was headed to the nearest watchtower."

The warrior saw her eyes well up when she mentioned her destroyed house. "Sorry about your home. It seems like we're all losing things we have grown attached to." He quickly glanced back to where his dead gryphon lay on top of the phoenix in the crater. "The watchtowers are probably closed up now. The monsters have advanced too far in. But I think I know a place where we will be safe. Follow me."

The two began to walk side by side, down the road, away from the wreckage of the plaza. "What's your name," the warrior asked his new companion.

"Kari Quinn. Yours?"

"Ty Canard, grandson of the warrior Jackson Canard, who died honorably in combat serving King Zoran," Ty said, pointing back to the broken, headless memorial statue.

"Let's get to safety before we end up like him," Kari encouraged.

"Yeah, I haven't done enough yet in my life to be worthy of getting a statue like his," Ty agreed.

"Then we'll have to stay alive long enough to change that," Kari said. "Where are we headed?"

"My brother Darren and his wife Cassandra live only a few streets over from this plaza. He is a warrior, so he won't be there. But she should be. I will escort you to the safety of their home before resuming battle."

Kari was about to begin arguing against his returning to battle comment, but thought it best to keep silent. Most warriors were too stubborn to stop fighting even if they were injured like Ty was. He still looked very pale and was walking with a limp.

Warriors. They would rather die battling alongside their brothers, saving the lives of citizens, than live on knowing they had been a coward. In a way, Kari admired the Elf. Sometimes stubbornness for the right reasons can be attractive.

Before they turned the corner, Ty stopped, turned around, and took one last look at his dead monster friend. It was only a brief second, but that was all he needed. Among the hundreds of memories he had made with his gryphon, this would be the last one. Ty filed the image of the scene in the back of his mind and said a wordless goodbye to his good friend Wildwing.

Ty used his sword to break the lock off a tall building. He and Kari climbed up the long spiral staircase and exited out onto the roof, being careful not to be noticed by any of the many flying enemy monsters.

He pounded his fist angrily onto the floor of the roof, holding back his screams of anger.

"What is it?" Kari asked in alarm, but then she saw his cause for frustration.

Ty knew the attack was bad from what he saw when he was atop Wildwing. But it wasn't until he stood on the building that he could concentrate and fully assess the siege. "We've lost Celestial," was all he said, seeing the overwhelming amount of monsters. *We're vastly outnumbered.*

From where they were in the southwestern corner of the Circle City, he saw no warriors, not in the air, not on the walls, and not in the streets. The closest watchtower was surrounded by monsters both on the ground and in the sky. Warriors and civilians had bunkered down inside. Leaving the security of the tower would lead to a quick death. All they could do was hope other warriors would eventually come and rescue them.

But it wasn't rescue warriors who made it into the watchtower first. Ty watched as the flying monsters broke a hole in the top of the tower. The stone tower was impenetrable to fire, and monsters were not patient enough to wait there until they starved. If there was one thing that monsters did not have, it was patience.

Three blue flying monsters began to fill the tower with their element of water. The warriors and civilians who were taking shelter in the tower were forced to open the doors to avoid being drowned. Hundreds of people, coughing and choking, spilled out into the plaza in a wave of water.

The monsters waiting outside killed them all.

Kari noticed that the last of the monster army was making their way into the city, through the breaches. They mostly came in groups of similar type creations, showing their clan affiliations.

Ty explained to Kari the stages of a typical monster attack. "The first stage of the monsters' goal of taking over Celestial is to break into the city and get to the castle or warriors' watchtowers. Since the watchtowers are an important part of the city's defenses, capturing them is a huge advantage. The second stage of their goal is to cause as much death and destruction in the streets as possible, killing every living thing they can.

"We are witnessing the third and final stage right now. See how the monsters aren't progressing into the city anymore? They are all gathering around the edges, on the inside of the inner wall. What they are going to do is work together towards the city center. They will comb every house and every building for people. If you don't come out and follow them, your home is burned with you alive in it."

"How do you know all this?" Kari asked him. "Monsters have never gotten past the inner wall in previous attacks."

"We were required to study attacks on cities of the past to learn monster strategies in Warrior Training. There weren't many case studies of large organized attacks like this one in the historical documents, but from what we do know, the three stages are generally the steps used. Draviakhan invented the system. He would have his army tear apart the city, finding every single person. Sometimes he let them all live as slaves, but most of the time he killed them all, usually in a cruel, torturous way."

"What are they going to do with all of us?"

"That is up to them. You know as well as I do that whatever it is, it will not be the pleasant and comfortable life we have come to know in Celestial."

"What can we do?"

"I don't know. But I'm not going to roll over and give up. If I'm going to die, then I'm going to go out fighting. I'm definitely not going to let them make me a slave. That would be even worse than death." Ty sighed in exasperation. It had already been a long, taxing day both physically and emotionally. The future held no hope of change for the better, but Ty refused to give up. "Don't worry, when the opportunity comes, we will strike back."

From his vantage point high on the tall building, Ty used his finger to trace the roads that would serve as the fastest path to Darren's residence. There was a crumpled building blocking the way he wanted to take, so he retraced the roads and found an alternate route.

Ty and Kari exited back out onto the street. They started down the path Ty had mentally memorized. The two had to be very stealthy and avoid making noise, which was not the easiest thing to do. Kari's arrows rattled against each other and Ty's armor pieces clanged together. There were a couple times they narrowly avoided being caught by monsters.

When they finally got to the street Darren's house was on, it was blocked by two orcs. Ty snuck up and threw a rock at one, making both turn around and chase him. Ty turned the corner into an alley, baiting the monsters. As soon as the orcs rushed around the corner, Kari released her already prepared arrow. At such close range, the arrow went completely through the head of the first monster and lodged deep into the skull of the one following it.

One of the orcs had been an archer. Kari excitedly grabbed the arrows in its quiver and added them to her own. She had been low on arrows, but now she had a little more freedom to be less conservative in her attacks. She would still try to keep as many as possible, lest she almost run out of ammo again.

Kari reached down and pulled the arrow out of the orc's skull. She used a ragged cloth the monster was wearing to wipe off the blood and then inserted it into her bow.

Ty led Kari to the door of his sister-in-law's house. On a normal day, they could have covered the distance from the building in a ten minute walk. It took them twenty-five minutes to get to her home because of the alternate route they had to take. Ty hadn't even been able to take the alternate route he had scouted from the top of the building because a dead dragon had fallen across one of the roads he was planning on using. He had to backtrack and go out of his way just to get on another path that would safely take him and Kari to their destination. *An alternate of an alternate*, he realized, annoyed by the wasted time.

Despite the encumbrance, they finally arrived at the only safe place he could think of. Ty rapidly knocked on the wooden door. Somewhere behind him he heard the growls of monsters who had just found the two dead orcs. Undoubtedly they would quickly be searching the area for the murderers. Ty charged his shoulder into the locked door, but it didn't budge. His furious knocking offered no return from the other side of the door. Ty began to call out the name of his sister-in-law, quietly at first, but louder with each call.

"Cassie! Open up, its Ty! Please open the door! Cassandra!"

"Hurry!" Kari cried, knowing there was nothing she could do to speed up the situation. She looked to her right and saw a group of angry monsters turn the corner and come out onto the street. There was nowhere to hide.

Ty and Kari were standing in plain sight.

Chapter 22

Finally, there was a clicking noise from the other side of the door as it was unlatched, and the door slowly squeaked open. Ty and Kari burst inside right when the monsters turned their heads to look down the street in their direction. A split second longer and they would have been spotted.

"Tyrus!" Cassandra smiled and immediately hugged Ty. Ty knew that smile would have been wider and that hug tighter if it had been her husband, Darren. Nonetheless, he was happy to see her and learn that she had not been one of the many victims of the siege.

Kari quickly closed the door behind them and latched it shut. She noticed the meat cleaver that had stuck into the floor when Cassandra dropped it to hug Ty. *She must be scared out of her mind in here, hearing the sounds of destruction all around her and smelling the smoke from nearby burning buildings. I can't blame her for delaying in opening the door. I would have been cautious too.*

"I'm so glad you're okay, Ty. Have you seen Darren anywhere?"

"No, I haven't, but I'm sure he's okay. He's one of the strongest swordsmen I know, much like our father before us."

Cassandra took a deep breath and nodded. Hearing Ty's strong belief in the skill of his brother gave her reassurance that her husband was still alive.

Darren was Ty's older brother by three years. Darren lived with Ty and Steve under Titus Thatcher's roof after their parents were murdered. After eight years, he turned sixteen, passed the warrior's test and entered Warrior Training. A couple years later he married Cassandra. One year later they were blessed with a son.

"Uncle Ty!" Lucan had nervously been peering around the corner from his bedroom, waiting to see who came through the door. As soon as he saw it was his uncle, he ran to Ty and jumped into his arms. Kari couldn't help but smile as she watched the two embrace.

"Did you fight on Wildwing?" the five-year-old asked.

Ty had forgotten how much Lucan loved the gryphon. He thought Wildwing was the coolest monster, and Ty was just as cool for riding him. Ty sighed deeply, debating if he should tell the sad news to the excited child. He bent down and looked Lucan in the eye. "Yes, I did. You should have seen how fast he was today!" Ty knew he couldn't break the heart of this wide eyed child.

His mother saw the expression on Ty's face and changed the subject as she looked at Kari. "Hi, my name is Cassandra."

"Hi, I'm Kari. Thank you for allowing us into your home. I realize how scared you two must be in here."

"You have no idea," Cassandra said, glancing quickly at the meat cleaver. "So are you one of Ty's girlfriends?"

Kari was somewhat startled by the question. "What? Me? No, no, we just met actually."

Lucan walked up to Kari and held out his hand like a proper gentleman. Kari shook it politely and complimented his manners with a wide smile. "I think you're beautiful," the boy slowly said, annunciating the last word of the sentence.

Kari's smile turned into an open-mouthed laugh. Cassandra and Ty joined in.

"You Canard's are quite the ladies men, aren't you?" Kari asked Ty.

"Lucan, go into the other room please. I need to talk with your uncle and his friend."

"Awww, but mom, I want to stay with Uncle Ty," the five-year-old whined.

"Mind your mother, nephew. Do what she says."

Lucan slouched his shoulders and slowly paced into the next room, closing the door behind him. He liked Ty so much he didn't want to disappoint his uncle by arguing with his command.

Lucan had left for his room, but Ty knew the boy's ear would be up against the door, as he tried to eavesdrop on the adult conversation. His mother knew he was doing so as well, so she talked in a softer tone as the three moved to sit down at the kitchen table. "Wildwing?" she asked.

Ty hung his head and shook it from side to side. Cassandra shook her head back and forth, understanding. Ty was too hurt to speak about it.

After a moment of reminiscing about the gryphon, which had become like a part of their family, she said, "Remember when you took me up on him to get to know me before I was going to marry your brother?"

Cassandra looked at Kari to tell the story since Ty's head was still bowed. "I was so scared. It was my first time flying, but when we got up there high above Celestial, and Ty told me I could look down...It was a sight I will never forget. Absolutely incredible. It was breathtaking."

Kari smiled at the picture she was visualizing. She thought the city was beautiful from the ground. *From a bird's eye view, Celestial must look amazing.* She had seen artists' paintings of Celestial from the Valpyrio Mountains, but paintings could never do reality justice. Celestial from above was a sight Kari wanted to experience with her own eyes someday.

"I wonder what it looks like now." Cassandra said. If she had had any idea how much damage had been done, she would have realized how morbid her question was.

Ty lifted his head up. "It's bad. Far worse than I've ever seen. Did Darren say where he was stationed today?"

"He said he was headed to Ostravaski's Tower. I only know that because he was complaining about how he was going to miss seeing Steve compete in the Joust."

Ty buried his face in his hands. His breathing increased rapidly.

"Ty, what is it?" Cassandra asked in a quivering voice.

"Commander Ostravaski's watchtower. It fell...I watched it collapse when I was in the air on Wildwing."

Cassandra stood up from the table and started to pace around, muttering to herself in denial. "Darren was in that tower. Darren was in that tower. He can't die. He can't be dead." Out of her mouth escaped the panicking thoughts as they crossed her mind.

Ty sat at the table thinking of how much his brother had been a role model to him and how much he always looked up to his brother, especially after the death of their parents. Ty's chin was quivering, but he held in his tears. Cassandra stopped pacing and collapsed to the floor, sobbing uncontrollably. Kari moved from the kitchen table and sat down and wrapped her arms around Cassandra. She didn't know how else to help the grieving woman.

After seeing his sister-in-law weep, Ty could no longer hold back his tears. He got up from the table and went over to embrace Cassandra. Kari let him take her place as she stood up and stepped back.

Even though she didn't know Darren, she felt her own eyes well up. Kari was a very caring and compassionate person. She hated seeing people in emotional or physical pain. *A beautiful family has just lost their leader. A wife is now a widow.*

Lucan is left fatherless. A child should be able to grow up provided for, in a loving home under a mother and father. I know what it was like not to have that.

Kari walked over and opened Lucan's door. His eyes were already red from the tears he was crying. He had heard his mother's sobs from his room. He knew he wouldn't see his father again. The boy sprinted to his mother and uncle and joined the emotional, huddled hug on the floor.

Kari left the grieving family alone, walked up the stairs to a loft, and then climbed up a short ladder out onto the roof of the house. Darren and Cassandra's house wasn't nearly as tall as the previous building they had climbed, but Kari could still see a good distance from the roof. She expected to be able to see, at least, the top of the inner wall. All she could see was a faint, shifting orange light that seemed to surround the curved, circular edge of the city. A wall of smoke filled the air above it. She thought back to what Ty had said.

If people don't come out of their locked homes, the buildings will be burned to the ground. Monsters didn't care to waste time going through every room in the tens of thousands of houses in Celestial. If no one came out of a locked house, it would be set aflame.

In the distance, Kari saw monster archers patrolling the rooftops of evacuated homes, searching for any people that may have been missed. In the streets, large groups of civilians were being herded like sheep towards the castle, the center of the city. It seemed like every main road had large groups of people on it. They were all heading towards the main road, merging with other groups and being led toward the castle.

Was Ty right? Will we really all become slaves? Or are they just gathering us to kill us all, ensuring a monumental victory in the ongoing war of people versus monsters?

Kari imagined what her life would be like in the coming days, weeks, and months. People in Celestial lived a very systematic life. Every day was exactly the same for most people. They woke up, ate, worked, ate, and slept before starting the process all over again the next day. They always traveled to the same city locations and interacted with the same people. People followed the same paths, gave the same greetings, and purchased the same products from the same merchants.

Everything we have grown so used to for so long will be gone. The people, the places. Some of it has already disappeared forever. We always go to sleep assuming the things we have will be there when we wake up. Why do we take so much in our lives for granted?

Kari wished this attack was all just a nightmare. She wished she could wake up and find out she had only been dreaming. Everything would go back to the way it had always been.

Unfortunately, all the horrors she had seen were real. Never again would she live the life that she had grown accustomed to. An unexpected attack on an ordinary day was forever changing the lives of hundreds of thousands of people on Element.

Kari heard screaming, causing her attention to focus in on a group two streets over. A monster had just ran his sword through the back of a child. The father attacked the monster with a dagger he had hidden in his pocket, stabbing the monster repeatedly in the chest. The child-murdering monster clutched its chest and fell to the ground dead. The father was still savagely attacking it with his dagger even though he had already killed it. An ogre pulled him off of the dead body and crushed his head with a spiked mace.

Kari didn't know how much more she could bear. *This day will be forever remembered. Mostly through the nightmares it is going to give all of us who survive.*

Ty climbed up the ladder through the hole in the roof. He gently put his hand on Kari's shoulder, trying not to scare her, but she jumped anyway. "They will be here soon. I'm not going to fight back. They will kill Cassandra and Lucan if I do."

"Who is to say they won't kill us anyway? I just watched them murder a child in the street the same age as Lucan for no reason."

"I know, Kari. This is horrible, all of this, but obeying their orders is the only option we have." It was hard for Ty to give in. He wanted to fight back, but couldn't because of his family. Ty had just lost his brother. He couldn't bear losing Cassandra, his nephew, or even Kari. *It's my responsibility to keep them safe, no matter what the cost.*

"Can you help me take off my armor? If they see that I am a warrior, they will kill me instantly," Ty requested of his new friend.

"Of course," Kari said as she moved in close to help.

"Thank you," Ty whispered as he gently stroked her arm. It was a thank you not for currently helping him with the armor, but for being so tender and caring to his family and also towards him when he was disoriented after crashing down into the plaza.

"You're welcome," Kari said back.

For a moment the two held each other's gaze. Kari felt drawn to Ty as she looked into his eyes that were still watery from crying. Warriors were known as strong men who never showed their emotions, but Ty didn't care about that stereotype. He was moved by the realization of Darren's death. His tears showed her how much he cared about his brother and the family the deceased warrior left behind.

Ty leaned in towards Kari.

He's going to kiss me!

She was equally scared and excited. But the attractive blonde-haired Elf only kissed her on the cheek; another way of showing his appreciation for her. A part of Kari wished he had kissed her on the lips. She was beginning to like him, the more

211

she got to know him, but she knew it wouldn't be a good idea to share that type of kiss. *We've already experienced enough drama today*, Kari thought as she helped Ty remove his armor.

Warriors typically wore a six piece metal armor set. The plate was the main and largest piece of armor. It protected the warrior's torso by covering their chest and abdomen. Gauntlets covered their leather gloved hands and part of their forearms. Spaulders covered a warrior's shoulders. Some styles covered the upper arm as well. Cuisses were armor for the thighs. Greaves were a thin metal shin guard. Steel boots, which came in optional low or high cuts, protected the warrior's feet. High cut boots had the greaves built in, so warriors who wore those only had a five piece set of armor.

Helms were optional (just like capes). Warriors tended to only wear the steel head-protectors when they knew they were going into a dangerous battle. Chainmail was rare and expensive. It was only worn by captains, commanders, knights, and the king. It covered the spaces the armor left and was incredibly difficult to cut through.

As Ty took off his blue gauntlets and leather gloves, Kari removed his spaulders. Then she unbuckled the leather straps that held the front and back pieces of his silver plate together. Ty slid out of the armor. He was dressed in a tunic drenched in sweat and blood and typical civilian breeches.

"Could you go get me one of my brother's shirts? Not even the most nervous man on Element would sweat as much as I have today if he wasn't fighting monsters. I don't want to give them a reason to believe I'm a warrior."

Kari saw the wisdom in his thinking and climbed down the ladder. She found a shirt of Darren's and brought it back up to Ty.

She could not suppress a smile when she climbed back up onto the roof and saw Ty standing with his shirt taken off. He was incredibly muscular. She could tell he didn't mind showing off his amazing physique to her.

Kari walked forward and handed Ty the shirt, physically unable to resist the temptation of admiring his body. *Stop staring Kari*, she said to herself.

"Thank you," Ty said as he overconfidently winked at Kari.

Ty left his armor and weapons buried under a pile of hay on the roof. He came down the ladder and walked down the stairs, looking like an average civilian. The disguised warrior, a still sobbing widow, a child, and Kari, all gathered in front of the door to the home. Ty analyzed how the four of them would appear to the monsters when he noticed a fault.

"Cass, I'm sorry, but you can't be holding Lucan in front of the monsters. When they see a strong love between two people, they will kill one of them to set an example. Having someone to love strengthens and empowers you. If you see a loved one murdered, it causes you to do something stupid and rash, which gets you killed, or it causes your heart to break. Either way, the monsters get what they want. You're either dead or defeated. That's why they break the bond of love by death."

Kari was surprised by what Ty had just said. *Having someone to love strengthens and empowers you. I had no idea he was that deep and poetic.* He was continuing to impress her.

Cassandra kissed her son on his forehead, "I love you so much, Lucan. Your daddy loves you too. He's watching over both of us at this very moment. Nothing will happen to you or me. I need you to keep quiet and do what you're told. Can you do that?"

Lucan was too scared to even say "Yes," but he nodded his promise to his mother. Cassandra stood up and let go of her son.

Ty looked at Kari. She was clutching her bow to her chest, knowing she could not bring it with her, but hoping no one would notice. Without him saying anything, Kari blurted out, "Ty, I cannot get rid of this!" She was on the verge of tears.

Ty considered her connection to the bow for a moment. "Leave the quiver in the house, but you have to offer the bow to the monster that collects us. Maybe it will be an act of good faith and none of us will be killed." As soon as he said that sentence, he saw the fear in Lucan's eyes as his nephew realized that any one of them might be killed within the next couple minutes. The boy started crying again, afraid he would lose his mother or end up dead like his father.

Ty knelt down next to his nephew. "Lucan, you are scared. I see that, but I want you to show these monsters that you..."

Ty was interrupted by screams coming from the next house over. The monsters were getting close. He grabbed his nephew by the shoulders to regain his attention since it had been taken by the awful sounds.

"Lucan, it's okay to be scared. I'm scared too. But you can't show the monsters that you fear them. Show them that you are brave. Monsters kill the weak without a thought. They feed off of fear. You can't cry in front of them. I know that you are strong. You can do this. Someday you will be a mighty warrior like your grandfather, like your father, like me. Being a warrior is in your blood. Harness the anger that you feel at the monsters for killing your father. Use it to fuel the fire inside of you, to keep pushing forward, to make you stronger. Like your mom said, your dad is watching over you. And the three of us will stand by your side as well. We won't let anything happen to you...I won't let anything happen to you."

Two loud thuds on the door made all four of them jump. KNOCK! KNOCK!

Ty gave one last word of encouragement to the group. "None of us are going to die today. Don't look at them. Don't do anything other than walk the straight line to wherever they lead us. We are going to make it through this."

KNOCK! KNOCK!

Chapter 23

Ty opened the door and was immediately grabbed by the collar and thrown down onto the street by a cyclops. Cyclops' were gigantic monsters, larger even than ogres. Because of their size, putting a weapon in their hands was an easy way to guarantee destruction. However, who or what was damaged was anyone's guess. The one-eyed brutes were incredibly dimwitted. Whatever was in their way was what they attacked. Their range of targets could consist of anything from a person, to another monster, or even to a tree.

Cassandra and Lucan cautiously filed out after Ty. Lucan almost bent down to help his uncle up, but a quick, strict glance by Ty made him reconsider. Ty picked himself up and joined Cassandra and Lucan in the crowd of about one hundred civilians that this group of monsters had gathered. There were twenty armed monsters surrounding the group.

Ty could feel the heat emitting from a house that had been set on fire just three buildings down. It was already fully engulfed in flames. He heard the wooden floor of the second story come crashing down to ground level.

Kari walked out holding the bow with her arms outstretched, trying hard not to show that they were shaking. Two orcs and a minotaur pushed past her and began searching through the house for any people, armor, or weapons. The huge cyclops roughly ripped the bow out of Kari's hands and handed it to a horse mounted, pale yellow orc.

Ty thought he recognized the black horse the orc was riding. It looked like Sampson, a massive percheron warhorse. Sampson was one of the largest horses in the warriors and had belonged to a warrior from Ty's watchtower. He knew the man's face, but could not think of his name. The warrior belonged to a large family who was known for breeding horses for warriors. The family was attempting to create a purebred line of the strongest horses ever seen. Each generation would be stronger than the last. Sampson was a sixth generation purebred. He was incredibly large and as strong as three regular-sized horses combined.

The orc admired the bow in his hands and spoke to Kari with only the few basic words he knew. "Where you get?" he asked her. When Kari didn't answer, the yellow orc nodded to the cyclops. The large monster backhanded Kari across the face, knocking her to the ground. Kari stood up and glared into the single, oversized eye of the giant cyclops. The entire side of her face was numb, but at the same time she could feel the sting from the blow. A trickle of blood fell from a cut across her cheek.

Ty was about to charge the cyclops who was over three and a half times his size. The only thing that stopped him was Cassandra's gentle hand on his arm. Ty hated seeing women get hit, especially Kari, who he was starting to like more and more. It didn't matter if they were hit by monster or man; women were meant to be honored and treated with respect. Seeing abuse awakened a fierce thirst for violence in Ty against the abuser.

As a warrior, he had dealt with the situation a couple times. A man (usually intoxicated) would get in an argument with his girlfriend or wife and talk with his fists rather than his words. Needless to say, when Ty was through dealing with him, it would take the man almost two full months to heal from his broken arms or hands.

"Where you get?" the pale yellow orc repeated, getting angrier.

Again Kari did not answer. Ty knew she was trying to show no fear, but there was a fine line between being fearless and intently stirring up anger. The orc nodded to the cyclops for the second time. This time Kari prepared for a closed fist punch that would likely break many of her bones wherever it landed.

Before the fist struck her, one of the monsters who had gone into the house came out with Kari's quiver of arrows and handed them to the orc. The orc took the quiver and put it around his shoulder, but only after he drew an arrow and notched it. He pulled back on the bow string and aimed it at Kari's head.

Kari stood bravely, awaiting death, just like she had done with the fire phoenix. Ty watched helplessly, unable to get to Kari because of the surrounding crowd. He reached down and picked up a stone and chucked it at the large butt of the massive horse. The horse bucked in surprise at the same time the arrow was released. It flew into the mighty shoulder of the cyclops. The giant monster felt the arrow enter into his body, but for him, it was only comparable to a bee's sting. Still, he didn't appreciate being shot. He angrily turned to the yellow orc.

The orc threw down Kari's bow and waved his hands, showing he didn't mean to shoot him, but his plea was futile. The cyclops grabbed the orc with one hand and squeezed. Kari heard an awful cracking and popping sound that made her wince as she imagined the pain she would have felt in the orc's position. The cyclops opened his fist and the orc fell motionless to the ground.

The minotaur who had brought the quiver out of the house laughed at the death. He walked over to the dead yellow orc, bent down, and took the bow and arrows from his lifeless body. He put them over his shoulder, mounted Sampson, and motioned for Kari to join the rest of the crowd.

The four of them made it out alive. None of them knew how much longer they would still be able to say that, but they held onto that truth nonetheless. They were led down the street, surrounded by monsters. They added about sixty-five more people by the time they finished off the rest of Cassandra's street and the adjacent one. The monsters set six more houses on fire in just those two streets.

The minotaur wordlessly declared to the other monsters that they had finished their designations and would head towards the center of the city, following the many other groups of people headed that way.

No one talked as they walked. One man had tried to strike up a conversation, but was pulled out of the crowd and killed for that action. Along the way, the group stepped over dead bodies, mostly of people, but some were monsters. Ty motioned to Lucan not to look down at them. The smell of burned flesh filled the air, making many in the crowd gag. It combined with the smell of smoke that had taken over the entire city. The Fluorite River was tinted red with blood, some sections a little more than others. Ty noticed many bodies floating in the slow-flowing river.

They exited out onto the main road and combined with a larger group of people. There were more and more monsters towards the center of the city, providing a guard in case there was a revolt with so many of the civilians together. None of the people had weapons other than their hands and feet, so the monsters weren't expecting any problems.

The group walked over Commander Ostravaski's tower, which had fallen across the Big Square Plaza. Many people fell and twisted their ankles on the uneven rubble. Ty mentally told himself not to look down at the bodies of the warriors they were stepping on and over. The last thing he needed was an emotional breakdown in front of these people and the monsters if he saw the dead body of his brother Darren staring up at him.

Instead, Ty looked up in horror at an equally haunting sight: the once magnificent castle of King Zoran. It looked like someone with a god-sized hand had torn off the top of the King's Tower. He could see where pieces of debris had crashed down into and around the castle.

The monsters had gotten through the iron portcullises of the castle wall and the castle itself. How they did that, Ty had no idea. He thought it was impenetrable. *They must have gotten someone to open it from the inside by lowering the drawbridge, allowing the monsters to enter.*

There were four drawbridges in total leading into the courtyard outside the castle. Just like the four outer warriors' watchtowers, there was one on the north, south, east, and west sides. The group was led over the south drawbridge, the main one that led to the face of the castle.

Lucan looked down at the intimidating moat as they walked past the incredibly high castle wall that separated King Zoran's castle from the rest of the city. They were led into the large circular courtyard.

The courtyard's south side was where the general public would gather to hear the king give a message or announcement to the city. People were free to walk along the beautiful gardens with flowers of every color imaginable and shrubs cut into the shapes of animals. All of this beauty had been trampled or destroyed.

Each group of people formed a square and was placed into a section of the courtyard. Squares formed into larger squares and soon the entire courtyard became one huge mass of people.

Ty's legs were sore. All he wanted to do was sit down. He couldn't believe that only this afternoon he had been laughing, joking, and enjoying the celebration of the Warriors' Tournaments.

Oh how things have changed. How many people have I seen die today? How many people died today that I didn't see? He didn't think he would be able to emotionally handle the number of civilian deaths in Celestial if someone gave him the true count.

The Elf looked upwards. The sky was now a pink and orange mixture. The day was winding down. Monsters had already lit torches and stuck them in the ground throughout the courtyard. In another three or four hours, it would be completely dark. Ty felt physically sick when he noticed a huge pile of at least three hundred dead civilian bodies piled on top of the courtyard's stone platform. A monster lit the pile on fire with a torch and added one more light for the onset of night.

Apparently the people in front of Ty could not hold in their stomachs' contents at the sight that Ty had just seen. He heard their retching, and it wasn't long before another putrid smell was added to the air.

People began to talk sporadically. Monsters had no way of enforcing everyone to shut their mouths. The chatter grew louder and louder as more people grew brave and used the ability that had been taken from them. Half of the people in the courtyard were broken down, crying over their lost family members and close friends. The other half were talking about the things they had seen and wondering about what was to become of them.

Ty heard crazy rumors everywhere around him: that the entire world was completely overrun by monsters and every city had fallen, that King Zoran was dead, and that they were all collected together to be executed. He tried to eavesdrop on as many stories as possible. Warriors were trained to listen intently and then piece together the information as best they could. But with all the noises and sounds, Ty was having trouble focusing. It was too much in one day for any man to be expected to handle.

He stood with Kari, Cassandra, and Lucan. They had worked hard not to allow themselves to be separated. Ty and Kari stood quietly. Kari was sneaking angry looks at the horse-mounted minotaur holding her bow. The monsters that had led their group into the courtyard stood around the people they had brought in. Cassandra was comforting Lucan even though the boy hadn't shed a tear since they left the house. Perhaps that was because he cried himself dry after finding out his father died. Whatever the reason, Ty was proud of his nephew for the strength he showed.

Monsters continued to bring cart after cart of dead bodies to add to the burning pyre of people. Ty wondered if they were killing people just for the sake of the fire. He eyed everything suspiciously, trying to take in all of the information presented to him. There was what looked to be twenty thousand people in the courtyard.

After the courtyard was filled, Ty began to hear the chatter of people beyond the circular castle wall. *Monsters must have gathered people all along the moat.* If there was a revolt, the monsters could just drive the people backwards where they would fall to a death of drowning, being impaled by spikes, or being eaten alive by vicious alligators.

The monsters had gathered everyone in the city as close as they could to the castle. *Maybe they are going to kill us after all.* The civilians on the other side of the castle wall would be able to hear, but unable to see whatever was going to happen in the courtyard. They were louder than the people on the inside. *There must be more people out there than in here; maybe twenty thousand in the courtyard and maybe thirty thousand on the outside of the castle wall*, Ty estimated. Celestial had a population of about eighty thousand.

He couldn't say for sure about how many casualties there had already been, but the number was probably as many as there were people in the courtyard, and that was being optimistic. Ty couldn't begin to estimate how many visitors were in town for the weekend of celebration. *Whatever the number is, most of them are probably dead because they had no idea of the defense protocol or where to go for shelter during the attack.*

Ty also thought about Celestial's force of 5,000 warriors. *I wonder if there are any left?* Ty would miss the laughs and company of his warrior brothers who had passed on. He hoped his brother Steve Brightflame had somehow survived, but reality told him to bet against his hope.

When he had first entered the courtyard, everyone had been packed in tightly, but now the space around him was even more compact. He felt like he was being pushed in from all sides. Kari was having trouble breathing next to him. Ty could tell she had a fear of tight spaces. She was focused on the emptiness and open area of the sky instead of the people surrounding her, crushing her ability to breathe.

Ty was able to reach up and rub her back. He tried to comfort her, but didn't think about the burns she had received from the phoenix. Kari winced and awkwardly flinched away from his touch. At first Ty thought he had offended her, but then he saw that he had hurt her. "It's okay," Kari said, before he could apologize. Ty felt like an insensitive jerk for causing her pain.

Kari felt bad that Ty felt bad. *All he was trying to do was help. He's caring and sensitive.*

The only thing Ty could do was keep encouraging Kari that it would all be over soon. The fact that they stood in the same claustrophobic conditions for two more hours proved him a liar. The huge yellow-orange sun was beginning to set behind where they stood.

Monsters were everywhere Ty looked. Probably two-thirds of their entire force was stationed around the courtyard. There were thousands of monster archers along the castle wall. Some aimed in toward the courtyard while others aimed toward the large group beyond the castle wall. A security line of all types of monsters with every weapon imaginable stood at the front of the crowd on the steps of the large stone platform that led into the castle. Featured front and center on the platform was a wooden gallows.

Ty's focus, along with everyone else's in the courtyard turned to the front doors of the castle when they were opened, and the portcullises were raised.

Ty knew the man who walked out the moment he saw the color of the armor. In a full suit of bright white armor, Prince Silvanus strutted out onto the platform. The Prince *always* wore white. Normal clothes, ceremony clothes; Prince Silas had ridden a white horse and wore white armor in every single one of his exhibition jousts, and today was no different. *He wears white so that he can look majestic, stand out, and be noticed by everyone.*

Ty heard a rumor that an elderly castle seamstress had asked him why he liked the color so much. Supposedly, he felt her tone was mocking him. He got angry and cut off the woman's hands so she could never sew again.

There is a legend of a White-Armored Warrior. Perhaps Prince Silas wants to steal that name for himself. The White-Armored Prince.

The physically strong prince that lacked charm and charisma walked forward with a brazen confidence. He stood next to the gallows and looked over the huge crowd of civilians. Everyone was able to clearly see him from anywhere in the courtyard. The setting sun caught the reflection of the golden crown he was wearing.

"Silence!" the prince yelled, even though very few people were talking. Ever since he was a child, Silas loved being the center of attention. He was a spoiled brat of a boy then, and now, at nineteen, nothing was different. His need to always be in the spotlight had only gotten worse with age.

"Silence!" he screamed louder. Other than a couple of people still quietly sobbing, there was no noise at all except for the crackling of flames. For no reason whatsoever, the prince made one swift motion to the monster archers on the walls.

Thousands of arrows rained down into the crowd. Everyone ducked down and covered their heads. The women and children started screaming in fear.

Ty covered Kari. Cassandra covered Lucan.

When the sound of arrows whizzing through the air and pelting into people stopped, everyone stood up. Luckily, none of the four had been hit. The woman standing in front of Ty had been hit, and she stayed down on the ground. Ty bent down to examine her injury, but she was already dead. The long arrow had pierced through her hand and penetrated through her eye and into her head.

After a couple minutes of screaming and crying from people who had lost loved ones, the crowd stopped and gave their undivided attention to Prince Silas. He unsheathed his golden sword and lifted it up for the crowd to see.

"The Aurelian Sword" Ty said out loud to himself. *If he has that it can only mean one thing...*

The prince poked the tip of the blade down into something round that lay in front of him on the stone platform. He held it up for the crowd to see. At first, only the people in the front part of the collected crowd could see what it was. Many of them screamed and yelled in shock, terror, and despair. Ty realized it was the head of a Human.

"I present to you, your beloved KING!"

Chapter 24

The middle and back part of the crowd gasped. Cries filled the brisk night air.

King Zoran, the one who singlehandedly killed Draviakhan, who built Celestial from the ground up, who reigned over his kingdom consisting of all the cities of Element, and who ushered in three decades of a global peace never known before, was dead.

"One man with one sword killed one five-headed dragon and suddenly the world changed. Celestial was built, and a kingdom was born. But that man is now dead. And with it you lose your city, your kingdom. How can the life and death of one man cause so much change? Did you know you were this fragile?" The prince shouted as loudly as he could to be heard by as many people as possible.

"I always knew this day would come eventually. I dreamed of it since I was a child. I don't know what makes me happier: the fact that he is dead, or the fact that I am now the king? I hated the man you people loved. How many times have we all heard the legend of his famous defeat of Draviakhan? I grew tired of hearing that story. Answer me this: What is the point of that legend if this is what it has led too?

"People expected that I, as the next king, would be just as noble and heroic as he was. At first, that's what I expected of myself too. I've always dreamed of myself as the future king, protecting Celestial from any and every monster. When I asked my grandfather if I could learn how to sword fight and join the warriors he said, 'No. It's too dangerous.' I was never allowed to do anything I wanted to do.

"Zoran kept me trapped inside the castle walls, forcing me to learn manners, relations between the four races, and politics. I just wanted to be king already and be the one in control of my own life. Even though I was the prince, I was powerless. So I spent my time gambling, drinking, and spending quality time with the willing ladies of this city. I figured if I had to wait for his death, I would have as much fun as possible in the meantime.

"And then one day, a couple months ago, I finally found a way to break out of the waiting. My father came to me. The man who Zoran told me was dead was still alive. No longer was his identity kept a secret to me. My father told me that the evil god believes that I am the one who will fulfill the ancient prophecy hidden in this very sword I carry." Silvanus waved the sword through the air to show off his newest prized possession.

"After meeting my father and learning about my part to play in the planned siege of Celestial, everything made sense to me. I realized the monsters were just like me. All of their lives, they too feel trapped and are only seeking a way to break out of their miserable lifestyle. I realized that my life finally had purpose. I would help lead monsters to take control of the greatest city on Element. I was given the ability to control the element of water and told that the more I serve the evil god, the more I will prove myself to him. He will give me more elements to control as I lead his forces to victory.

"And so, today, I carried out the plans my father gave me. Myself, Visuvis, and a small group of trusted monsters murdered the warriors in the four outside towers, with help from Nightstrike, before they could sound their alarm. Our monsters were able to breach the outer wall and get all the way to within one thousand feet of the inner wall before we were noticed. By then, it was too late for you. We attacked with wave after wave of monsters, overrunning the warriors on the inner wall. Then we broke through and got into the city, just as we planned. And then finally, I did what I have wanted to do every day of my life. I killed the king."

Prince Silas swung his sword upwards, launching the head of the king off the tip of his sword and into the crowd. An angered man yelled out from the crowd, "How does it feel to betray your kingdom?"

"Kill him," the prince calmly commanded nearby archers. The archers sent a fleet of arrows into that section of the crowd. Since most of them were not experts with the bow, they ended up killing the man, along with twenty people standing near him. The prince issued a warning to the crowd. "You do not have to like me, but you will respect my authority. Or else you will die."

A woman on the other side of the courtyard had seen the man die, but chose to be equally defiant. "We will never respect the man who murdered our king!" The monster archers looked at their leader. The prince annoyingly nodded in the woman's direction. Arrows rained down on that part of the crowd too, killing more innocent civilians. Ty prayed that no one around him would be fool enough to say a word.

A man dressed in a hooded black cloak, with pieces of silver armor, appeared on the castle's balcony, high above where the prince stood. Ty realized that this was the rider of Nightstrike. The huge obsidian-scaled dragon landed on the top of one of the front castle towers and let out a blood curdling scream. It seemed to Ty like the whole crowd took one giant step back in fear.

It wasn't Nightstrike the people were mainly afraid of. It was his rider, the Hooded Phantom. His ominous presence stood above them all. The man was pure evil and commanded the full attention and silence of everyone without having to ask for it. Even babies and children seemed to stop crying as the

Hooded Phantom began to speak. His voice was slow and raspy, but very strong. It carried across the courtyard with more command and power than the prince's voice had. Ty questioned whether or not King Zoran had even had this powerful of a voice. The Hooded Phantom spoke in a tone of hate, malice, anger, and disgust.

"I was once like you. I grew up among you. I was raised in this city. I know how you people think. I know how you act. You care only about yourselves. You think monsters are the evil ones? No! You are the evil. You are selfish. You horde food for your winters. You fill your stomachs three times a day while the monsters starve. It shouldn't be that way! Why should you be allowed to live a higher quality of life than the monsters? You are no better than them.

"For them, it's a cutthroat world, survival of the fittest. They live in inescapable misery, constantly fighting for food and shelter. They fight for their lives. They live every day not knowing who to trust because the monster next to them might betray them at any second, just to live to see the next day.

"You people live in your fortified cities with no worries at all: your health, your gold, your safety, your food. You take every day and everything for granted. You don't know what it is like to live in constant fear. It's time you learn what fear is. It's time you feel the pain the monsters have endured for so long. No longer will this imbalance stand.

"The evil god has opened my eyes to these truths. He has allowed me to see things for how they really are. He has made me the most powerful creation to ever walk this planet, above even the powers that the great Draviakhan once wielded. I control all five of the elements. I will use my abilities to enforce justice on those who deserve it. Monsters will finally learn the peace that justice brings when the four races are held accountable for their actions.

"There is a reason why the monsters, I, and your new king can control the elements of this world and you can't. There is a reason why you can build, hunt, and cultivate food, but we can't. You were created with the abilities to serve the ones with power. We are stronger than you, and you are inferior to us. It is time that you finally learn your purpose. From this moment on, you are our slaves. You will build us our houses and our cities. You will cultivate our food. You will fight and die for our entertainment. Anything we command you to do, you will do it."

The Hooded Phantom spread both of his arms out toward the thousands of monsters in the crowd, on the walls, and hovering overhead. "Celestial has fallen. It now belongs to us. Today is only the beginning. The evil god and his creations will rule over all of Element."

The prince continued to explain the terrible future which was in store for the civilians of Celestial. "What my father says is true. In this very sword I hold now, I saw the prophecy with my own two eyes. Monsters will be victorious, and I will be their leader. I will rule over Celestial as your new king as my father leads the majority of his endless army to take over any city, town, or village they come across. The reign of Draviakhan was nothing compared to what is to come. The kingdom will be ours. Every living, breathing creation of the good god will be held accountable. Everyone is beneath the height of my throne. You cannot run. You cannot hide.

"With father and son working together, under our organization and direction, empowered by the evil god himself, we will conquer all. The success of our siege on the capital city of this kingdom will motivate monsters worldwide and show them that if they band together, they can take over their local cities and no longer live in misery.

"All that I require from everyone is your respect. It does not matter to me whether you are person or monster. This is my command, and it will be followed by all. No one respected me as prince. BUT YOU WILL RESPECT ME AS YOUR KING, or the consequences will be severe."

Prince Silas thought that by screaming his command, it would be more effectively enforced. All it did to the civilians was make them hate and disrespect him more than they already did.

Another civilian yelled out from the crowd, knowing in doing so he would die like the man and woman before him. There was no quiver in the man's strong voice. His last words were spoken clearly and confidently. "You wanted to leave the shadow of King Zoran, but you've stepped into the darker shadow of your father." A couple of people chuckled throughout the crowd and more joined in once the reality of his statement set in. The defiant man's last sentence proved to be both literally and ironically true. The prince's face began to turn red in embarrassment and anger.

Another man in the crowd yelled out. Little did he know, the name he was about to call Prince Silas would be what everyone in the kingdom would refer to him as until the day the prince died. "You will never be our king! You are the Prince of the Shadow. The Shadow Prince!" The man laughed in the face of his upcoming death. A couple more people in the crowd laughed as well, but most were too scared of what the consequence would be for even showing a smile. Everyone respected the two men for speaking out without fear, but felt bad for what they knew was about to happen to them.

Instead of the Shadow Prince signaling for arrows, it was the Hooded Phantom above him on the castle balcony who provided the punishment. He held his sword up to the sky. Everyone watched as it turned a bright, sparking yellow. A dark cloud menacingly appeared high above the courtyard. The dragons, gryphons, and phoenixes hovering around speedily flew out of the way.

Ty knew something bad was about to happen.

With a tremendous crack of thunder that deafened everyone's ears, ten giant blinding flashes of lightning shot down all throughout the crowd. Two of the blasts impacted the areas where the men had spoken out against the prince. The rest hit random spots of civilians. Each blast created a tiny explosion and launched anyone in its general vicinity flying lifelessly through the air.

There were minutes of more screaming and crying, but finally people began to settle down and were forced to give their focus to the newly titled Shadow Prince. No one else was willing to speak out and take the chance that the next elemental strike would be targeted in their direction and kill everyone around them.

The Shadow Prince's voice was softer and the red shade of his face simmered as he continued speaking. He had calmed down along with everyone else.

"I have already ordered my servants to cut out your tongues if they hear one word of slander. If one finger is angrily pointed in my direction, then all of your fingers will be chopped off. If you hear someone disrespect my name and do not tell your monster superior, but they find out about it...then your children will be killed. To go along with opposition against me by not confronting it is the same as agreeing to it. You are just as guilty as they are, and I will not have the next generation of your family defy me.

The prince allowed a moment for all the information to sink in before continuing on.

"Today you mourn the people that you have lost. At times, you will wish you had died in the attack today, so you will not have to learn the meaning of true suffering and fear. Every day you will ask yourself, will I survive this day? Do I want to survive this day? Will my wife be murdered today? Will my children be alive at sunset?

232

"It would be most profitable for you to you obey me and follow my commands to avoid these worries. I know that when you do, you will begin to feel an inner peace as you realize you are fulfilling your true purpose. However, if anyone should feel the need to fight back, flee the city, or disobey any of my or your superior's orders, you will be forced to watch your entire family be tortured. Then you will be killed and end up just like your precious King Zoran and the many others who have died today."

The Shadow Prince motioned behind him for a person to be brought out from behind the castle doors. "To show you what I mean, we have our first victim of insubordination. This warrior will be hanged for trying to assassinate me in my throne room."

Ty watched as a warrior in red armor was led to the gallows. After he tried fighting back against his captors, the Shadow Prince tied a rope around his neck. After squinting his eyes to get a better glance at the warrior, Ty exhaled one word as he saw who it was.

"Steve."

Memories raced through his mind of the two brothers growing up together. Here was his best friend, standing before everyone, being prepared to be killed. Ty would not be able to physically watch the hanging. There were some things in life that were best left unseen because of the endless nightmares they would cause.

After a minute of Ty breathing heavily, trying to keep his composure and holding in his emotions, something amazing happened. People began to notice that this was Celestial's jouster standing before them in his suit of red armor.

Sporadically around the courtyard, people began to put up two fingers. Lucan was the first one around their area to join in. His mother, Kari, and then Ty soon followed after him.

Within seconds, every single person in the crowd had their arm raised and their two fingers pointed high.

It was the most amazing feeling Ty had ever felt. A cold chill moved through his body from the awesomeness of the spectacle. Ty looked next to him and saw that both Kari and Cassandra had tears streaming down their cheeks.

Two points. That was all Steve needed to make it to the championship match. But then he was interrupted by the attack. Now his life will be interrupted. Gone too soon, before it should end.

Kari reached out and gently rested her hand on Ty's arm. She saw how shaken he was from seeing his friend in the gallows. She wanted to help comfort him.

Ty looked at her and forced a smile, trying to show he was okay; but he wasn't. He needed to do something to help Steve, but he didn't know what he could possibly do.

He is hanging there, so close to death, with no escape. He is helpless.

Ever since they were kids, the two of them talked about death. They always assumed if it didn't come with old age, it would come when they died fighting valiantly against monsters. They both wanted to die in the midst of a hard fought battle, ending their lives being brave and courageous and saving the lives of the civilians. The two even pledged to sacrifice their lives for each other if the situation called for it.

Ty knew this was not how Steve wanted to go out, and Ty didn't want to see him die this way either.

The last thing he would want to be remembered by is as a lesson that Celestial's civilians should serve evil.

Ty knew if he was in Steve's position, Steve would do anything in his power to try to save him. In that moment, the Elf knew what he had to do as he looked to Kari and told her his intention.

"I lost one brother today. I'm not losing another."

Chapter 25

Ty blocked out Kari voicing her opinion at the stupidity of his idea and studied his surroundings to formulate a plan. Near him was the minotaur who had taken over the orc's position as the leader of the civilian group the four of them were in. He sat on the muscular purebred Sampson, smiling as he waited for the rebel warrior to be hanged. His attention was not on the crowd as it should have been.

Ty's eyes connected with the eyes of a tall, strong-looking fisherman about fifteen feet away, who was also observing the unaware minotaur. Ty nodded to the man and then glanced to the minotaur. The man made the same motion, showing that he understood and approved of the nonverbal cues.

Ty turned back to Kari and rudely interrupted her ongoing rant about how this was the worst moment to pick a time to "strike back." Ty asked her a simple question. Her answer would change the rest of her life.

"Are you in or out?"

Before Kari opened her mouth to give an answer, the Shadow Prince pulled the lever that dropped the board beneath Steve's feet. The red warrior fell, violently kicking the air, twisting and turning in his noose. Steve's life was being suffocated out of him.

It was at that moment that the revolt began.

The entire crowd erupted in pandemonium. There was shoving, screaming, crying, and shouting. People picked up rocks and whatever other items they could find in the courtyard and threw them at nearby monsters. They also aimed them at the monsters guarding the platform and the Shadow Prince, cowering behind them. It was a clear act of defiance against all of these evil monsters and showed that the people would not give up their city without a fight.

Just like the previous people who voiced their opinions, there was a consequence for the actions of the civilians. Arrows and elemental attacks poured down into the crowd. Mothers tried to shield their children's bodies as their husbands fought against the monsters. Every man and some of the women were fighting back. In the midst of all the chaos, Ty forcefully pushed his way through the swaying crowd. Kari took his hand and followed close behind.

The muscled fisherman had reached the minotaur before Ty. Sadly, the minotaur had seen the large framed man coming towards him. He used Kari's bow and an arrow to shoot the fisherman in the chest. But one arrow wasn't enough to stop the large man. The fisherman still pressed forward, only falling after taking two more arrows. He bought Ty enough time though, as the Elf was able to close in on the blindside of the minotaur.

The monster saw Ty and Kari, but didn't have enough time to draw back the arrow he loaded before Ty reached up and tore him down from Sampson's saddle. Ty put his foot in the stirrup and mounted the huge horse. Kari ripped her bow and quiver from the fallen minotaur's hands. She was about to release the loaded arrow into his body at close range, but a group of civilians swarmed around the monster and started stomping him to death.

With one hand on the reins, Ty reached down and grabbed Kari's outstretched hand. He used his large warrior muscles to quickly yank her up onto Sampson behind him. Ty grabbed the reins with both hands and snapped them hard. Sampson charged forward through the crowd.

People were just barely able to dive out of the way before being trampled. The crowd parting before them was like a heavy fog. Ty could see what was ahead and thought he wouldn't be able to avoid it, but just like the fog, it parted as he went through it.

Some members of the crowd, who had disarmed and grappled the monsters near them, pushed the monsters out into the open path, where Ty's huge, charging warhorse easily trampled over them.

Kari clutched the back of the shared saddle tightly between her thighs as she drew arrows and fired at monsters. She impaled four as they rode, allowing the civilians to easily finish them off.

Kari realized that she and Ty were putting a large target on their backs as they rode forward towards the platform. An arrow was shot at Sampson and his two riders from a monster archer on the wall. It sunk deep into the purebred's shining black coat, but also gashed Kari's leg. Luckily, a civilian ahead of them had disarmed a monster and taken its shield. He tossed it up into the air as the horse rode past. Kari snagged it with her expert hand-eye coordination. She put the bow over her shoulder and held only onto the circular wooden shield. She had a better chance of surviving if she defended against the archers rather than attacked.

She wrapped her free arm around Ty's waist and pulled herself tight against his body as Sampson began to pick up speed. It wasn't three seconds after Kari grabbed the shield that a nearby archer shot an arrow right at Ty's head. It would have killed him if she hadn't intercepted it with the shield. She blocked two more shots aimed in their direction, but most of the arrows were inaccurately shot and hit innocent people in the crowd.

From his heightened view, Ty watched a man rush to climb the platform that Steve was on. The man looked to be around fifty years old: old enough to have lived a life that had undoubtedly saw friends and family die at the hands of monsters, but young enough to still have a fighting spirit. He didn't even make it up two of the steps before a cyclops in the security line of monsters hit him so hard with a spiked club that he was instantly dead. He sailed through the air, far back into the crowd. A splatter of his blood rained down on civilians as his body flew over them.

This elicited a response from many people standing in the front rows of the crowd to also charge the platform. The line of monsters was only able to kill four or five people each before they were overrun by others. A couple of people broke a hole in the line and ran past the monsters. Once the hole was created, it only got larger and larger as more and more people funneled through it.

Some ran up the steps while others stayed at the base of the platform to finish off the monsters in the line. Everyone in the crowd wanted to get to the Shadow Prince, so they could wrap their hands around his throat and squeeze. But the coward turned and ran back into the castle as soon as he saw the revolt begin.

The first man that reached the blue-faced Steve hugged his body and lifted him up, taking the tension off the rope around the warrior's neck. The people behind him attacked Visuvis, who did all he could to fight them off.

A Giant was given a dagger acquired from a monster. He easily reached up and cut the rope around Steve's neck and then the rope that was binding Steve's hands together. The ropes were quickly pulled off of the warrior.

Although his neck and wrists had rashes of purple and red, Steve was free. He could breathe on his own. Celestial's jouster gasped for air, filling his lungs with life.

Stephen Brightflame was alive.

Ty rode Sampson right onto the platform. Steve was patting the backs of the people who had risked their lives for him as he made his way towards the horse. Some of the people reached out and patted him back too, encouraging him to continue on and hopefully escape. They all wanted the hero of Celestial to survive.

Before Steve got halfway to the horse, he stopped and turned around. *Brightflame. How could I forget?* Steve turned back to get it, but one of the civilians must have known the story of the magnificent sword's creation. The man had already wrestled it away from the horned minotaur and was handing it down the line of men to the warrior it belonged to. Steve was handed Brightflame by the people who saved him.

This sword has never felt more comfortable in my hands. Because of the pain from the beating and torture Steve had sustained, Ty and Kari had to lift him up onto Sampson while the men on the platform helped push him up onto the horse. They sat him in the middle part of the saddle, facing forward, in between Ty and Kari. Kari handed him the shield. Steve felt ready for a fight now that he was holding his typical battle weapons: Brightflame and a shield.

Ty turned around and charged back the way they came. From the top of the platform, he saw everyone. The entire crowd was before him, moving and fighting like tens of thousands of ants crawling over scattered pieces of broken bread on the ground.

Kari turned around on the back of the horse and was sitting the opposite way of which Sampson was sprinting. Once again she equipped her bow. She fired at the archers, since the people on the ground had no way of attacking them. Even for being on a sprinting horse, she was incredibly accurate. Archer after archer fell off the wall after she shot an arrow. If the arrow didn't kill them, the crowd below did.

239

Steve had his back against Kari's. He was deflecting arrows with the shield in his left hand and swinging at any monsters that the crowd pushed towards him with Brightflame in his right hand.

Ty sat in the front, ducking low on the horse's neck to avoid the arrows Steve couldn't block.

Stephen Brightflame, the Human; Tyrus Canard, the Elf; and Kari Quinn who shared both features of their races escaped through the revolting crowd. The crowd was still parted down the center as the three heroes rode through the easy lane they created. People cheered all around them, spanking Sampson's muscular rear as he charged past.

"BRIGHTFLAME! BRIGHTFLAME!" The chorus of chants for Celestial's jouster and his two companions was the single ounce of hope everyone in the shattered city could put their faith in. What happened in the courtyard was a small moment of victory on a day of utter defeat and destruction.

The monsters all abandoned their attack on the civilians and instead moved to attack the three riders on the black warhorse. They knew if they killed the people in whom everyone placed their hope, they would regain control. A large group of around one hundred monsters emerged from inside the castle and chased after the three heroes. The crowd was able to slow the monsters down by coming back together in the center where they had parted.

More monsters came out after the first hundred. These ones were all mounted on horses, dire wolves, and other four legged beasts. For them, it was much easier to power through the crowd, but they were still not as fast without the open pathway the three heroes were charging through.

A crack of thunder followed by lightning smashed into the crowd right next to Sampson, sending people flying in every possible direction from the center of the blast. No doubt the Hooded Phantom was directing his attack at the rebel leaders.

Another blast came down right in front of Kari (behind the horse), blinding her vision and causing her to see bright spots. Two monster archers were spared because of her temporary handicap.

The lightning was followed by a wall of fire as a phoenix and a gryphon swooped down from opposite sides and ignited seven rows of people with their element. The attack failed to contain the heroes as Sampson showed off his amazing strength by jumping over the seven rows in one gigantic leap. The people had collapsed down onto the ground, screaming from being burned alive.

When Ty heard the loud sound of the drawbridge being raised, he snapped the reins and verbally encouraged Sampson to press on faster. Two more arrows plunged into the purebred's body to join the five that he had already been impaled with. The pain made Sampson angrier, which also made him accelerate. For bearing the weight of three people, Ty could not help but be amazed at the speed of the amazing horse. The percheron went even faster as he raced to make it over the rising drawbridge in time.

The monsters were trying to trap them inside the castle wall. Had they known how to remove the locks of the portcullises and raise the draw bridge, they may have already achieved their goal. But it was beyond most monsters' abilities to understand mechanical procedures. The drawbridge was not so difficult; it only required the two spokes on either side of the drawbridge to be simultaneously cranked. This they had managed to figure out.

The heroes passed the castle wall, but five monster archers were standing on both sides of the path before the rising drawbridge. In close quarters, they launched eight more arrows into the side of the horse. Ty caught three on his shield. One cut open a gash in Steve's leg, matching the one Kari had received a couple minutes prior.

Sampson's knees instantly buckled, but the strong willed horse regained his composure and continued sprinting up the rising wooden drawbridge. When he got two-thirds of the way up, there was a dramatic slowdown in the horse's speed from the increasing slant. The three riders felt like the horse was going to rear and bail them all off. They would slide back down the drawbridge into the awaiting arms of the monsters.

But the mighty horse had an inner strength as strong as his muscular appearance. He slowly pulled himself and the weight of the three people on top of him to the tip of the drawbridge. The hard, cobblestone street on the other side was twenty feet away and eighteen feet down. Without wasting time to let the fear of the consequences of failure stop him, Sampson jumped across the spiked moat.

He cleared the massive jump successfully.

But it was the landing that wasn't successful. The moment he decided to jump, Ty, Kari, and Steve knew what would happen when the horse landed.

All four of Sampson's legs snapped. The horse whinnied in pain as he fell to his side and spilled the heroes onto the cobblestone road. It had taken fifteen arrows and four broken legs to kill what was arguably the world's strongest horse.

At least he didn't suffer in death, Kari thought.

Ty thought just as positively, *He died a hero, an inspiration.*

Then Ty got a better look at the horse as it lay on its side. He had thought that Sampson was the horse owned by a warrior he knew who's family had been breeding warhorses for generations. Ty was only partially correct. Sampson did belong to that warrior, but the horse lying dead in front of him was not Sampson. It was Sampson's sister.

The crowd on the outside of the castle wall was also revolting, although not as successfully because they were backed up against the moat. A couple people ran over and helped Ty and Kari get to their feet. Ty and Kari then helped Steve get up.

Now that Ty was able to see his brother up close, he noticed how extremely pale and weak he was. Steve had a line of dried blood from his right ear to his jaw. One eye was badly swollen shut and he had dirt, bruises, cuts, and blood all over his face and body.

Steve saw that Ty and the woman were staring at him with a look of concern. "I'm fine," was all he needed to say. As soon as they helped him up they were all off and running. The three of them sprinted through the streets as monsters converged on them.

The drawbridge was re-lowered, so the hundreds of monsters from the castle and courtyard could join in with the monsters already on the chase. Dozens, if not half a hundred flying monsters were starting to come down from high in the skies to see what was going on.

Ty took the lead, Kari followed behind, and Steve was the caboose. Behind them was every type of monster (and more) that each one of them had faced in the siege earlier. It was hundreds of monsters versus three.

There was no way to lose the monsters, despite taking every turn and back alley they could to lose them. The only advantage that the heroes had was that Ty, Steve, and Kari had memorized most of these streets from all having grown up in Celestial.

"Do you have a plan or are we just winging it?" Steve called out to the warrior in front of him.

"Do you really think I thought this far ahead?" Ty looked back as he talked to make sure Steve heard him.

Suddenly, they found themselves caught on a road with monsters chasing them from behind and monsters coming at them in the direction they were running.

"Get down!" Kari yelled to Ty in front of her. She strung two arrows as Ty ducked, and Steve stopped behind her. Kari let the two arrows fly at the same time. Each one of them impaled the monster they were aimed at through the head. Steve's mouth dropped wide open.

Ty looked back at Steve and nodded with his eyebrows arched as if to say, "Yes, it's true. She can shoot with incredible accuracy."

Kari ran past the Elf, hurdling over the monster bodies with arrows sticking out of their heads. "Come on! What are you waiting for?" she said, grabbing Ty's sleeve and pulling him along.

Some of the faster monsters quickly closed in on them, clearly not as winded as the heroes were. They hadn't spent the entire day running, fighting, and holding onto their lives by a thread.

Steve slashed with Brightflame at the leg of a cart of pumpkins. The imbalanced cart tipped and spilled its contents, covering the alley floor behind them. "There's a couple extra seconds," Steve called out sarcastically, knowing the payoff would barely last longer than the breath it took to swing his sword.

"Every second counts," Kari encouraged him. "Delaying them makes our escape more possible." Kari knew her words meant nothing given their chances, but she had to do everything she could to keep up their motivation. The second they gave that up and were captured, would be the second that marked the end of their lives. Deep down Kari was just as pessimistic as Steve.

It wouldn't matter if we had all the time in the world. We have nowhere to go. We'll never be able to create enough separation to sneak into a house and hide from them. Even if we did manage that, the Shadow Prince will tear this city to pieces looking for us. He always gets revenge when he's made to look like a fool, she thought.

A group of ten monsters came towards them in a narrow but long alley. Kari reached back into her quiver. Her hand felt around for an arrow, but there were none. She was out of ammo.

"We've got company!" Steve warned the two in front of him. A green phoenix was flying above the building tops behind them. They stopped in the alley, surrounded on all sides. Ty tried budging through a door locked from the inside. After two failed attempts, Steve and Ty shouldered through it together.

They heard the inhaling of its breath as the phoenix unleashed what felt like a tornado ripping through the alley behind them. Kari hadn't yet come through the door and grabbed onto the sides of the doorframe, trying not to be carried away with the wind. Steve reached out and grabbed her by the front of the shirt. He pulled hard, leaning back, and brought her into the house they had broken into. Steve fell backwards onto the floor, and Kari fell down on top of him. Her chest lay on his. Their faces couldn't have gotten any closer unless they were kissing.

"Sorry," Kari said, blushing, but also smiling at the warrior she imagined herself with dozens of times.

"Don't be," Steve said back with a flirtatious smile of his own.

As Kari pulled herself off Steve, he kicked the door closed with his foot while still lying on his back. He heard the screams of all of the monsters that had been running towards them as they were carried through the air and blown away.

The monsters that were slightly delayed by the pumpkins would not have been caught up in the phoenix's element. Since the lock on the door was broken, those monsters could come in at any moment. The three heroes ran out the front door of the house into an empty plaza.

"I suppose you want another point for saving my life?" Steve asked Ty, reaching forward to put his hand on the Elf's shoulder. The question itself was a thank you to his friend. *This is twice in one day he has saved me,* Steve realized.

"Let's make it out of this city alive, and then I'll gladly take the point," Ty promised. That would give Ty six points while Steve remained at four.

This point will be one I'll never forget earning, Ty thought as he still couldn't believe they were still breathing after the events of the past five minutes.

"Horses!" Kari called out. McGregor's stable, where civilians could rent or purchase horses to gallop through the city, was located in this plaza. McGregor's was the largest stable in Celestial. They usually had about seventy-five horses on hand.

Half of the stable was burned down. Between seven and ten bodies of horses lay under its black and gray charred wood. It was hard to give an exact number of the dead animals. The others had probably been rented by tourists and were out in other parts of the city when the siege hit, or they were currently being used by monsters.

There were about fifteen horses left. All were individually tied to one long, half burned, half collapsed wooden fence. They were nervously jumping around, trying to pull free, as they had probably been for the past few hours. All were too spooked or too injured to be ridden.

Kari was sad to see them in such distress. *The poor animals haven't been able to escape the sight of their charred friends lying near them.*

At the same time that Ty, Kari, and Steve reached the stables, monsters began pouring in from every exit of the plaza. The three heroes all let out a sigh of defeat.

"We're surrounded," Ty said.

"By three hundred," Steve estimated. It was an optimistic guess. They were really surrounded by more than five hundred monsters. The number grew every second as more and more showed up. Dozens of dragons, gryphons, and phoenixes hovered in the air. Hundreds of archers took positions on the top of every building surrounding the plaza. The rest of the monsters were on the ground. Many were mounted on horses.

All of the exits were blocked: the four roads that led into the large plaza, as well as the two narrow alleys. Extra monsters formed a shoulder to shoulder line around the buildings in the plaza, so the Human, Elf, and halfling could not sprint and break through a locked door and escape out the building's rear. The colors of every element could be seen around them.

The three heroes all came to the same conclusion. *There is no way out.*

Steve had Brightflame, but had discarded his shield because of the damage it had taken from arrows and the fact that it slowed him down when sprinting. Ty and Kari both drew their weapons as well, although Kari had nothing to shoot out of her bow. Ty felt half unarmed with only one of his two swords. The monsters were staring with no emotion at the three Celestial civilians. Steve, just like Ty, would rather go out fighting and die honorably than just give up be killed.

"What are you waiting for?" he yelled at them all.

He got his answer when the Shadow Prince came down into the center of the plaza, riding the green phoenix that had just attacked them and almost killed Kari. He leaped off it and stood in the center of the monsters in the middle of the plaza. Prince Silas's sword turned blue and into the element he possessed, ice. He was ready to fight.

Every evil thing the prince had done ran through Steve's mind when he saw the betrayer. *If it wasn't for this man, Celestial would not have fallen into the hands of monsters today. Clyx, Thatcher, the Supreme Commander, King Zoran, and thousands of civilians would not be dead.*

Steve started smiling. They may have been surrounded by monsters, but there was nothing standing between him and the Shadow Prince. Steve looked down at Brightflame and then to Prince Silas. All these archers could poke his body full of arrows. These monsters could burn, freeze, paralyze, or poison him. He was an open target that could quickly and easily be disintegrated.

But Steve knew none of those attacks would be fast enough to kill him before he charged forward and plunged Brightflame through the small heart of the Shadow Prince.

The Story of Evil will be
continued in...

THE
STORY OF EVIL
Volume II

Tony Johnson

Coming Soon!

Official Website:
www.thestoryofevil.com

Social Media:
Like *The Story of Evil* on www.facebook.com

Follow on www.twitter.com @thestoryofevil or
https://twitter.com/thestoryofevil

CELESTIAL JOUSTING QUALIFIERS

Warrior Finalists:
*1 warrior representing each of the 12 watchtowers. Every warrior jousts in at least two matches. If they lose both, they are out of the competition.

- Stephen Brightflame
- William Callahan
- Tyrus Canard
- Rylon Gordick
- Michael Greyson
- Mar Hudson
- Matthew Kane
- Zachary Ostravaski
- James Reese
- Kyle Reid
- Spencer Reid
- Robert Wright

Round 1:
*Opponents paired by random draw
*Losers goes to Round 2 Loser's Bracket

- Stephen Brightflame
- Rylon Gordick
- Matthew Kane
- Robert Wright
- Mar Hudson
- Michael Greyson
- Tyrus Canard
- James Reese
- Zachary Ostravaski
- Kyle Reid
- Spencer Reid
- William Callahan

Round 2:
*Round 2 seedings based on difference of lances from Round 1 joust
*Winners automatically advance to Round 4
*Losers move to Round 3

- (1) Rylon Gordick
- (2) Robert Wright

- (3) Michael Greyson
- (4) Tyrus Canard

- (5) Zachary Ostravaski
- (6) Spencer Reid

Loser's Bracket:

- (1) James Reese
- (2) Stephen Brightflame
- (3) Kyle Reid
- (4) Matthew Kane
- (5) Mar Hudson
- (6) William Callahan

Round 3: Loser's Bracket
*Round 3 seedings based on difference of lances from Round 2 joust

- (1) Michael Greyson
- (2) Stephen Brightflame
- (3) Robert Wright
- (4) William Callahan
- (5) Spencer Reid
- (6) Kyle Reid

Round 4: The Ladder Round
*Round 4 seedings based on difference of lances from Rounds 2 and 3
*Matches start from the bottom, with the 6th seed challenging the 5th seed to take their spot and climb the ladder. 5th seed challenges 4th, etc.
*NO MORE LOSER'S BRACKET. If you lose both, you are out of the competition.

Celestial Qualifier's Champion:

Stephen Brightflame
*Represents Celestial in the Warriors' Jousting Tournament

Seedings from Winner's Bracket:
- (1) Rylon Gordick Stephen Brightflame
- (2) Tyrus Canard Stephen Brightflame
- (3) Zachary Ostravaski Stephen Brightflame

Seedings from Loser's Bracket:
- (4) Robert Wright Stephen Brightflame
- (5) Spencer Reid Stephen Brightflame
- (6) Stephen Brightflame

THE LADDER

Acknowledgements

Thank you to my editor, Jennifer S. Burrows, JSB Writing, LLC.

Thank you to my cover artist through crowdspring.com, Patrick Kerkhof.

More than anyone, thank you to God. Thank you for sending your son to die for me and take the penalty of my sins. Thank you for allowing me to realize that you are the true purpose and meaning of life. Help me to honor you by trying my best to obey your commands and make the right choices.

This world is growing darker every day. Help me to shine with your light, that through me, people may see the beacon of hope they have in your son, Jesus Christ (John 8:12).

Thank you for making me the person that I am and blessing me with the creative mind I used to write this story and the ones to follow. None of this would be possible without you.

For all have sinned and fallen short of the glory of God (heaven). – Romans 3:23

For God so loved the world that he gave his one and only Son, that whoever believes in him should not perish, but have eternal life. – John 3:16

Jesus replied, "Very truly I tell you, no one can see the kingdom of God without being born again." – John 3:3

If you declare with your mouth, "Jesus is Lord," and believe in your heart God raised him from the dead, you will be born again. – Romans 10:9

Made in the USA
Lexington, KY
15 March 2013